COME BACK, YES

Before Tamara reached home, she experienced a crazy and dangerous desire to turn back and find her way to Axhurst Mews. She wanted crazily to surprise Paul. She wanted to see him again — if only once more. She argued with herself. It wouldn't affect her too badly even if she did see him. Long ago — oh, so long — he had become the focus of her existence. Not now. Why not just pay him a visit, out of sheer curiosity. Besides, he might like to see *her*, and hear about her present life. The prospect of this propelled her towards him. It would be interesting, if nothing more, to find out what he thought of her after so long . . .

Come Back, Yesterday

Denise Robins

CORONET BOOKS
Hodder and Stoughton

Printed and bound in Great Britain for
Hodder and Stoughton Paperbacks, a
division of Hodder and Stoughton Ltd.,
Mill Road, Dunton Green, Sevenoaks,
Kent (Editorial Office: 47 Bedford
Square, London, WC1 3DP) by
Richard Clay (The Chaucer Press), Ltd.,
Bungay Suffolk

ISBN 0 340 22001 5

For Virginia

Come Back, Yesterday

Last night I went again to our hotel
Where once we stayed and always loved so well.
They gave me the same room — the same key
But nothing seemed at all the same to me.

You took the magic from me when you left
I felt so crushed and lonely, so bereft.
How gay we were, how crazy, you and I!
But you never saw my tears or heard me cry.

Why did our love and laughter have to end?
How long does it take a broken heart to mend?
I turned away and I left our room again
Nothing was there but the memory of my pain.

But I want you still — oh, come back, Yesterday!
Just once again, just once — you need not stay.

DENISE ROBINS

I

"IT ISN'T TOO late to change your mind, Tam, and if you're really not sure you're doing the right thing by marrying Quentin . . ."

Virginia Robinson, the maid-of-honour — there were to be no bridesmaids at this wedding — broke off. She felt a little embarrassed. She was usually most diplomatic and she didn't want to upset her best friend on this Great Day.

Tamara Whitfeld turned from her reflection in the long mirror and interrupted. "It's all right, Virginia, I am sure I'm doing the right thing. I am terribly in love with Q. so don't worry any more and — " she added, "even if I did have a single doubt, it's too late to do anything about it."

Virginia put her tongue in her cheek. She said no more but she was not altogether satisfied. She hadn't been from the start. She knew her Tamara (Tam to most of her friends and family), quick to act, over-impulsive, but so sweet, so utterly charming. Most people adored Tamara. Virginia reflected that the bridegroom must be already at the church with the best man, waiting for the bridal entourage to arrive. He was crazy about Tamara — perhaps a little too crazy for Virginia's liking. Would it last? With either of them!

Virginia was second cousin as well as trusted friend to Tamara. She really did know her well. They had played together as children and had only gone their separate ways once Virginia, who was of studious mind, went to University. She wanted to read history. Tamara settled at that time with her parents in the large country house down in Haslemere where the Whitfeld family lived before Mrs. Whitfeld died.

Virginia also knew that there was just that quirk in Tamara's nature that made her want the thing she couldn't get. Once she had got it, she didn't seem to want it any more.

Virginia could only pray Tam wouldn't go that same way once she was married. She'd certainly got Quentin, body and soul, Virginia knew that. He had used all his particular charm — and he had so much of it — in order to get through to her heart. That in itself was an achievement. At the time of their meeting, when Q. — most people called him this — first joined Whitfeld & Hansford, the firm of stockbrokers in which Tamara's father was senior partner, Tam had been hopelessly infatuated with another man.

Virginia felt a little ashamed because she was allowing the memeory of that other man in Tamara's life — Paul Pryce — to disturb her on Tam's wedding day. But after all, Tam had, only a short while ago, been frantically in love with Paul. She was a bit frightened, too.

Virginia, herself, was a stable, reliable sort of girl, Three years older than Tamara, she had been married to an attractive doctor, much older than herself. He had died tragically, not long after their marriage, from septicaemia due to an infection following an operation. It had borken Virgina's heart. Although it happened two years ago, she still mourned for him under the cheerful façade she showed the world. Much as she loved Tamara — and they saw eye to eye in so many ways — she could never quite understand Tamara's over-emotional side. Tam had already had so many love-affairs in her lift. But Paul had been the one she seemed truly to have loved, and grieved over for a long time. It was an affair Virginia had never understood — and Paul had ended it — not Tamara that time.

"It's my Russian blood," she would say with that urchin-like grin which was one of her many attractions. "I'm like Mummy and, as you know, she was a Slav through and through. I know I've also inherited some of Daddy's practical side — but he's always assuring me I'm poor darling Mum all over again. She was an extremist — mercurial, the novelists call it! Either up in the heights, or down in the depths. A bit dangerous, although let's face it, Mum finally settled down with Daddy and never loved anybody else."

Virginia hoped and prayed this morning that Tamara would settle down with Q. She was so much more Slav than English, and looked it, with those high cheek-bones and marvellous eyes, deep, brown and haunting. The long straight blonde hair made a fascinating contrast. She had inherited that fairness from her father. All the Whitfelds were blonde. As for the wide teasing smile, and that beautiful mouth, they had a stunning effect on men. They fell in love with her. Tamara loved love. She equally liked to be cherished. Q. was an unselfish man and he usually let her have her own way.

Never had Virginia seen Tamara look as beautiful as she did this morning. It was of course the day on which a girl should look her best. Tamara might have stepped out of any man's dream. Instead of the orthodox satin gown and lace veil, she had chosen a delicate spot-muslin dress, frilled, in layers, down to her small satin shoes. The bodice was tightly stretched across her small breasts, and because she had a long neck she was able to wear that high collar with a stiff ruche under her pointed chin. The sleeves were wide and edged with ribbon. A few moments ago, Virginia had fixed a cloud of apricot-tinted tulle on the blonde head, floating from a half-circle of orange flowers and seed-pearls. She was to carry a bouquet of creamy roses and stephanotis. The exquisite flowers with their delicate green leaves waited for her downstairs. Q. had sent them. The card that came with the bouquet Tam had shown to her cousin. There were few secrets between them.

My Tamara, with all my adoration,
  I loved you yesterday. I love you even more today. I shall love you more and more in the days to come.
Q.

"Isn't that divine?" Tam had exclaimed, a hint of tears on her fabulous lashes.

Virginia agreed. Quentin Marriot was a very delightful

man. Men and women both liked him. That in Virginia's opinion labelled him a winner. Yet she still worried about this marriage. Wasn't it all a little *too* perfect — too impossibly romantic? These two starting out with absolutely everything — looks, good health, and money? But Virginia realised that there was no time now to think in this way. The die was cast. A voice called from the front hall. John Whitfeld calling for the bride.

"Hi there — it's getting late, Tammy, my darling. Aren't you ready, and where's Virginia?"

Virginia glanced out of the bedroom window down at the shining blue Arrow — Q.'s adored racing car. Mr Whitfield's private chauffeur was standing by waiting to drive the couple to Heathrow immediately after the wedding.

It was a summer's day. The sun was shining. Everything glittered. Tamara was so lucky. Virginia walked up to her, picked up one of the beautiful slender hands and laid it against her cheek.

"All my love and blessings, darling. See you in church. I must run. I ought to be there now."

"Have the ushers gone?"

"Long ago."

"I'm awful to be so late."

"You always are," Virginia teased, and departed.

Just for a moment Tamara remained standing in front of the mirror, as though posing for a photograph. She was having quite a few doubts. Why did she always think this way after reaching any kind of decision, she asked herself. It was awful. She had felt happy and unhappy in turns ever since she woke up. In no time at all she would be Mrs. Quenton Marriot and have to say goodbye for ever to Tamara Whitfield, daughter of this house. She hated leaving her father. Mrs. York, his sister, was coming to take over from Tamara, so everything would change. Her mind seethed with visions of the future. Of course she knew she ought to feel glad to be handing Daddy over to such a good person as Aunt Elizabeth.

A widow in her late forties, Mrs. York was a cheerful, essentially nice woman who enjoyed being a housewife. She was also a good cook, which was lucky for Daddy in these days when hired cooks seemed to disappear as fast as they appeared. Daddy had put up with a lot from her, his Tamara, although he never complained, and stoutly maintained that he preferred his daughter's company to that of any other woman.

Would Q. understand her as well as Daddy did? *Or as Paul had done?* Those were questions that worried Tamara even at this eleventh hour. He was so easy, he seemed to make allowances for her excitability and selfishness. She was ashamed of her own failings but never quite able to overcome them. *Would Q. always be so kind and tolerant?* This morning, deep down in the recess of a confused young mind, Tamara realised that it was Paul Pryce's memory that was actually haunting her, rather than doubts about Q. Ever since the date of their wedding was fixed Paul had started to creep insidiously back into her mind. She felt that his ghost was actually here this instant, standing just behind her with the old attractive mocking smile on his lips — and a look of disbelief in his eyes which used at times to upset her. It had so plainly indicated that he had little faith in *her*. He was much more difficult to deal with than Q. Yet during the good moments they had been so *close,* and so deliriously happy. Certainly she loved Q. in a fashion. But where was the delirium, the marvellous madness of the passion she had shared with Paul?

For an instant, Tamara's whole face creased into an expression of absolute anguish. It should have been Paul, not his ghost, standing here, waiting for her to turn and throw herself into his arms. *He* wouldn't have been careful of her veil, or her hair, or her exquisite bridal gown. Q. would — he was so considerate. Paul, if he had been in the mood, might have torn the delicate dress and veil from her and covered her bare shoulders and throat and lips with kisses. She could even hear his voice — lazy, mocking like his smile.

13

"You love me. You want me, don't you, Tammy, baby? You've got me under your skin, haven't you? Well, you're under mine. Checkmate, lover!"

He used often to call her baby or lover — a little pseudo-American perhaps, but she didn't care. Anything he did for her was right *then*. Now Tamara tortured herself a dozen times with more memories. He had finally rejected her because he had broken through the little girl façade to the real woman; the real Tamara who became utterly dependent on him. Then he had moved away from her. He had let her down and gone to another girl. Gone right out of *her* life. Perhaps, Tamara mused unhappily on this her wedding day, she had loved him too much, and she had still got him 'under her skin.'

"Paul! *Paul!*" She called his name, then swung round as though she actually believed he was in the room. "Go away! Go away, for God's sake. Don't stand there laughing at me in that devilish way. You are a devil. I hate you. I'm just going to church to marry Q. Oh, *go away* — leave me alone."

The mocking ghost vanished. The room, so full of June sunshine, seemed to grow suddenly chill. Tamara drew a deep breath. She felt she was struggling up from the swirling waters that threatened to drown her.

She heard her father's voice, "Tam — *Tam* come on *down!*"

She took a deep breath, drew on her long white gloves, and slowly walked downstairs. Her father, tall, imposing in conventional morning dress, grey topper and gloves in hand, was anxiously waiting for her.

Mr. Whitfeld's eyes were full of pride as the beautiful bride came slowly down step by step, one hand sliding down the polished banisters. He handed her the gorgeous bridal bouquet. She took it, a set smile on her lips.

"You look wonderful, my darling," he said, "and more than ever like your mother this morning. You know, I've often told you, our wedding day was the happiest in all her life. I want you to feel the same."

14

Tamara closed and unclosed her eyes. She made a supreme effort to banish the ghost of Paul, and suddenly that sad bad ghost vanished and with it her doubts and indecisions. Why think about him? Why have a single regret? She had chosen Q. He was the man in her life now and he was marvellous and she loved him. She lifted a face to her father. She felt calm again and she went on smiling.

"I know this *will* be my happiest day too, Daddy, darling. Thank you for being so good to me and for everything. Let's go."

She took his arm and walked with him out of the house to the waiting car.

2

MR. AND MRS. QUENTIN MARRIOT were 30,000 feet up in the sky in the Trident which was flying them to Nice. Q. preferred driving, but he knew Tamara wanted to get to their destination quickly so he was letting the chauffeur take the Arrow down to the South. For the next two days until the car arrived, they would be staying in the fabulous villa which had been lent to them for their honeymoon by Prince Savarati — one of Mr. Whitfeld's wealthy Italian clients.

Tamara was delighted at the mere thought of the 'staff' awaiting them — an Italian man and wife. Q. knew the villa and had described it — gorgeous and luxurious, he said, with access to a little private beach, and a perfect swimming pool. Later in the week he intended to take Tamara for long car drives along the coast and up to the mountains above Cannes.

"I must show you France as I know it," he told her, "I spent two years at Grenoble and so many holidays with my parents on the Côte d'Azur. It should be a wonderful change for you, my darling. We'll eat at my favourite restaurants, and we'll swim and sunbathe and make love and be quite alone in the villa when we feel like it. It will be perfect."

It sounded perfect to Tamara. She felt relaxed and dreamy as the Trident flew steadily over a bank of snowy cloud under a brilliant sky of blue. Everything in her life seemed at this moment to have become brilliant. The past had faded with the shadows that had darkened her mind before the wedding. The horizon had cleared. She took off her jacket and pushed back her long fair hair. She was glad she had chosen to travel in a cool summery suit, palest yellow. She wore a long gold twisted necklace and carried the big white bag Veronica had given her. It was warm in the plane. Tamara liked warmth and snuggled like a kitten against her newly-made husband. Rid now of her ghost, she was happy, and by the knowledge that she was at last a married woman — and Q. was her husband.

He turned his head. Their gaze met in a long ardent exchange. She liked it when Q.'s gold-flecked eyes had that look in them. She liked his clean, smooth skin, his thick hair as fair as her own. They had a lot more to discover about each other, and of course, Tamara was aware that there were also things they didn't share. Q. liked all sports — particularly car-racing. He was also enthusiastic about bridge and backgammon. Cards bored Tamara, but he was determined to take her one night to the Palm Beach Casino in Cannes. He wanted to teach her how to gamble. It would be fun. 'Chemmy' was the game he liked best. She agreed to try it out. Not only would she be a willing pupil but the Palm Beach Casino was, she felt sure, a good place in which to show off the marvellous dresses she had brought with her. Daddy had not stinted her over the trousseau.

She turned now to Q. and reminded him that Chris St. John, his old Eton friend who owned a small villa in Beaulieu, had a yacht down there at the moment. She hoped they could contact him so that he could take them for a short cruise around the coast. She would so adore that. She liked Chris. It was sad he hadn't been able to come to their wedding, she said.

Q. nodded. "He has some girl-friend lined up and she didn't want him to leave her, but once Chris knows we're in Cannes, I'm sure he'll contact us."

"Super," murmured Tamara, and nestled her cheek against her husband's arm. He picked up her left hand and began to play with her wedding ring. He twisted it gently round her finger. Tamara had long slender hands. They always thrilled him. To him she was in some ways very young, yet deep down, he was convinced she was also a passionate woman. The combination was nothing if not exciting. He kissed her finger-tips. The oval nails had been varnished a pale apricot-colour — her latest craze.

Q. pictured her lying in a bikini by the jade-green pool in Savarati's villa. After a few days in the sun, that small perfect body of hers would turn to gold, like her hair. She would look more seductive than ever.

How lucky he was to have won this entrancing girl for his wife. Q. had not meant to marry until he was over thirty, but now here he was, tied down at the age of twenty-eight, and liking it. Lucky he wasn't jealous. He was well aware that there had been other men who had found Tamara attractive — one in particular — a serious affair. She had been honest about that. But it had ended, and Q. was sure that now she belonged wholly to him. He was determined their happiness should last. He would try to give her everything within reason that money could buy. He was comfortably off, if not as rich as his father-in-law. But even now, at the back of his mind, he couldn't entirely erase the memory of that business talk he had had with his father-in-law only yesterday. Inflation was on the way, so John Whitfeld had told him gloomily. Labour was fast taking over from the Tories, and a recession was certain. They'd had a good time on the Stock Exchange so far, but it certainly might not be so good in the future. John Whitfeld was a generous man and he had bought the lease of an attractive penthouse for his daughter, as a wedding present. It was in a large newly-built block of luxury flats overlooking the river. Tamara was quite in love with it. As for cars, Q. had his Arrow and Tamara her own small Fiat. They would start in clover, but Q. couldn't altogether ignore Mr. Whitfeld's words of warning. However, "*Don't worry it may never happen*" was Q's favourite quotation. After all, *why* worry too much about world affairs and a probable financial crisis, while he was on his honeymoon? Sufficient unto the day, he reflected happily.

The flight to Nice was easy. A few hours later Mr. and Mrs. Marriot walked into the big arrival lounge at Nice airport. Blue skies — sunshine — palm trees and flowers — and the whole world seemed to be at their feet.

Tamara watched her husband as he walked off to find a porter. She was so proud of him. He always looked super, she thought. Today he was, as usual, so well-dressed. She liked him in those brown and cream check linen pants, with the cream and brown striped shirt. He carried a casual sports-jacket over his arm.

They drove to Prince Savarati's villa in a hired car and were there received by his excellent middle-aged Italian couple, Luigi and Maria. The Italians welcomed the young English honeymoon couple with all the warmth and charm of their race. They had been in the employ of the Savarati family for many years. Marvellous, Tamara thought, after the domestic difficulties at home.

Villa Loretta was one of the most beautiful places she had ever seen. White and turreted, it resembled a small marble castle, built on the rocks with a terrace running along the edge of the cliff. The villa windows and sheltered patio overlooked the blue sea, and secluded beach. The garden was vivid with scarlet flowers and shaded by cypress trees.

Tamara was enchanted with the whole place. The interior was elegant, typically French. Huge bowls of roses and carnations welcomed the bride and bridegroom in every room.

18

Champagne in a silver bucket of ice with a special card of welcome from the Prince himself was waiting for them in the salon. Savarati wrote that he hoped to catch a glimpse of Q. and his wife before they finally left the villa. He was for the moment hung up with urgent business in the Middle East.

Once in their splendid bedroom which had a balcony with a superb view of the curving coast, Tamara took off her jacket and skirt and slipped into a short cotton dressing gown. She was thankful the journey was over, and all that had gone before. It was late afternoon now. She had had an exciting and tiring day so far and she was still thankful that she and Q. had skipped the usual long-drawn-out wedding reception. After changing, they had been driven straight to Heathrow.

She threw herself on the big wide bed — arms outstretched and eyes shut. Q. was standing at the open french windows, looking down at the sea.

"Q," she called his name drowsily. "Oh, darling, isn't it all *super*! I feel I'm in a sort of dream and I don't want to wake up."

He came to her side and looked down at her, so sweet, so lovely, and very young in that gay, flowered wrap.

"It's more than 'super' and I refuse to wake up," he said and kissed her hungrily. "And oh, God, I do love you, Tamara! I can't believe you're my wife. I'm in a sort of dream, too, — my darling."

She lifted her lashes and smiled at him in the way that made the blood mount to his head.

"We *are* married, I assure you, lover," she said softly.

And after that they both knew this was no dream. They shared the thrill of vital, delicious reality.

Later, the servants brought tea and cakes and more champagne. They left the tray on a table by the window. But Q. and Tamara wanted neither. They slept, utterly fulfilled and content, in each other's arms.

Tamara woke up to find herself alone. A note was pinned to the pillow beside hers,

You're the most alluring wife a man ever had. Please go on loving me. Let's never be any different. I'm going down to the beach for a breath of sea air. Wait till I come back. Don't run away, will you, my love?

Yours Q.

Run away? she thought. No, dear Q. I am happy with you. Why should I want to run away?

Yet now that she was alone, a queer feeling of guilt began to spoil the perfection of this new relationship. Q. adored and idealised her. She didn't really know whether or not she could live up to his ideal. She was too vulnerable — at times too exacting. She was frankly aware of this. The strangely different happiness that had been hers all the time she was with Paul, *and* the catastrophic ending of their affair had left a mark on her. Time could not easily eradicate it.

Just now in Q.'s arms Tamara had experienced the physical pleasure and fulfilment any woman could desire. Wasn't it enough for her? *It had to be.* That restless craving for other things in the depths of her being, must be completely annihilated. She wanted so much to give all she could to Q. Paul no longer existed in her life. She must remember that now and in the future. All her yesterdays could not come back.

It had all been so different. The memory of Paul suddenly began to materialise — to flash in front of her, as clearly as though she was watching him on a T.V. screen. Yes, he was there, right there in front of her, his lips curved in the old sardonic smile even while he possessed her body — and sometimes she had thought, her very soul. He could be gentle, careful of her feelings at times. Then so casual — even sadistic — caring little how he hurt her. Even when he went wild with passion she had realised in despair that she could never really reach his heart and take complete possession of him. She had felt that he had been hers only for a brief crazy moment. And for that moment she had been willing almost to give her life.

Paul was so utterly unlike Q. in every way. And she had loved him with a blind passion which she seemed capable of feeling only with him. The mere thought of this frightened her today. Yet just now she had believed herself satisfied in Q.'s arms. But she knew it was different — more gentle — more lasting perhaps but something was missing.

Recalling the panic, she had felt just before her wedding, she trembled. She was feeling it again now.

Could she love two men at the same time? Or was it only Paul who had been capable of rousing her to absolute passion and fulfilment?

She tried desperately to reorientate her feelings. Paul was dead to her. Done with her and she must be done with him. She was Q.'s wife. She would never see Paul again.

Yet she went on remembering with an unquiet mind.

This alarming disturbance must be annihilated. It was sheer fantasy, she told herself. The sooner she settled down to the kind of loving and giving that Q. gave her, the better.

She went into the bathroom and ran a cold, chilling bath. Frantically she towelled her glowing beautiful body and brushed her hair until it shone. Then she slipped into a white bathrobe and drank a tall frosted glass full of orange juice. She felt better, and ashamed. Once again she banished the memory of that other man, and fastened her mind and thoughts on the one she had married. She couldn't wait for him to come back. She needed his quiet strength.

But she knew in the deep recesses of her mind that she could never forget Paul completely — no matter how hard she tried.

3

PAUL PRYCE FIRST and foremost was a musician — pianist, guitarist and composer. A boy who, in his late teens, started to write songs — and later joined a small group. He sold some of his compositions — one at least had been included in 'Top of the Pops,' but his life remained a struggle. Several times, Tamara knew, he had had to live on National Assistance, and had once or twice been in hospital with some kind of blood trouble.

As a man he bore little resemblance to Quentin Marriot. An odd character — a misfit, perhaps, with a touch of genius. Tamara, who loved music — his sort of music particularly — fell hopelessly in love with him. Everybody knew about their affair. But her father and friends, even Virginia, deplored it. They admitted that Paul Pryce was, in his way, an attractive, gifted young man. But he was scarcely the type John Whitfeld hoped his daughter would marry. He was afraid of the association. Paul came from a totally different social world.

John Whitfeld, although old-fashioned, was not stupid enough openly to discourage the friendship between Paul and his daughter. He was a lenient man. But he worried more as the affair seemed to continue and become more dangerous. For a whole year Tamara spent a great deal of time in Paul's studio in Chelsea, and saw less of her family and friends — with the exception of Virginia, who remained her devoted confidante.

On her wedding day, Tamara not only remembered all that was wonderful about Paul, but that other side to him — the queer, bitter streak that made him difficult, and suspicious — sometimes impossible. He constantly reminded Tam that she belonged to a society in which he had no place. She in return reminded him that class distinction in this day and age was supposed to have come to an end, but in Paul's opinion Tamara was out of his reach — smart, cultured and too sophisticated. He could not live up to her. He was proud, self-sufficient and preferred the company of people in his own set.

He was the son of a man who, in his youth, had worked in a piano-factory for a low wage, and had never bettered himself. His wife had died after Paul was born and he had largely had to fend for himself. Paul's education had been neglected. Only after he left the state school in which he had learned what he could, he found a job in a shop that sold musical instruments. He stayed there until he had taught himself as much as he wanted to know about the piano and guitar. He spent holidays and his evenings paying an old retired musician to teach him how to write the songs that crowded into his mind, waiting for expression.

At the age of twenty, he met a guitarist who knew all the ropes and introduced Paul into the group that found a market for his work. During the years of poverty and struggle — never willing to abandon what he knew to be a genuine gift — he also learned to take his place in the world in many ways. He read hungrily. He went to concerts. He improved his vocabulary, and his general knowledge. But the innate bitterness of the one-time poor against the rich, remained, sullenly smouldering. Once he fell in love with Tamara, he had battled against all his instincts in order to surrender some of his pride and take Tamara into his heart and his life. But not for long.

On his twenty-first birthday his most popular song 'I Loved You Best' was accepted and produced by the group. That was his real beginning. From then on it had meant more hard work — and a combined effort by himself and those who played with him, to get anywhere near the top. In his profession there were too many struggling for success.

When at length he left the group and struck out on his own he worked late into the night until he was almost blind with fatigue. More often than not, he tore up the music he composed and began again. Perhaps it was the deep-rooted class-hatred in him that spoiled Tamara's happiness once she had accepted him as her lover. He was first with her;

23

she wanted him to feel the same way about her. She made no difference between them because of their social positions. She was no snob. She could well remember one day when she had begged him to forget that she had a rich father, he had given a sardonic smile.

"You're Upstairs, I'm Downstairs, my love," he said, "and there I'll probably stay, no matter how popular my songs become." After listening to such protests, for she made them often, he would close her lovely mouth with the sort of kisses that left her weak and gasping and completely enslaved. With him she couldn't win. No man had ever been able to make her feel as he did. Pride, dignity, convention, vanished when she was with him. She became part of his life, and once the quarrelling ended and she was in his arms again, she was deliriously happy.

All her heart's delight lay in Paul's studio in a cul-de-sac just off the King's Road — too hot in summer, cold in winter, it had none of the attractions of her own luxurious home. But there with Paul she experienced all the excitement and sensuous pleasure she needed. Her chief delight was to sit on a cushion at his knee, or curled up near a small one-bar electric fire that did little to heat the room — listening while he played to her. Such sessions generally ended with a song he had written expressly for *her*. She liked to croon these lines, and he would turn his head and smile, and sing with her:

> *They all loved you — all the rest*
> *But I was the one who loved you best.*
> *Loved you best.*

"Okay, I do love you best, Paul — better than anybody in the world," she would whisper later when they lay together on the divan. So the dingy studio became a paradise — for a few hours. Then she had to say goodbye. She had not yet reached the point of leaving her father's home — and coming to live permanently with Paul.

What days those had been! Unforgettable! The memory tore at Tamara's heart. Yet she had also to recall that often after a few blissful hours Paul could change completely, slide into one of his dark, slightly malicious moods. He would then tell her, abruptly, to get dressed and leave him to work alone.

"Go back to your own centrally-heated pricey pad, baby, and have an evening out with one of those jet-set guys you used to know — Sir-This — or The Hon. That, or even a belted Earl. Any one of them can buy you diamonds, take you to the sunny South, or drive you in a Mercedes-Benz. I'll never be rich nor will be anybody but the lad who wrote a popular song and gave most of his earnings to the Treasury." Then he would laugh because she looked so unhappy. She would leave him in silence. Sometimes she almost hated him. As she left she would hear him playing his piano loudly — almost rudely. Yet she went back.

He was not even as handsome as Q., let alone as kind.

Q. had recently become a junior partner in her father's firm. He fell deeply in love with her. He had money and position and a lot more to offer. Why did she still want Paul? What held her? What drew a woman to a man despite the many ways in which he hurt her? She wondered at it, and at herself. She had always thought she had more pride. But Paul had only to put out a hand, touch her hair with sudden tenderness, then take her in his arms, and she was lost — conscious that he was essential to her. His very songs, sentimental and poignant — full of feeling — were as powerful to her as a drug and she had become a hopeless addict.

She wanted to break away, yet could never give him up. She knew she was upsetting her father, and that even Virginia advised her to finish the affair, but she did nothing about it — wanted nothing, nobody, but Paul.

What a strange thing love could be. Sometimes she compared him unfavourably with Quentin Marriot. Paul was short and stooped a little.

He was a year older than she was. She had been nineteen

when they first met. She had glowed with youth then, and when he was making love to her he used to cup her face in his hands and tell her she was the most beautiful girl he had ever known.

It was his eyes that fascinated and drew people to him — so like Tamara's in shape and colour — dark brown, brilliant and intense. He on the other hand looked prematurely old; thin and forehead lined.

Life had taught Paul many hard lessons. So she forgave him for all his faults and failings. She wanted to make up to him for all he had suffered. And at that time, although she had come to admire Quentin Marriot and found him charming she was not particularly attracted. To her he was a little too smooth, and too sure of himself. Paul was the opposite — nervous, lacking in confidence, uncertain of his own abilities, yet he fascinated her.

In a strange way she and Paul resembled each other. They might have been brother and sister; both so dark eyed, so swift of movement, so impetuous. They shared a feverish gaiety, the capacity to enjoy life to the full — to extract all that could be drawn from the torrential passion they had roused in each other — just the two of them alone, shut away from all outside influence. Yet from the beginning there was that secret nagging fear in Tamara's heart that one day he would want no more of her.

On this day of her marriage at the very start of her honeymoon — the memory of Paul hit her suddenly — like a physical blow that left her stunned.

How wrong she had been to think she had forgotten the pain and anguish of her parting from Paul. It was here — all with her — terrifying her. The vivid memory of that awful February morning when she had left her home in Eaton Terrace, walked down the King's Road in a sudden flurry of snow and finally climbed the narrow dusty staircase up to Paul's studio.

Often she would hear the sound of music coming through that door long before she reached it. This morning, all was silence. Perhaps, Tamara thought, he had gone out to buy something for their lunch. She had promised to stay with him all day today. She used sometimes to bring expensive sandwiches from home — prepared by Daddy's cook — but Paul nearly always complained about this. Sometimes he even rejected the food.

"To hell with your charity. If I ask you to have a bit of nosh with me, *I* shall be the one to buy it."

Not very grateful — yet she could forgive his rudeness and admire his independence. At least Virginia was wrong in her belief that Paul was mainly interested in the handsome allowance her father gave her, and that he sponged on her. She had almost quarrelled with her friend about this. Paul was *not* that sort of person. Never on the make, she argued hotly — on the contrary — it was because he was proud and hated to let her pay all the time that he sometimes behaved so churlishly.

It was pride in the end that was his downfall and finally *hers*. On this, the very day of her wedding to another man she felt the sharp pain of remembering.

When she had reached the studio door that morning, the first thing she saw was the large envelope sticking over the bell, and marked '*Miss Whitfeld*'. In Paul's rather small writing. She felt sick. At once she knew that Paul was not only out, but that he would not come back. Yes, she had been suddenly, horribly, heart-rendingly sure that the end had come.

She slit open the envelope. While she read what Paul had written she leaned against the wall, sick and shaking. Oh God, if only she had come yesterday! But she had had to cancel her usual date with him because Aunt Liz, Daddy's one and only sister, had elected unexpectedly to turn up for lunch. She particularly wanted to see Tamara, who was a great favourite with her. Tamara had had no option. She had put Aunt Liz off twice before lately. She couldn't tell her she was going out. So perforce, she had rushed around to Paul to make her apologies. He had smiled and nodded.

Now — standing in that draughty freezing hall, she recalled the fact that he had only said briefly, "Okay", and suddenly roughly held her close, kissed her and said, "I must get back to work. Thanks." Then he shut the front door.

Thanks for what?

Just for coming round to see him for five minutes? And he hadn't ended with the usual "See you". At the time it had merely struck her that his manner had been a little strange, but it so often happened that she didn't worry for long.

Now she knew it had been goodbye, and perhaps the 'thank you' was for all that had been between them in the past.

In his note, rather badly written (Paul's writing was not his best point, neither did he spell as well as he should), he told her frankly that everything was over. He wouldn't be seeing her any more. He had spent yesterday packing up and two of his friends from the old group had helped him shift his things — including the mini-piano — and taken them all in a van to another flat. He didn't give Tamara the address.

I'd better tell you straightaway I'm moving in with a girl who used to sing with our group. She's a success and she's always been keen on me. I still think the world of you, Tammy, and honestly I'm grateful for all you've done for me but we can't go on. You belong to the Jet Set, my love, and that's where you should stay. I belong to my work and my crummy friends.

I'll always remember you. I think the hell of a lot of you, and I know I've never been all that easy. Anyhow one thing I swore I'd never do was to marry you. I was bloody sure your Dad would say I was after the cash. I'll never forget you, I swear it again. I didn't have the courage to tell you outright. But with me it'll always be true — 'I loved You Best — your song, Tammy, and mine. I expect you'll find some terrific chap to get hitched up

28

with and soon get over me. Thanks for everything, darling...

Then his signature. She knew it so well. A big flourish on the P. A double loop on the l. They used to laugh over that signature. Tamara had once called it the sign of an inferiority complex which made him write that way. *Inferiority complex* — yes, that had been Paul's trouble. There wasn't supposed to be any class distinction these days but he had allowed one to come between them.

Tamara had stood out in that bleak hall (it smelt of fried fish and chips), and stared blankly at the closed and locked door which would never open to her again. Along with her nausea, there came a wave of anger — and a sharp bite of jealousy. That other girl — that group singer — oh, God, how dared she live with Paul now? Paul had mentioned her once, casually. Said what a good voice she had and such presentation. That was the word he used. A red-haired girl — from Vienna, he described her, and he called her Liesel.

Now he had gone to Liesel. She earned good money, and she would be sharing it (and herself) with Paul. He wouldn't be too proud to take things from her as he had been when Tamara was generous to him, because she was 'his kind'. Someone who had nothing, but had made good, as Paul meant to do, given time and opportunity.

Tamara's nausea increased. She shut her eyes and tried to stop shivering. Hopeless, defeated, furious with Paul, whatever else she did, she would never try to get him back. His pride had come between them. She would be proud now, and let him go without a struggle. She would never see him again.

Yet her thoughts continued to circle around him. She could even picture him lying on his divan with Liesel as he used to lie with her. A lock of Liesel's red hair would be in his clenched fingers. He used to like pulling *her* hair while he made mad love to her. Remembering it she bit her lips till they bled.

Suddenly she turned and ran down the stairs. Her anguish intensified as she walked through the swirling snow towards her own home. She had never dreamed it would be so terrible to lose Paul. Walking back to Eaton Terrace, she kept hearing his voice. In tender mood, he used to look at her, his brilliant eyes half-shut, and croon '*I Loved You Best*'.

It had taken her a year to get over her bitterness and grief when that affair ended. They had neither met nor communicated with each other since. He went completely out of her life. Eventually when she had hardened up, she tried to convince herself that she did not care any more.

She never said a word about it to her father. Virginia was the only one who knew the whole story. Daddy knew, of course, that the affair had ended. He paid for her to go abroad with Virginia who had friends in Rome. They stayed in Italy for a month. Then Tamara returned to England and felt able to face life again. But she kept away from Chelsea and the King's Road. She refused to go anywhere near her old haunts.

It was on the rebound from that fatal affair that she began to fall in love with Q.

She half-guessed that her father used to bring his junior partner home to dinner rather frequently in order that she would see a lot of him. Dear, scheming Daddy! How happy he had been when she told him she had re-discovered love and the joy of loving — this time with Quentin Marriot.

Yet even tonight, waiting for Q. to come back from his 'breath of fresh air', vivid pictures of the old affair with Paul thrust themselves back into Tamara's mind.

She looked at herself, naked and beautiful, in one of the long mirrors. She spoke angrily to her own image. "You're mad — round the bend. Why let the thought of Paul spoil today? Q. is really much more worthwhile. You love *him*, idiot Tamara!"

But her lashes were wet as she made up her face.

When Q. came in, he found his wife ready for the evening, in an enchanting white crepe dress that showed the curves of her small figure off to perfection. He took her hands and held them against his cheeks.

"My little love — you look like a Grecian nymph. I say — I like that dress! I adore the way that cowl-thing, don't you call it, falls down at the back."

She giggled. "I like the cowl-thing too. It isn't my most expensive dress, but I must say I took to it when I first saw it."

"The most expensive things are not always the most beautiful," said Q. loftily.

"That puts *me* out of the running," she chuckled again. "You're always telling me I'm beautiful, and I know I'm frightfully expensive. Daddy says so. I've got to start being more economical."

"No — go on being *bien-chic, ma chérie*," he said. Q. liked his French. "I'll buy you anything you see in any shop," he added recklessly. "We'll comb the Croisette."

She took one of his hands now and held it against her flushed face. The thought of Paul had vanished as though by magic. She had absolutely no doubt in her mind that Q. was one of the nicest as well as one of the most attractive men she had ever known, and that she had chosen wisely.

"Don't be so reckless, darling. The best dress shops in the Croisette — so I've been told by my dear Virginia who knows her Cannes — are outrageously expensive. Besides which, I really did go to town on my trousseau. I don't need another thing."

He kissed her, moved away and looked through the balcony window. The gold of the sun was fading. The sea had turned purple. Bright stars already flickered in the sky. He could see lights twinkling from the hotels and villas along the curving coast. Then he turned back to the girl in the Grecian dress.

"I enjoyed my walk," he said, "and what I liked most was coming back to this villa — to my wife."

Tamara did not speak for an instant. There was something about Q. and some of the things he said, that gave her a pang. She felt guilty because she had allowed the ghost of Paul to haunt her — even for a second. Now, as Q.'s wife she would never have to feel as unhappy and insecure as she had done so often when she was with Paul.

"Q. darling!" suddenly she exclaimed, "Isn't it *gorgeous* here?"

"It is, and you are the most gorgeous thing of all," he smiled.

She hugged him, loving the now familiar tang of his cigarette smoke, and the faint aroma of his hair. It was smooth and shining and beautifully cut, a little long at the back. She liked it that way. She raised a glowing face to him.

"I'm awfully proud to be Mrs. Quentin Marriot. It's fantastic," she said.

"So are you, my love."

Now he was sliding a fold of the white dress down from her shoulder and kissing her with passion. He was the warm possessive male — the type the average woman would want to give herself to without reserve, and Tamara was no exception.

For both of them now this was to be a wonderful memorable night.

4

THE HONEYMOON WAS an undoubted success. Q. and Tamara enjoyed every moment they spent in Cannes.

From Q.'s point of view, perhaps, it was even more of a success than from his wife's. He was devoted to sport and particularly crazy about water-ski-ing. Tamara tried to share his fun but found herself a slow pupil. Her balance was poor and she often fell, so finally lost confidence. Came the time when she returned to the villa in tears, which made Q. decide that water ski-ing in the Mediterranean wasn't 'her thing'. She must give up trying, he said laughing. She encouraged him to go on with it and sat quite happily watching him on his skis skimming behind the boat over the blue water. It thrilled her to see the tall graceful figure, so perfectly balanced, pulled at speed. His precision held Tamara breathless. She felt proud of him. He was good at so many things.

Q. ran into an old tennis-friend in the Carlton Bar one day and spent a few hours on the tennis-court with him. Once again Tamara sat and watched. She played tennis but not well enough, and she never begrudged her husband a moment's amusement. Neither did Q. allow her to feel bored, or abandoned. Frequently he turned his head to smile or wave at her, and he always apologised for leaving her there alone. She protested that she didn't mind and that she enjoyed watching the game. She was pleased, too, when his friend who had been at Eton with him, smacked Q. on the back and said, "You're a lucky old bastard, Q. Your wife's beautiful, and unselfish into the bargain. My wife's a great girl, but she can't stand watching me play tennis or any other game. Women can be difficult, you know. Tamara is super."

Q., delighted, agreed with this. Tamara, walking between the two men back to the Carlton Bar for a pre-lunch drink, was made to feel good.

She didn't however feel quite so good at the concert they eventually attended in Monte Carlo. Rubenstein, the fantastic, ageing pianist, was playing Beethoven. Tamara had a particular penchant for Beethoven *and* for old Rubenstein. Back came the thought of the past — and Paul. Although he composed light songs, and enjoyed pop-music, the great composers always fascinated him. Tamara remembered one

33

particular concert at the Albert Hall. They had sat close together, hands locked, while they listened to a Mahler piano concerto.

Q., on the other hand, committed the unpardonable crime of going to sleep during the concert in Monte Carlo. Of course, she knew he had only brought her to it because she had wanted him with her. She supposed she shouldn't have taken advantage of his good nature. She knew he was not musical. Once, in an unguarded moment, he had told her gaily that he would rather listen to the thrump-thrump of a superb car engine being revved up just before a race than to classical music. At the time she had thought he was joking.

She turned her attention from Rubenstein and glanced sideways. He sat with arms crossed, eyes closed and mouth a little open. Yes — he was asleep. Tamara felt hot and bothered. He wasn't snoring, but wake him up, she must. People near them would notice. She couldn't bear it. She hated him not to *want* to hear Rubenstein play. She patted his knee. He opened his eyes, grinned at her and mumbled an excuse. But long before the concerto ended he was dozing again.

He was wide awake once they were in the Arrow driving through the magical starlit night down the curving coastal road back to Cannes. He laughed and chatted animatedly. But not about the concert, although he had apologised again when they came out.

"I found it a bit too hot and stuffy for me in that hall," he excused himself. "Do forgive me for the shut-eye, Tammy, darling."

Of course she forgave him, but she found herself lying awake that night, feeling rather ashamed because she began to wonder what *Paul* would have said about old Rubenstein's incredible performance.

Then Q. opened his eyes. His eager tender hands explored her mouth and her breasts. She gave herself to him willingly. She was all his again.

She wrote to Virginia that next morning,

34

Our honeymoon is nearly over. We'll be back in town by Saturday. We'll take over two days' driving to Boulogne and I only hope darling Q. doesn't rush it. That's something I'll have to insist on — he must slow down in the Arrow, because although I can take a steady eighty, I really hate it when the clock touches a hundred even on these autoroutes. I'm not as keen on speed as Q. is.

In your last letter you asked me if everything had been absolutely all I'd hoped for, and I assure you it has. I don't think I ever imagined a man could be as kind as Q. He just spoils me hopelessly, and I'm sure we'll always be terribly happy. Mind you, we don't always see eye to eye about certain things, but they don't matter really. I admit I find it sad that I have to walk around the bookshops alone or listen to good music, knowing that he doesn't really hear a note of it. But we don't differ over the important things which is what matters. Anyhow you warned me that in your own marriage you found it necessary to carry out this give and take business. One mustn't expect one's better half to agree with everything, and I daresay I'm occasionally a disappointment to him. We knew each other pretty well before we got married, but it does seem it's really only afterwards one finds out the discrepancies in taste. I think Q. and I are both inclined to be a bit selfish. But we certainly haven't disappointed each other seriously. He's super the way he gives in to me and, Virginia, darling, I'm glad, terribly glad I married him . . .

And in her heart she was, and she was completely happy until the glamorous honeymoon came to an end.

They drove back most of the way on the autoroute — ninety miles of straight road. It suited Q. and his Arrow.

They stayed the night in Aix-en-Provence — in the Hotel Roi René. The next day the weather changed, and as they neared Boulogne it began to rain. Tamara was glad of the warm jacket she had brought with her but never once had to wear while she was in the South of France. She sighed, and turned up her small nose at the sight of the grey skies. "Even in June — just look at it, Q! Grim after Cannes and the Villa Loretta."

He looked and grinned, a half-smoked cigar between his teeth. He needed no coat. He was happy in his light summer jersey and linen pants. He never felt the cold. But he knew that Tamara did. Q. was full of health and vigour. His whole body was now richly tanned. He felt fine.

Once they were on the car-ferry, he tried to persuade Tamara to go up on deck. She preferred to stay in the lounge and get warm. He looked at her a bit anxiously, "You haven't caught a chill, have you, pet?" She looked suddenly pale and depressed — unlike herself.

"No. I think it's just the sudden drop in temperature. You know how I feel it. It's so damp after Cannes."

He nodded, looked out at the roughening sea, then at Tamara. She was huddled up in her seat, her coat wrapped tightly around her. He often spoke without thinking, and he did so now.

"What you need is more exercise, my love. Why not come on deck for a stiff walk with me?"

That annoyed her. Her expressive eyes glowed up at him resentfully.

"Sorry, but I'm not the outdoor type as well you know, darling! I don't rush madly over golf links and don't want to go mountain-climbing. And in my opinion, I walk quite enough — certainly in town. Or do you think I ought to sell my Fiat?" she added on a sarcastic note.

It was the first time she had ever spoken to Q. quite so coldly. Aware that he had blundered, he tried to make amends. He bent and kissed her quickly, but her eyes were still resentful.

"Tammy, my *darling* of course you mustn't sell your own little car, and I'm sure you take enough exercise."

"That's not what you said."

"Darling, don't be silly, I didn't mean that."

"Then you should say what you mean."

There was a couple in the seats opposite them. The woman tittered. Q. became suddenly self-conscious and rather annoyed. He and Tamara seemed to be having a small quarrel — the first since they had known each other. He was also aware that she drew away when he tried to take her hand. That really upset him. He whispered to her, "*Darling,* so stupid of me not to see you're shivering. Look — I'll go along to the purser and get you a cabin. I would have booked one, but it being such a short trip —— "

She interrupted, "I don't want a cabin, of course not. We're nearly at Dover."

"Hardly, but if you want a cabin even for ten minutes you can have one."

"Of course not. I'll be all right. I don't really like Channel-crossings. Just leave me alone."

Now it was his turn to feel resentful, and much as he adored his beautiful wife he felt it necessary to defend himself.

"Darling, I meant absolutely nothing against *you* — and I certainly did not suggest you should rush round golf courses or climb mountains. Oh, darling Tammy, *don't* be cross with me. You know I adore you."

Tears sprang to her eyes. She bit at her lips angrily. She was angry with herself rather than with him. She knew she was being unreasonable. The whole thing sprang from the fact that she was extremely tired. They had been in the Casino until three o'clock this morning (having sworn to each other that once they got to Aix they wouldn't go near the place), but Q. couldn't resist a final effort to run a bank at his favourite game of chemmy. The trouble was that he had already lost rather more than he intended at the Palm Beach Casino — before they left Cannes. He had been stupid and he, too, was tired.

Tamara gradually thawed. They had had such a wonderful honeymoon. It was absurd of her to be so childish. Spoiling everything. She put out a hand, and as she felt the warmth of his strong fingers she began to lose her irritability. She pressed his fingers in response.

"Darling, I adore you, too. Don't worry any more about me. I'm feeling warmer every minute and it's getting hot in here. You go up alone and get a breath of sea-air. I know how you love it."

"No," he said firmly, "I won't leave you," and he sat down beside her and suggested they should order coffee. So they were in harmony again.

Now the woman on the seat opposite announced loudly that she wished to go and eat in the cafeteria and the couple departed.

Left alone with Tamara, Q. put an arm around her. She did what he called her 'snuggling up act' — the atmosphere between them cleared completely. He felt that she belonged to him again. His eyes glowed and he raised her hand to his lips repeatedly.

Drinking their coffee they began to discuss plans for the future. The office and work awaited Q. Tamara said she would be busy in the penthouse.

"There'll be an awful lot for me to do. It'll be terrific fun," she said, and no longer felt unhappy, while she and Q. made lists of the things she would have to buy. It would be very exciting — their very first home. Daddy had given them some lovely pieces of furniture. The decorations were complete and the curtains and carpets in place. It was just a matter of putting the finishing touches Tamara liked the idea of that. Also there were all the wedding presents, many of which they hadn't yet had time to open. And hundreds of thank-you letters to write.

"I'll get Virginia to help me," Tamara ended happily.

"You're very fond of her, aren't you?"

"Yes. We've always been tremendous friends. She's so sweet and sympathetic, and so sensible, too. The perfect friend in fact."

"I hardly know her, but I'm sure she's a great girl," nodded Q.

"So easy to get on with too," added Tamara.

"Please, *please* say that I am, too," Q. begged with mock drama.

She burst out laughing. "Idiot!"

"I am certainly idiotic about you, darling. But a bit tactless at times, I fear. I remember when I was a boy, my poor mother used to tell me that somehow I always managed to put my foot in it. But I do mean well!"

Tamara laughed again and squeezed his hand. "As far as I'm concerned you mean *very* well, and I'm mad about my handsome husband. Darling, we *did* have a wonderful two weeks together."

"Gorgeous, and I'm never again going to tell you to take more exercise, I swear it."

"Q. darling, *of course* you can say what you like to me. It's not at all important and I must have been out of my mind to feel annoyed, even if you do think I'm a bit lazy. I expect I am."

"I don't think so at all. You're my lovely, lazy girl, and I don't want you ever to change."

"You mustn't change either."

They continued to exchange frivolous, tender remarks, and make plans for their future life. Tamara was in high spirits by the time they disembarked and were in the Arrow. Q., happy to be in his beloved car again, drove smoothly towards London.

Tamara was silent after the first few miles. Quite privately she realised that a tiny seed of fear had been sown at the back of her mind — very tiny, but it was there all the same.

A disagreement could arise between husband and wife over something quite infantile. It was true she had never been an 'outdoor girl' or thought much about walking or swimming, or enjoying cold fresh air before she came in contact with Q. Was she going to disappoint him? Still more important *was he already disappointing her*?

Nonsense! Of course she would never be anything but content and happy with him. He was so marvellous to her and if he said anything she didn't quite like, she must in future accept it and act less like a spoiled baby. It was time she stopped lapping up flattery like cream and taking umbrage at the slightest criticism. She felt ashamed of herself. Suddenly she said, "Q. darling, let's give a marvellous cocktail-cum-reception party in the penthouse soon after we get home."

"Yes, it'll be tremendous. You shall arrange it all, my pet."

"I'm rather good at parties and making eats. And you're awfully good with drinks. It should be a super combined effort. And we'll only ask our dearest friends and the people we really want to know."

They laughed and indulged in a mock argument as to who they would invite and who they'd ignore.

It was, perhaps, a little ironic that when they were halfway to town, Q. suddenly switched on his car-radio. After a moment they heard a girl's voice, accompanied by a guitar,

> Oh, I know they loved you, loved you, loved you,
> All the rest.
> But I was the one, oh, I was the one
> Who loved you best.

Q. switched off. "Ghastly stuff — I just can't take it. There's never anything worth listening to on this darned radio."

Tamara automatically made a movement to switch on again, but fell back. Q. was busy now passing a pantechnicon on the double lane. He kept his eyes on the road and didn't notice Tamara's sudden silence.

She had gone quite white. Her whole body was taut. The slight sickness she had felt on the boat came back. But this time it had nothing to do with being either tired or nauseated. *That song!* Paul had written it. Paul had written it for *her*. He had played and sung it to her before anybody else heard it, and long before the group took it up and made it popular.

I was the one who loved you best.

Suddenly the presence of the man at her side — he had just laid a hand lightly on her knee — became almost unwelcome. But Q. slowed down and went on chatting gaily. The thought of the flat and the reception, and the whole happy picture of her future life, was temporarily blotted out for Tamara.

Why in the name of all that was holy did Q. have to turn on the radio just at that precise moment? *Why* did it have to be *that song*? A hateful coincidence, of course, but enough to make Tamara realise yet again that Paul's memory still had the power to hurt.

Q. was amusing and charming for the rest of the journey. She tried to relax and stamped on the memory of that all-too-familiar haunting song. Gradually the memory of Paul was banished from her mind. By the time they reached London she was once more gay and sparkling, thrilled at the prospect of seeing her father. They had always been devoted to each other.

An hour later a few relatives and friends dropped into the penthouse for a drink, and to bring 'welcome-home' flowers. Everybody said how well the bride and bridegroom looked *and* how happy! They went out to a family dinner later on that night with Mr. Whitfeld, his sister, Elizabeth York, and, of course, Virginia, who had been invited by post while Tamara was in France. Virginia looked at her friend's glowing face, and came to the conclusion that Tam had surmounted her difficulties. Obviously the honeymoon with Q. had been a great success. Virginia was immensely relieved.

5

DURING THE FOLLOWING week Tamara had little time for anything but her new home. The penthouse was air-conditioned. Even on a warm June day it was pleasant, although both Tamara and Q. missed the glamorous Villa Loretta, and particularly the swimming pool. Tamara, with Virginia to help, was soon involved in turning the beautifully decorated and furnished flat into a real home. She only gave a pleased thought occasionally to Cannes and her honeymoon, and none to Paul.

That next day Q. returned to the city, not forgetting to telephone Tamara during his lunch hour.

"How is my beloved wife?"

"She is very well and very busy, making the penthouse perfect for her beloved husband," was Tamara's gay reply. "And how are you, Q.?"

"Up to my eyes. There's a lot doing. The market is up. Maybe I'll buy you some more shares and make some money for you, darling."

"Oh, never mind about that, just come home as soon as you can. I miss you!" was Tamara's reply.

"You're a gorgeous girl. I miss you, darling!"

They continued the conversation in this happy mood.

So the honeymoon spirit remained with them for several days, and days lengthened into weeks. Tamara had no time for anything much outside her penthouse. Whatever she had said about money not mattering, she had to admit the pounds and pence were vitally necessary. There was so much still to buy. Q. was generous to a degree. She felt herself to be very lucky. He was away all day but they had wonderful re-unions when he came home. They behaved as though they had only just fallen in love.

Mr. Whitfeld was delighted. Every time he saw his daughter he was sure she had made the right choice. She seemed completely recovered from her crazy infatuation for the boy he called 'that impossible fellow who wrote sickly songs'.

Virginia, rather more intuitive than Tamara's father, was only fairly happy about Tamara, and as summer drifted into autumn, various things began to worry her again.

In October, the central heating was switched on in the penthouse. It was warm and comfortable, and always bright with flowers. Virginia often lunched with her friend. One dull autumn day as they drank their coffee, Virginia looked hard at Tamara and her secret fears about what might be going on behind all the outward gaiety, returned. Tamara looked pale and thin. The delicate skin under her beautiful eyes had a bruised look, now that her tan had faded. She hadn't been sleeping well.

"Is everything all right with you, Tam?" Virginia suddenly asked outright.

"Everything's great," was Tamara's answer. "By the way Q. and I are thrilled with our domestic help."

The 'help' was a Filipino boy who came in daily to cook and clean the flat.

"His being a Filipino is an asset," said Virginia, "they're so well trained, and make such good cooks."

"Panay is sweet, anxious to do everything he can and a good houseman, too. Can't do enough for us. Q. appreciates him because he valets so well. He's worth his terrific wage, and the only fear we have is that he mightn't get permission to stay much longer in England. His time is really up."

Virginia looked at her closely.

"And is dear Q. still the idol of your heart?"

An instant's hesitation — not lost on Virginia.

"Oh, of course." But Tamara's tone of voice hardly convinced her friend. Virginia knew her too well. That cool note and the little shrug and giggle that followed the 'of course' — what did that mean?

Tamara met Virginia's gaze and glanced quickly away.

"I suppose it would be ridiculous to say *everything* is the same as it was on our honeymoon," she admitted.

"For some couples marriage is one long honeymoon right up to the Golden Anniversary."

"Oh, I think that's a tall order!"

"Unusual for you to be a cynic, Tam, darling."

"I'm not. But I just think that one has to settle down and learn really to know each other, don't you?" And now Tamara laughed again, but she did not meet her friend's gaze this time.

Virginia stayed silent. She could only think of the husband she had lost — the man she had adored and who had so cruelly been taken from her after two years. They had remained passionate lovers, absorbed in each other, right up to the time of his death.

Then Tamara spoke quickly, "I'm terribly happy with Q. and he is with me, I haven't a thing to grumble at. These last few months have been super. I can't think how many what Q. calls 'second honeymoons' we've had. Weekends on the river — staying at heavenly little hotels — always being treated like V.I.P.s wherever we went. You know what Q.'s like. He expects the best and gets it. Head-waiters have only to see him coming and his snap of the fingers, and it's the best table for Mr. Marriot."

Virginia lit a cigarette. "You're a lucky girl, darling. Personally I always thought Q. very attractive all round."

"He's super — but —"

"But?" echoed Virginia enquiringly.

Tamara stood up. She moved away from the lunch table, walked to the window and stared down at the river. Fog was creeping up; the river craft moving slowly were already shrouded in mist. She felt suddenly uncomfortable and sad, unable to go on making bright remarks to Virginia. She turned round and changed the conversation.

"Did you think Daddy seemed okay when you dined with us the other night?"

"Perfectly, and Mrs. York — your Aunt Liz — looks after him so well — they both seem happy."

"I thought so, too. I don't think he misses me at all."

44

"Just as well now you're busy looking after your husband."

"Oh, it's Q. who looks after *me*, really, but —"

"But what?" Virginia felt suddenly that she wanted to probe further. She must know the real reason of Tamara's despondency which she was obviously trying hard to hide. "Out with it, love! What's on your mind?"

Tamar stubbed her half-smoked cigarette in an ashtray. She avoided Virginia's gaze. Those big blue eyes saw far too much.

"Oh, *well*, one has to live with someone for a bit before you discover what they're really like, doesn't one?"

"What's that supposed to mean?"

"Well, really Q. and I have only been together a short time, haven't we?"

"Four months," smiled Virginia.

"Well, it's hardly time enough to learn a bit what someone's really like."

"H'm, has Q. suddenly found out what a spoiled brat you are?" Virginia asked affectionately, and received an answering smile.

"Oh, that's for sure. But I think *he's* spoiled, too."

"Did you expect anything else? I'm sure he's got a very nice kind side and nobody in the world would doubt that he adores you, but he's always had his own way and done everything he wanted to do until he met you. I think when a man's been a rather popular bachelor — like Q. — he's apt to feel a bit caged once he's married."

Tamara frowned and lit another cigarette. She was smoking too much these days. She must cut down.

"I don't think Q. feels caged," she said slowly. "I've often suggested he should have an evening alone with one of his friends and let me go round to Daddy, or you, or something. But he seems to prefer to stay at home or take me out."

"And does he always choose the fun and games and the places you go to, or do *you* do the choosing?"

Tamara shrugged. "I suppose it's mutual. We both decide,

but, my dear, I have no right to criticise darling Q. even if he *is* spoilt. I know I am!"

"Two spoiled people are apt to clash."

"You're always right, aren't you?" Tamara laughed, although she didn't think Virginia had said anything very funny.

"Well, *do* you two often clash?" persisted Virginia.

"No, he generally gives in to me when there's an argument."

"And do you have many arguments?"

"I suppose not. I mean not any more than most married people."

"And what are yours over, as a rule?"

"Oh, I don't know. Our tastes differ at times, you know, Virginia. I didn't quite realise that Q. was so absolutely *down to earth*. I mean he hasn't what you sort of call a spiritual side."

"And what may I ask is *your* spiritual side?" Virginia asked, her large blue eyes twinkling.

Tamara shrugged her shoulders again. "Oh, well, I'm not intellectual but I'm not always frivolous. Q. just doesn't care about good music, books, or serious conversation, except about money matters. He's terrific in that way, but he gets bored with good T.V. plays, though he'll sit for hours watching Rugby football, or that beastly wrestling on Saturdays!"

And that ended the conversation. Soon afterward Virginia left.

Tamara switched on her television. She broke into what must be the middle of a session of pop-music. She stared fascinated at the boys who were playing. The gaily coloured jackets and flared velvet trousers, the dazzling flickering background of black and silver — the usual sort of beat band show — and they were playing a slow rather sentimental ballad which was being sung by a boy with a beard and a shock of long black curls. It was upon him that Tamara's gaze fastened, fascinated. He wasn't really like Paul, yet that thick hair and that attractive voice was so like Paul's — it was quite uncanny.

Tamara's whole mind rushed back to the past. The beginning of their association when Paul used to be so much attached to his old pop group. As Tamara stood there, transfixed, it was as though she was not in her luxurious penthouse but the old studio in which she had spent so many stolen hours. She and Paul were lying side by side on his big divan. They were both smoking — not touching each other — just lying there in complete harmony, watching this kind of show on television. Paul was criticising the singer. "Thumbs down — they're crummy. Do you dig that tune — or the lyric?"

"No," Tamara had agreed, "I don't; it's a bit too religious. I never like these sort of words — a mix-up of sacred things, and earthy passions and all that."

Paul laughed aloud, got up and switched off the T.V. Tamara in this hour, all these years later, could see him quite plainly, looking down at her. It had been a hot day in London, in the middle of the summer. She remembered the yellow cotton sleeveless trouser suit she had been wearing. Paul had nothing on but a pair of favourite floral Bermuda shorts. He looked, she thought, very young indeed, with his tousled dark hair and that impish grin on his face. She wasn't sure she liked the grin. It meant he was going to say something provocative.

"So you're anti sacred music, are you?" he sneered. "My wicked Tamara prefers the earthy lyrics. Songs of passion, relating to sex — and —"

She had interrupted, "Oh, don't be horrible Paul. You know I adore the right sort of sacred music like *The Dream of Gerontius*. You liked it too. Remember when we went to the Albert Hall to hear it? But I don't like the mix-ups, like *'Jesus Christ Superstar'*. God and Christ and sex as you put it."

Paul picked up a carton of cigarettes and flipped one out at her, but she shook her head, "I don't want to smoke any more."

"What's the matter with you, baby? You've come over queer as my Mum used to say."

"Maybe, but don't let's argue. It's too hot."

"I enjoy arguing with you."

"What else do you enjoy?"

And she had looked up at him with huge dark liquid eyes — so like his own, feeling her whole body quiver with the intense feeling he aroused in her. Why this boy had such power to excite her — to possess all her thoughts as well as her body — she did not know. But she took the cigarette which he had lit for himself, out of his fingers.

"Don't smoke any more. Come and lie down again. I know I'm mixed up at times, but I do love you so terribly, Paul."

He laughed and flung himself down beside her and ran his fingers through her long fair disordered hair, pulling it until she cried out, "*Don't*. You hurt."

"I like to hurt you sometimes, haven't you noticed it?"

She had shut her eyes tightly, feeling his cheek — rough because he hadn't shaved today — against her own smooth one. She locked her hands behind his neck. "I keep noticing things about you, Paul, that I don't particularly like. Yet I'm mad about you, and I don't know how much longer I'm going to be able to live apart from you — I mean I want to leave home and come here for good and all."

He stopped smiling. It was his turn to grow serious, although he went on mocking her to cover his own feelings. Yes, he had made it obvious in those days that he cared about her as much as she did about him, but that his life as a composer came first, and so did his dislike of her social status, and his absolute conviction that once she left home for him she would regret it. Of course, he did not want to be made to feel guilty. He had his scruples. But physical contact with her — the touch of her hands, her mouth — never failed to turn him into the lover she had grown to love so frantically. He began to draw strands of her hair across his lips, kissing them, then brushing them away from her hot face and between laughter and kisses, whispering to her.

"So this is your spiritual side, lover — well, it's okay by me."

Later when they were calm again she had said, "Let me tell my father that I want to come and stay with you for good and all, please Paul."

When she said that sort of thing, his reply was always the same. "I'm all yours, beautiful, but not as you want it. I'm not really your sort whatever you say and you're not mine. You can keep your so-called spiritual side, but what you really mean is that you're a crazy romantic mixed-up kid — nicely brought up and enjoying what you get with me because it's so different from your upbringing. You find it a wonderful change. Let's leave it at that. If you left home and came here for good it would cause such an upheaval — it wouldn't only end in trouble for you, but for me. And don't argue."

The old protest — the old feeling he gave her of being utterly insecure with him, yet passionately needing the security of permanent union with him.

All these years later in her luxury home, Quentin Marriot's wife could still feel her body tremble and her heart beat with the old agony of losing Paul. She was ashamed of it, and remembered suddenly that there was something else on her mind — something much more important.

She rushed to the telephone. She must speak to Dr. Fisher. She had seen him a week ago. He had promised to call her today, but he had obviously been too busy. Now there was something she must know.

That mental flashback to the day when Paul had made a mockery of her so-called spiritual side, had been so vivid, following upon the question that Virginia had asked her with slight sarcasm, but her usual sweetness — "And what is *your* spiritual side, darling?" — that all thought of Dr. Fisher had vanished. Tamara phoned the doctor's surgery.

"Ah, Mrs. Marriot, I tried to get you this morning but your number was engaged, and I've been out all day. I'm coming round to see you tomorrow but I wanted you to know.

at once that the result of your test is positive. You *are* pregnant."

They spoke for a few moments, then Tamara put down the receiver. She was going to have a *baby*. The ghost of Paul and that mad period of her life with him receded into the background. She sat down and began to laugh weakly.

When she recovered she ran up to her bedroom, made up her face again and stood for a moment staring at her figure in the old Victorian pier glass that Aunt Liz had found for her.

Slim, not a sign of pregnancy — but of course it was too early. But soon she would lose that slender line. She would have to buy maternity clothes. They could be very attractive these days but the morning sickness wasn't very nice. She hoped Dr. Fisher would give her something for it when he came.

Now what would Q. say? A sudden excitement brightened her eyes and brought a flush to her cheeks. Of course he'd be thrilled. They hadn't meant to have a child so soon but it would be a link between them — a new link stronger than all the others.

She gave Virginia time to reach home and then telephoned her. After she had blurted out the news, Virginia gasped,

"Oh, congratulations, my dear, it's too wonderful."

"You think it's a good idea?"

Actually Virginia thought it would be the best of ideas because it had been made obvious that she didn't see eye to eye with Q. but it wouldn't matter now they were going to have this child.

"It'll be wonderful and the whole of your life will be richer," Virginia said, "and you're not to worry about one little thing, and I'm going to be the godmother and no arguments."

All the tiny niggling doubts about Q. as her husband vanished that day. It was as though they had never existed and for the first time since her marriage she forgot Paul completely. She was young and strong and quite ready to bear a child and was going to tell Q. so.

When he come home she was there in the hall to meet him; she had heard the key turning in the lock. She had a look in her big melting eyes that he had secretly missed for a little while. It dazzled him.

She walked with him up into their bedroom. "You'll never guess," she said, "I've just heard from Dr. Fisher that my test is positive."

"*What* test?" Q. asked, mystified.

"Pregnancy test!" she said, and suddenly wanted to cry. But she controlled herself. She told Q. what the doctor had said to her.

Q's expression changed from surprise to pleasure. "Well, *well*, so we've been and gone and done it, have we? It must have been that night when —"

"Don't let's go into details," she broke in, and moved over to the windows. The fog was creeping down the river. It was quite dark now in the flat. She switched on the lights. She then gave Q. a quick kiss and pulled him down on to the bed beside her. "Are you pleased?"

Q. answered excitedly. "Pleased is putting it mildly. I can't believe it. Tamara — to be a mother! It sounds fantastic. November ... December ..." He began to count the months, but as he reached the following April, Tamara interrupted him again.

"Don't let's get so far. It's all a bit much, isn't it? Ought we to have let it happen? Would you rather I went to one of these clinics and had a —"

"No, I wouldn't," he broke in before she could complete the threat, and Tamara thought he looked quite angry. But she was pleased. She gave him her widest smile. So he didn't want her to get rid of the baby — good!

"Do Father and Aunt Liz know?" he added the question.

"Yes, and they're both absolutely delighted."

He ran his fingers through his hair. He had felt tired when

he left the office — now he felt terrific. He put his arms around her and kissed her.

"Darling, you're marvellous and the news is fantastic, I must say that I'm more than pleased that *you* want it."

"You can't go on calling it 'it'," she giggled.

"Will 'it' be a boy or girl?"

"We won't know that till it's born, honey."

His brain worked overtime. "We can't live in the penthouse any more — I mean after he, she, or it arrives. Think of taking a pram up and down in a lift and walking it along the Embankment instead of in nice country air. We'll have to find something out of town."

"Okay," she said airily.

Now as they walked toward the sitting-room, Tamara felt an impish wish to tease him. "Okay, we'll have to sell the lease and *you'll* have to sell the Arrow and we'll buy a nice family car."

"Sell the Arrow," he repeated. There was a note of dismay in his voice that reached her. Suddenly she felt cool and her happiness evaporated.

But the evening was good. Her father and aunt had been invited to dinner. Mr. Whitfeld, already dubbing himself 'Grandpa', brought out a bottle of champagne to toast the coming event. Tamara was the 'prima donna' of the evening, and Aunt Liz, when she could get a word in edgeways, began to caution her niece not to smoke so much or eat the wrong things. They all laughed a lot. Tamara's pregnancy seemed to be the subject for general rejoicing in the family.

It was only when she and Q. were alone in their bedroom that night that the gaiety evaporated again. While Q. undressed he began to wonder about finance and whether or not Tamara would really appreciate all the responsibilities of motherhood. *And* if she had really meant it when she had said he would have to sell his car.

6

As THE WEEKS slipped by, it seemed to Tamara that her whole life had altered on account of the fact that she was pregnant. Her own outlook underwent a subtle change. It was almost as though she was not the same person. So much was happening — perhaps too quickly. She felt that it was all a little too soon after her marriage.

Events crowded down upon her. Her father assured her constantly that he was delighted by the idea of becoming a grandfather. Liz, enraptured, started to knit furiously. Tamara's friends seemed even more excited about the baby than she herself. But she also underwent what seemed a complete physical change. She was not well — she had always suffered from nerves and tension and now she felt worse. She often talked to one of her friends who had recently had a baby, and experienced such aggravations as morning sickness. And vain as she was, she felt particularly self-conscious because of her thickening figure. As for wanting to sleep more than usual — these things were all natural signs of her condition.

Yet somehow Tamara felt her mind was changing, as well as her body, and it was that which worried her.

"I'm just not *me* any more," she told Virginia one day when the girls were having one of their salad lunches together. "I feel odd."

The Marriots were still in their penthouse. After a family conference with her father and aunt, Tamara backed by Q. thought that it was convenient for Q. to stay in town at least for the present. They were not far from Westminster Hospital where Tam had booked a bed for her confinement. Why not enjoy her beautiful home at least for a few more months. Meanwhile she and Q. spent weekends looking for a suitable house not too far from the City. If they found it soon, they could get it ready and move when Tamara had returned from hospital and felt better able to cope.

Virginia, as usual, consoled her temperamental friend. "You'll always be *you*, Tam," she said, and her eyes were full of sincere affection. Sweet and impulsive, Tam was at times a little too introspective — yet always lovable. "You'll never really change."

"What's so good about that?" Tamara sighed, and twisted her lovely lips. "I wish I *could* be really different."

"We all like you as you are, darling. And the physical change is to be expected."

Tamara shook her head. "I've changed in other ways."

Virginia lifted an eyebrow. After a brief period of married life, Tam was bound to be restless. She was still too intense and unpredictable. Yet that emotionalism — that fervent desire to live life to the full — made her unusually attractive. That was what endeared her to her relatives and friends, and of course, particularly to Q. Now, mused Virginia, inside that beautiful young body another life was growing. Motherhood was sure to calm her down in some way. But what really worried Virginia was the fact that she was depressed these days. She seemed on excellent terms with her husband. What, then, was wrong, Virginia asked herself uneasily.

Virginia's admiration for Q. had increased. She had never quite thought him the perfect man for Tam but she had to admit he was good for her — so tolerant and good-humoured. No matter what mood Tamara was in, he had coped with it successfully.

"There isn't anything you haven't told me, is there?" Virginia asked suddenly, and received a definite answer in the negative. No, Tamara assured her, there was nothing wrong except that there were moments when she got into a 'thing' — when she just felt she couldn't come to terms with life — or her husband. So Virginia, the wise and watchful, decided that what her friend Tamara really wanted was to avoid responsibility.

Yet at times Tamara had found her attitude to Q. and their marriage a paradox — she said she didn't really want Q. to give in to her so completely. Perhaps in a perverse sort

54

of way she felt overwhelmed by his selfless loving and wanted a man who could master her, both in body and mind. Perhaps she even disliked the fact that Q. said 'yes' instead of 'no' most of the time.

Now Virginia turned her thoughts wholly to Q. "How do you think he'll enjoy being a family man?" she asked Tamara, and at once her sharp eye noted the shadow that crossed Tamara's beautiful face. But she answered casually,

"Oh, okay. He says he's looking forward to being called Daddy in due course."

"Let's hope it's a boy. I think a sportsman like Q. would adore a son," remarked Virginia.

Now Tamara grimaced and the grimace was not lost on Virginia. But she went on, "Oh no — he says he likes pretty girls and would like a daughter. He's positive she'll be a perfect dream. Of course she ought to be with two such handsome parents," Tamara added.

But this jocular remark did not entirely satisfy Virginia. Despite the fact that Q. was all kindness and so attentive, Virginia wondered if he would give up all his old habits; his sports clubs, his racing car and next winter, ski-ing? Wouldn't these two have to think twice now before they went to their usual sports-hotel in the Alps — with an infant? Perhaps they wouldn't go away this year at all. But would that suit Q. who had never, since he left University, had to miss his ski-ing, nor in the summer his gay life in some sophisticated sea resort — or on a friend's yacht.

Before she left the penthouse, Virginia stopped worrying. She pushed her fears to the back of her mind. She did regret, however, that she would not be able to help Tamara once the baby was born. At the end of April, Virginia was flying to South Africa to stay with a married cousin. It was a holiday she had long promised herself, and could not cancel. It had been arranged before she was told about Tamara's condition.

She left England at the beginning of April — a cold unattractive month. Tamara missed her friend and confidante enormously. When the ninth month came, she began to feel quite lost and lonely when Q. was not with her. She relied more and more on his love and attention.

Nowadays when she looked at herself in the mirror, she found it a comical sight. She really was like a little barrel. As to her pretty modern maternity clothes, she hated them. She would give the lot away as soon as the baby was born. She never wanted to see them again. She would never have another baby. One was enough.

One cool April evening when Q. arrived back from the City, he gave his wife the usual hug, washed his hands and returned to pour out drinks. Tamara, sitting on a high-backed chair which she preferred these days, fancied that there was amusement in his eyes as he smiled down at her.

"Do you think I look a sight?" she grimaced and flicked her long lashes at him.

"A sight? Of *course* not. You look sweet — as usual."

"Hardly your gorgeous girl with her twenty-four waist," she grumbled.

"Well, you'd be a mutation if you were on the verge of producing an infant and still had a twenty-four waist, my love," he laughed at her.

"Oh, I shall be so glad when it's over, Q.!"

"I shall, too, but I don't feel anything for you but enormous love, knowing that it's our child who has made you lose your waistline, my love."—

She felt warm and happy again, and held out a hand. He took it and sat beside her, sipping his sherry.

"When do you think you'll take a drink again, darling?"

"Well, Dr. Nye said I could have one whenever I wanted it, but I just don't."

"Never mind, darling, any day now it'll be all over and we'll open a bottle of champagne the day you come out of hospital, if not before."

"I want to feed my baby," she said suddenly.

Now Q. put down his glass. His expression changed. He couldn't deny that it was right and proper that Tamara should feed the baby but he could see in a flash what that would mean. She mightn't get back that fabulous figure so quickly and she would have to be on call at all hours of the day — even during the night (so he had heard from one of his married pals at the office). *He* recommended bottle feeding if a chap liked to have his wife around and not be absolutely tied by breast-feeding, or the nappies, and all the rest of baby paraphernalia. Q.'s rather long silence made Tamara feel suddenly uneasy.

"Don't you *want* me to feed our baby?"

"Well, it'll pin you down a bit," said Q. clearing his throat, and not wishing to say or do the wrong thing.

She bit her lip but agreed. It *would* tie them both down. It was one of those things. Indeed, it would alter their whole lives and take away some of the glamour, and most of the freedom, even after only one year of marriage. Tamara felt a sinking sensation. Then Q. put an arm around her.

"Look, darling, not to worry. I was talking to your father the other day and he said we've got to have a nurse for the baby for six months at least, no matter what it costs. I agree, don't you?"

She opened her eyes wide and looked doubtful.

"You've no idea what trained baby-nurses ask for these days, Q., darling."

"I don't intend you should economise in any way," said Q. in a lordly fashion. "Your father endorses this."

"Daddy's given me so much already."

"Well, what about me? I can cope. At the moment things are okay on the Stock Exchange. The market is still in our favour. Honestly, my pet, we needn't worry too much about cash until the baby's at least finished with feeding."

Now Tamara burst out laughing. "Will you start starving it fairly soon after that then?"

"Idiot, I mean finished with having to be fed by *you*!"

"Oh, well, then I suppose we could get hold of a nanny and perhaps an *au pair* later on."

He stood up. "I want you to have exactly what you need and I'll fall in with any plan, my love."

Now she looked up at him, her eyes starry with gratitude. How kind and generous he was! Maybe on second thoughts she wouldn't feed the baby — for Q.'s sake, really. How long would his patience last if she were instrumental in robbing him of all his old fun and companionship with her? Hundreds of babies were given bottles and did well. Tamara decided that she did not want her marriage to become *too* domestic in design. She liked gaiety and having a good time as much as Q. Their shared recreations were really just as important as their love. 'Togetherness' was, in her mind, essential.

Q. walked to the big picture-window and now stood looking over the fabulous view to which he would soon have to say goodbye. A pity — they were so happy in this delightful penthouse. They both loved the busy historic river. A baby was certainly going to make a difference. Q. alternated between being excited at the prospect of fatherhood and fearing just a little bit that it might decrease the tempo of their lives so much that boredom would crawl in. Above all *that* must not be allowed to happen. But move they would. Even Q. could see that it would be too awkward here whether they had a nurse or not to help Tam. It would be so much more simple if they had a place with even a tiny garden in which to put a pram. It could be foggy too often close to the river.

One of Q.'s friends at the office had just bought a very attractive little house with a garden in Hampstead. They seemed very pleased with it. Why not look there?

Tamara, spreading her hands to the firelight glow, spoke to him. "Q. darling, do you think our baby will inherit my nature or yours? Will it look like me and not you? There is my Russian grandmother, and our child will be an eighth Russian, you know."

That made Q. grin. He came up behind her and stroked the blonde silky head. "I'd adore to have a little Russian girl with your tempestuous beauty and your grandmother's almond-shaped eyes. You know — like that portrait in the dining-room at your father's."

"H'm, well, *I* want a boy and I hope he'll look very English like his Dad."

"My nose is too long."

"It's aristocratic. I like it."

Suddenly he pulled her out of her chair up into his embrace. The laughing was over. He began to kiss her very gently and tenderly.

"My love — still so much my love — I can't yet believe that you are going to be a mother. I'm really rather thrilled, you know."

"Me, too," she whispered, and felt warm and happy — happier than she had felt for a long time. It seemed a secure sort of contentment — far removed now from the feverish delight of their honeymoon.

She came to one definite decision. She would get rid of the Fiat. She hadn't driven while she was having the baby for all kinds of reasons and to sell it would be an economy. When Q. tried to argue that she need not economise to this extent, she was quite firm about it. Amused and gratified he accepted her decision and Tamara found that she did not really mind a bit. She was going to change. She was going to stop being extravagant and become the perfect wife and mother.

That same night, when Panay brought in one of the fish and rice dishes he cooked so well, Q. opened a bottle of champagne. Panay watched attentively and respectfully as his master uncorked the bottle. The loud 'pop' made him smile all over his triangular, golden-skinned face. He clapped his hands. He was very happy with Mr. and Mrs. Marriot and was enjoying this job to the full. What they were celebrating with the bubbling amber liquid he did not know, but he presumed it *was* a celebration, and was delighted to join in. But of course he did not understand when Mr. Marriot said, "To my almond-eyed beautiful daughter," and Mrs. Marriot laughed and raised her goblet and added, solemnly, "To my fair-haired handsome son."

7

TAMARA'S BABY WAS born in the middle of May. She had dreaded the affair but the birth was quick and easy, and Tamara was quite astonished to find that she got through without much pain or trouble.

Early one morning Q. drove her to the hospital. The baby was delivered two hours later. Soon after she made her appearance Tamara held her in her arms and looked at her with some astonishment and a lot of pleasure. This was her daughter. She weighed seven pounds and was perfect in every respect. Claire was to be her name. How wonderful!

Claire was exceptionally pretty with a golden down on her round little head, very blue eyes and quite long lashes for a new-born infant. She also had perfectly-shaped oval nails. Tamara kept looking at them in ecstasy. The child was, in fact, like a Marriot and not a Whitfeld. Tamara was pleased about that. Let my Russian blood die out, she told herself, and felt a sudden rush of patriotic desire that her daughter should grow up to be as British, sports-loving and as good as her father.

Q. was at his best during the succeeding weeks. Babies, bottles and nappies were scarcely in his line but he was enchanted by his daughter. He and Tamara had agreed to the name 'Claire' — first and foremost because it was after Q's mother, and secondly, because they looked it up in a book of names and found that it meant 'bright and clear'. Rather nice to believe these words would apply to the life of their daughter.

A week later Tamara was back in the penthouse, with a hospital nurse to attend to Claire for a few weeks. After this a Norland nanny had already been booked. In spite of the fact that Tamara's doctor, and both her husband and her father were against her doing too much too soon, her homecoming developed into one long party.

Friends and relations poured into the flat. John Whitfeld,

soon to prove himself a doting grandfather, sent the young parents a dozen cases of champagne. He could see that his son-in-law's store was rapidly dwindling.

Panay cooked furiously for all this entertaining — little dinners, cocktail parties, women's lunches. To make it perfect, beautiful weather suddenly gilded the scene. The June days were mild. The sun poured through the big windows and sparkled on the river. Q. rushed home every evening to embrace his wife and daughter. Claire sucked her thumb contentedly, and seemed to approve of her father. Tamara was as happy with her baby as the Norland nurse allowed her to be. She was apt to be possessive. Tamara's happiness was intensified because she no longer wanted to look over her shoulder at the ghosts of the past.

On rare occasions her thoughts turned to Paul. Nearly always if she heard a particular tune or nostalgic song that had once meant much to both Paul and herself. Then came the day once she was out and about again, when she met one of hers and Paul's mutual friends — Christine Shore — who worked in a boutique in Knightsbridge. Christine hailed Tamara, stopped to chat with her, congratulated her warmly on her marriage and motherhood and then asked if she ever saw Paul.

Tamara's answer was "no that's absolutely over. But how's he getting on? How's his love-life?" she had added, with a short laugh.

Christine shrugged her shoulders and said that she didn't really know, but had heard Paul and Liesel were still together. They talked casually, then parted.

Tamara walked on, her lips curling a little. Paul and his mistress — still together! A stab of jealousy, of old pain, and remembering the anguish she had suffered when Paul left her, reminded her now not very happily that she had by no means forgotten Paul.

Christine had told her he was doing well with his songs, and was in fact entering the latest for the next Eurovision Contest. Tamara fastened on that thought, and was glad for him. Then told herself firmly that his love-life didn't really interest her at all and wondered why she had ever asked about it.

At home with Q. and the baby, Paul's ghost was definitely laid. By the end of June, the Marriots left their riverside home and were installed in the new one, known as The Little House. It lay at the end of a tree-lined cul-de-sac quite near Hampstead Heath. Small, whitewashed, newly-built in the Georgian style, it was charming, with green shutters. And best of all it had a small walled garden at the back, ideal for the baby, and Tamara interested herself not only in making the house perfect but in becoming an enthusiastic gardener.

There were just the requisite number of rooms. A large double reception-room at the back with french windows leading on to the tiny lawn; three good bedrooms and a dining-room, *and* an attic which they turned into a bed-sitting room for Panay. He had insisted on coming with the family as a resident cook. He was still very devoted and very necessary.

Virginia returned from South Africa towards the end of June. Although too late for the baby's christening, she was godmother, and completely fell for the beautiful little girl. Claire was a good placid baby and Tamara wondered why she had ever feared bad nights, perpetual crying or having to be tied down to domestic chores. The nurse was efficient. Tamara was able to lead the life she and Q. had always led. At weekends they could leave the excellent nurse to manage both baby and house, with Panay to cook for them. So life for the Marriots flourished.

There was little economy, apart from the sale of the Fiat. Money flowed with extravagant regularity. Tamara never worried about finance and Q. rarely discussed it with her. He was one of those men who liked to come back from the office and forget about his job and income. Tamara gleaned only from conversation with other people and reading newspapers, that storm-clouds were, in fact, gathering over the country both politically and financially. She had grown up with a father who was ready to supply what she needed. Why worry now? Q. was very generous and only now and again Tamara saw him lift an eyebrow when she handed him one or two of her largest bills. He did venture once to ask how long she wanted to retain the services of the Norland nurse who was very expensive. Why not an *au pair*? That would be cheaper. But nothing came of these remarks. Tamara agreed in her happy-go-lucky way that she would look for a foreign girl, but felt no need to hurry or worry. She was so well satisfied with the present set-up. Everything was swinging in The Little House. She really did not want to make a change. Panay, of course, was also a big expense. There was his pay *and* his food, and he was an extravagant cook. But he was *so* good. Tamara couldn't imagine life without him now. As for Q. he liked good living as much as she did, if not more. So Panay stayed.

Nowadays, Tamara saw less of her friend Virginia. The main reason was because a new thrilling interest had suddenly entered Virginia's life. During the flight to Cape Town she met a retired Army man — Colonel Henry Randall. He was young for his age but some fifteen years older than Virginia. It proved a fateful meeting. He continued to see her while she was in South Africa and once home did not allow the friendship to peter out. In due course, the Colonel fell deeply in love with her, and she found herself responding with an ardour she thought she had lost for ever.

Tamara and Q. both liked and approved of Henry Randall. The age difference between them seemed of no account. He was a charming man, still good-looking, fit and upright. A bachelor of moderate means, his chief interest lay in horses. Virginia liked riding and had always done a lot of it herself. She took a great interest in Henry's stables which he had recently bought with the intention of starting a riding school. The property was situated near Beaconsfield and included an attractive Tudor farmhouse. Virginia was charmed by it all. Henry asked her to marry him and she accepted. Virginia's good looks and amiable disposition put an end to any wish he had had to remain unmarried. They announced their engagement soon after Claire's first birthday. The marriage was to take place later in the summer.

It was the best thing that could have happened to Virginia, Tamara knew that, but she knew also how much she would miss the close friendship which they had enjoyed for so long. Things between them could not in future be quite the same. But Virginia argued, "They will be *just* the same, darling. Henry and I will come up to town and use your spare room, and you and Q'll come down and spend weekends with us. It's just wonderful that you and Q., and Henry and I, all like each other. We do get on well, don't we?"

"I'm not sure your nice Henry approves of me," Tamara said with a slight laugh.

"How can you say such a thing! He thinks you're one of the most attractive girls he's ever met."

"Except you!" Another laugh from Tamara. Virginia laughed with her. "Oh, I'm so glad it's all happened," Tamara added, "I'm sure Henry will make you a marvellous husband."

"And is all well with you, darling?"

"I'm having a fantastic time," was Tamara's airy reply.

"I know that. Are you as truly happy and fulfilled as you expected to be with Q?"

"Yes, everything's great with us, Virginia darling. And I adore Claire. She's made us both completely happy."

Why, Virginia asked herself, did she doubt the truth of this? Tamara had not mentioned Paul's name for a long time. She seemed to have settled down at last.

But Virginia had recently had a long chat with Aunt Liz and this had slightly alarmed her. Naturally they had discussed Tamara. Aunt Liz said, "Tamara's father and I are both pleased Tammy married Q. He's such a very nice young man and John thinks the world of him as a business man. He's so clever with investments. John relies on his judgment. But there is this other side of Q. which perhaps John doesn't see as clearly as I do. He's a bit weak with Tammy. She calls the tune and he dances to it. They spend money like water. In confidence, my dear Virginia, when Q. was talking to John the other night he let out that he was behind with his tax-payments. John told him not to be foolish and to keep the spending under stricter control. You know, a lot of people are worried about what might happen to us all. We have a Labour Government and we hear all these sinister warnings on T.V. *and* read in the papers about capital gains and transfers, and this and that and how none of us will be able to leave anything to our children because of death duties, and so on — "

Miss York paused to sigh, then continued, "It's really a bit worrying when two young people like Tamara and Q. behave like millionaires, which they are not, and never count the cost. Sometimes they amaze me the way they carry on. Mind you, for one thing, I blame our sweet Tam for keeping that expensive nurse so long. Tam does practically no work, except for a little washing and ironing. She always manages to get someone to do *something* for her. It isn't good for her. What about the *future*? Am I just stupidly worried, my dear?"

Virginia shook her head. She agreed that sooner or later there might have to be an end to the way Tamara and Q. were living. Virginia shared Aunt Liz's forebodings. It wasn't even any good warning Tam about the insecurity of the whole country. She and Q. had already lined up a super summer holiday in the Seychelles, in a party, including one of Q.'s wealthy clients and his wife. No talk of a quiet English sea-side hotel with little Claire. That wouldn't be in either Q.'s or Tam's line.

"I wish," Aunt Liz sighed, "if you ever get a chance, Virginia, you'd just murmur to Tam that her father is not happy about the financial future. They must stop spending capital. It's most unwise."

Virginia came away from Eaton Terrace realising that her private fears for Tam had merely been echoed by Miss York. She was happy enough but living in a fool's paradise. Yet today, sitting in the little sunlit garden of the Marriot's home, Virginia found it hard to worry too much about her much-loved friend. She was bubbling over with good spirits.

It must be wonderful to be born with such a carefree nature, Virginia reflected. But that reckless streak — and both Tam and Q. possessed it — that was dangerous! Virginia had stayed silent while Tamara talked of a weekend in Paris if Q. could get away. He wanted to meet a particular friend who drove an Alfa-Romeo. Tam was disinterested in cars but shopping in Paris might be fun, she said, her eyes dancing. With the pound falling and the franc rising, Virginia thought, troubled, it was typical of Tam, and Q. ought to curb his own inclination towards over-spending. But it was not her business. How could she interfere? It makes me feel Henry and I are elderly and stodgy, Virginia reflected.

The Norland nurse, who had just taken Claire on the Heath, now returned with the little girl. She was being wheeled into the garden in her small push-chair. Virginia's attention was riveted on her god-daughter. Beautiful, Claire certainly was, with her golden head a shade darker than her father's and a good deal more curly, and her lovely long-lashed eyes that were no longer blue, but growing like Q.'s — grey, flecked with hazel.

"Just look at all those toothy-pegs!" exclaimed Virginia, entranced when Claire smiled at her, "I see a new one every time I come."

Tamara picked her daughter out of the push-chair, and seated her on her lap. Claire was quite heavy these days.

"You're going to be a bigger girl than your Mama," she murmured, and pressed her lips against the child's cheek which was as glowing and pink as a sun-kissed peach.

How adorable she was! Really — it was bliss being a mother.

Before Virginia said goodbye to the family at The Little House she decided that she need not worry about Tam and Q. Perhaps Aunt Liz herself, was unnecessarily worried — even about the question of money. But about one thing,

Virginia was quite satisfied — Tam no longer seemed to remember Paul's existence.

Virginia at dinner with Henry that night told him that all was well with the Marriots.

It was on the tip of Henry's tongue to say "Early days, my dear," but being a cautious man, he said nothing of the kind. But enchanted though he always was by Tamara — and what man was not — he did not altogether trust her to settle down for ever.

She was not like his Virginia — not at all.

8

ONE NIGHT TOWARDS the end of October, Tamara and Q. received an unexpected visit from John Whitfeld. They were just drinking coffee when Tamara's father arrived. She was pleasantly surprised, but after their first hug she drew back and was less pleased because she thought he looked dreadfully tired and even a little colourless. However, he gave her his usual fond smile and asked tenderly after his granddaughter. He also remarked that The Little House on this autumn night was delightful. Scarlet and yellow dahlias coloured the small garden, and the button-chrysanthemums, rose-pink, with a background of purple Michaelmas daisies, made a splendid show. Mr. Whitfeld congratulated his daughter.

"You've turned into quite a little gardener, my sweetie."

'It's not only me, it's our gardener as well," said Tamara modestly.

Q. who had watched his father-in-law manoeuvre his big

Rolls up their rather narrow entrance, said, "We really ought to widen the drive especially for you."

Mr. Whitfeld smiled and shook his head. Seated comfortably in his favourite armchair, he thanked Tamara for the coffee and Benedictine, and began to look tired and depressed again.

"I doubt if I'll be able to afford to run the Rolls much longer," he said.

"Why not, Daddy?" Tamara was horrified. Something must be very wrong. She was quick to guess that her father was upset because things were taking a turn for the worse in the City. Q. had in fact spoiled their dinner by talking non-stop about the serious decline of business. The Stock Exchange was in real trouble. Q. did not as a rule discuss the office with her. Why depress her? Especially, he had once told her, as she had so little interest in stocks and shares. She had felt more and more gloomy tonight as he warned her of impending world recession.

Now she seated herself on a stool at her father's feet and laid a hand on his knee.

"Darling, don't say you've only come to spread doom and gloom. I've had enough for one night from Q."

He ruffled her hair and gave a faint smile. "Darling, I don't want to be gloomy but I've a lot on my mind, and I'm sure Q. has too. So many of us may find it necessary to sell things like large luxury cars, and cut down expenses generally. One has to listen to what we're told from most governmental departments about affairs in this country, and treat what they say with a certain amount of respect, no matter whether we're Left or Right."

Q. looked from his wife to his father-in-law, removed his cigar from his mouth and glanced uneasily at the fine pale ash. He felt a bit guilty because he hadn't so far told his wife to cut down. Mr. Whitfeld continued.

"As a rule I'm an optimist, you know that, and I've always told you that I believe in the young enjoying their lives as fully as they can and *while* they can. But I fear, Tam, that we *are* possibly heading for disaster. The market today has dropped to its lowest. The pound is depreciating. It's grim. I don't say we're at rock bottom yet, but this world recession and lack of confidence are just about rocking the boat."

"Only too true," muttered Q. and sat down with a deep sigh, and stretched his long legs in front of him.

Tamara felt suddenly frightened. She'd never known either of these two — her husband or her father — to be quite so grave or apprehensive. Gradually the frightened sensation developed into one of guilt. She knew that she was extravagant (not that Q. wasn't almost as bad). They encouraged each other to spend money. But she was intelligent and introspective enough to realise that sometimes her conduct had, perhaps, been irresponsible. She didn't give enough thought to the more serious aspects of life. And was that because she hadn't the courage to face up to trouble? No — courage was not what she lacked. It was foresight. She never liked looking too far ahead. She lived only for the moment. And because she had for so long been happy and pampered, she had accepted such things as her right. At the time of her mother's death she had known grief, but she had never been as close to her mother as she was to her father.

Nina Whitfeld had been a beauty in her day. Her husband had idolised her, but she had inherited the worst traits of jealousy and vanity from her Russian mother. She never gave the love and tenderness to Tamara that Tamara lavished on her own small daughter. John Whitfeld had suffered a stormy few years of misunderstanding and unhappiness with his attractive wife. Her attraction for him had waned in consequence, and latterly only compassion remained. Then Mrs. Whitfeld developed an incurable disease which sent her to her grave when she was still only in her early forties.

It was Tamara's unhappy love-affair with Paul which was the first thing to bring her face to face with personal tragedy.

Tonight, however, as she listened to the two men telling her, each in turn, about the shadow that hovered over most of the moneyed families in the country, she told herself she had better sit up and take notice.

She turned from one to the other. Her father's fingers were still threading through her silky hair with a kind of protective tenderness which was comforting. But her husband wasn't looking at her, and suddenly she wanted him to. She needed to find reassurance in those handsome eyes which so far had never failed her. But Q. was examining the share-index in the *Financial Times*, completely absorbed in it and Tamara felt suddenly quite absurdly cast out — abandoned by him — left to drown in these dangerous financial waters alone and unaided.

Her father kept on talking. "I have to admit, my darling, that our own family shares — mine *and* the ones I made over to you when you got married — have more than halved in value."

"I didn't know," said Tamara in a whisper.

"Of course you didn't. Why should you? Q. and I never wanted you to bother your little head about such things. You were never one to care about the Stock Exchange; eh?" He smiled indulgently.

She nodded, and bit her lip. "You make me feel ashamed. Perhaps I ought to have paid more attention to what was happening."

"No, no, of course not," Mr. Whitfeld tried to soothe her. "And I don't want to suggest that you should immediately sell your house, pawn your jewellery or do anything drastic, my darling girl. But you must realise it's necessary for you to be a little more economical — a little less careless with your money. I couldn't raise a penny more for you if you got into debt. This ghastly increase in taxation means the whole lot of us have got to pipe down."

Now Tamara lifted her beautiful head and turned to Q. He was still immersed in his paper.

"Q. have I been absolutely awful? Am I always the one to run up the bills?"

Immediately he dropped the *Financial Times* and held out

a hand to her. "Of course not, darling. Where money is concerned it's up to me to call the tune."

"Well, *your* tune's a bit on the high note. It's not only mine, is it?" she asked on a slightly reproachful note, then laughed and turned back to her father. Her lashes were wet. She was near to crying. "Q's very generous, Daddy. He's never said 'no' to anything I've wanted. It *is* I who have been the most extravagant."

"Don't let's start trying to find out which one of us has spent the most money," said Mr. Whitfeld, and his tired eyes looked at her with great tenderness. "Just let's agree that we'll think twice before we dip into any more capital. You see, my darling Tammy, what with crippling interest rates, *plus* inflation, and a total lack of confidence in the business world as regards the future, we must in the long run feel the pinch. I'm sure Q. hasn't told you this but we're even finding it quite hard to pay office expenses. Our partners all share in those, so it affects Q.'s income as well as mine. There's such a gigantic tax on unearned incomes, *and* so much capital tied up in the business — we're all short of cash flow. You do understand, don't you, Tam?"

Tamara stood up. She understood only too plainly. And suddenly her lovely little house and this warm lamplit room, full of flowers, and the full life she had been leading with all its luxuries and amusements, seemed to cave in, as though a bomb had demolished it. But she did not lack courage — or humour — and she exhibited both these virtues now. She looked from Q. to her father and held out a hand to each of them.

"Take hold of me and tie me up, you two. I need tethering. I want to be a prisoner so that I can't get near another shop. Q. we'll cancel our next trip aboard and I'll get rid of that Norland nurse at once. Then I'll ring up the agency who supplies *au pairs*, and tell them to find me one at once. I'll share the job of running the house, and Claire — with her."

"I don't think you need to be as drastic as that —" began Q. but she interrupted.

71

"Now don't try and make things easy for me. It's quite plain from what Daddy's just said that I have been living in a sort of cocoon and you've both wrapped it round me. But I'm just not going on as I was. I want to share whatever's coming with both of you."

John Whitfeld looked at his daughter's face, and the strength that he suddenly saw in the set of her lips and the sparkle in her eyes both surprised and delighted him. "That's my girl!" he exclaimed.

"And that's *my* girl, too," said Q. and put an arm around Tamara and murmured close to her ear, "I love you for being so good about it."

For some reason or other this annoyed Tamara. She moved away from Q. "Don't! Why pretend I'm doing something big just because I realise how stupid I've been. But I assure you and Daddy I'm determined to economise."

"Darling, it is not that. I just don't want you to feel you are the one to give up things — " began Q. but she interrupted,

"I'm not quite as irresponsible as Daddy and you think. I repeat — I shall tell nurse in the morning that she must go. *I* can tackle Claire. And there is Panay to think about, too. He costs us one hell of a lot. He'll have to be given a month's notice."

Panay at that moment knocked on the door, and entered, his face bland and smiling as ever, tray in hand.

"Take coffee away. Bring whisky," he said.

Nobody spoke. After he had bowed and retired, Q. rubbed the back of his head, and threw Tamara a quizzical smile. "Oh, come off it, love, do you think we ought to sack him? He is such a treasure. One doesn't find a Panay everywhere."

"I agree, but I can tackle the cooking and save twenty-five pounds a week," said Tamara firmly. "You'll have to put up with an amateur, that's all, and I'll make a study of haute cuisine instead of haute couture — " she giggled.

"But you must have help in a house like this," put in Mr.

Whitfeld. "Even if you get a good *au pair*, she won't cook if she's engaged as Claire's nurse."

Tamara's large dark eyes sparkled at him, "And how do you think we're going to be able to go on paying and keeping Panay if things are as bad as you say? I presume Q. is short of money now, and like you, Daddy, diving into capital. That can't go on just to allow me to live in luxury."

Q. admitted this reluctantly.

"Come, come, there's enough left that you need not be so drastic," exclaimed Mr. Whitfeld, smiling at this new thrifty-minded daughter, "you must keep some kind of domestic help, darling."

Tamara glanced at the tray with the whisky decanter, syphon, and beautiful set of crystal goblets which had been Elizabeth's wedding present. Then Tamara turned to a silver-framed photograph of herself with her baby in her arms, and muttered, "Poor little Claire — she didn't realise we were all going to be on National Assistance when she entered our lives."

"National Assistance, my foot," growled Q. "Things will take a turn for the better."

Again Tamara interrupted, her cheeks pink from the warmth of her feelings.

"No! Don't soft-soap me any more, darling, *please*. Daddy's told me the facts and you can't suddenly start to smooth me down by saying everything will be all right, I refuse to be a sort of fiddler while Rome burns, and I insist on starting an economy campaign. I'm not going to be diverted until things really do take a turn for the better — *if* they ever do!" she added, and rolled her eyes dramatically.

They all laughed. Secretly Q. was proud of Tamara, and not a little relieved that she had taken the bad news so well. He didn't like it just now when she drew away from him and spoke so curtly. He was also disturbed by his own depressing thoughts. National Assistance — no, but what about luxury cars? Nobody had mentioned the Arrow. It stood out a mile that he might have to sell his powerful, petrol-draining racing

73

car if he were to do *his* share of 'cutting down'. He could hardly bear the idea. The Arrow was really one of the great joys of his life. He recalled his father-in-law's warning that it might be difficult to sell an expensive car, and felt a certain sense of relief. But not for long. Of course *someone* would eventually buy it. Even now, when petrol was such a price and world conditions so frightening, one must not forget the possibility that a rich car-lover from one of the Arab States might like the Arrow. Then Q. put it right out of his mind.

Mr. Whitfeld refused the whisky his daughter had offered him. The Benedictine was enough for him, he said, besides which he had promised his sister he wouldn't be late home.

"She's been lecturing me about going out in the night air because of my damned chest. Dammit, the woman's making me feel old, with all her care and coddling."

"Well, I intend to start feeling old," Tamara grinned at him, "I've been acting the baby far too long."

Good nights were said and kisses exchanged.

When Q. opened the front door for his father-in-law, John Whitfeld said, "See you at the office in the morning, Q. Don't let your young woman take too much on her shoulders just because she feels she *ought* to. And you, Tammy, kiss my grand-daughter for me, and don't worry about *her*. It'll be a different world when she's your age, and could even be a better one. One never knows."

Tamara gave her father a special hug.

She went up to her bedroom and telephoned Virginia. Q. was still downstairs. He had a letter of sympathy to write to a friend who had just lost his wife in a car accident. Tamara told Virginia about this catastrophe.

"It makes my blood run cold every time Q. goes out in the Arrow. I hope he'll sell it."

Virginia's calm voice answered,

"I shouldn't worry, dear. He's a fine driver. How did your evening with Papa go?"

Tamara gave Virginia a résumé of the depressing conversation with her husband and her father.

"I'm not surprised," was Virginia's comment, "I know you never read the *Financial Times*, but I often take a look at it. I suppose it's because Bob used to like a flutter on the Stock Exchange and I got used to discussing share prices with him. And, of course, what little he had to leave me was in shares. Fortunately most of them went up high before this inflation, and I sold the lot. Now Henry advises me to keep it all in the bank. That will be — or should be — safe."

"You're lucky. From what I've been told, Daddy and Q. are far from feeling safe."

"Of course the Stock Exchange has been hit," Virginia agreed. "I don't know much about Q.'s affairs, but if I know Uncle John I'm sure he'll tackle the situation."

"I'm not so sure, Virginia. Darling, I've never seen him look so upset or hand out so many grim warnings. Between them those two tonight almost made me feel sorry we've brought another human being into this mad bad world."

A laugh from Virginia. "You know that's nonsense. You wouldn't be without my god-daughter for anything in the world. Is she okay?"

"Very much so. Nothing wrong with Claire but I've got to do a lot of planning for our future. And my first move is to sack the Norland nanny tomorrow and find a less costly *au pair* and I'll help mind Claire more myself, even if it ties me down."

"Are things really so bad as that?"

"M'm. I think I ought to get rid of Panay too."

"No, *not Panay*! He's unique and he adores his job. It'll break his heart if he has to leave."

"Well, we can't really afford him any more. Q. says he's going to halve the amount we drink, too. Wine only when we entertain, and the odd sherry before dinner, and so on. And if things really get as bad as Daddy prophesies, we might have to sell The Little House. Daddy's given it to us, I know, but he's paying a big mortgage for us. I think it's our duty to sell up and repay him."

An instant's silence from Virginia, then she said, "Darling,

I don't think you need go to such extremes. Besides, all this cutting down won't suit you at all —"

"I don't like you to say that," Tamara spoke quite crossly. "You all seem to think I enjoy being wrapped in cotton wool or something, but I'm quite capable of facing up to reality and doing my bit when times are bad."

"I'm sure you are," said Virginia. "Don't get me wrong, honey. You've always had guts."

"Well, my Russian blood plus my British phlegm are both up in arms," said Tamara with a bleak laugh, "and perhaps it will do me a lot of good having to put up with a few hardships. Certainly, Q. and I can't go on having everything we want without counting the cost. Virginia — What do you think would happen if the firm did go smash?"

"It won't. Whitfelds are big stockbrokers The few firms that have been hammered were smaller and less cautious, I'm sure."

"We'll see. Anyhow I thought I'd let you know that I was going to start my economy campaign as from tomorrow."

"Then I shan't come and lunch with you any more if I'm only going to be given a poached egg," announced Virginia.

At this they both giggled and their normal exchange of humour and the understanding that had made them such close friends for so long, was restored. Just before Tamara rang off, she said, "Incidentally, after Daddy left us, Q. made a tremendous fuss of me and said that he'd work his fingers to the bone before he let me give up my particular luxuries. He was really rather sweet."

"He's always sweet to you."

"But I'll tell you one odd thing, Virginia, not one word was said about the Arrow. My adoring husband won't be all that anxious to say goodbye either to his car or some of his other favourite sports. I know."

"Naturally not, but I'm sure he'd sell the Arrow before he'd let *you* make any great sacrifices."

"H'm," said Tamara, sighed and added, "oh, it's all such a bore. Goodbye, Virginia darling."

That ended the conversation.

Later, in their bedroom, Q. again touched on the subject of the recession and its consequences. Tamara was sitting against her pillows, mirror in hand, wiping night-cream from her face. She was naked and very lovely, Q. thought.

She said, "This sort of affair makes one nervous about all sorts of things that one hasn't even questioned before. For instance, this cream I use is horribly expensive. Up to now I've hardly noticed the price. I shall have to mend my ways and live in the supermarkets, won't I, darling?" and she put down mirror and cream pot and gazed sadly at Q. from beneath her fabulous lashes.

Q. was sitting on the edge of the bed, looking not at his wife, but at a sore toe. Now he glanced up. "Have you got a bit of plaster, my love?"

She grimaced at him, "You'll find a tin of air-strip in the cupboard over the basin in the bathroom. But did you hear what I *said*?"

"About your having to use cheap face-cream — yes — but I honestly don't think you need panic to this extent."

"Well, I shall," she almost snapped.

Q. gave a protesting laugh. "Darling, really that's nonsense. Papa merely cautioned us to go easy. We're not bankrupt."

"But we might be soon. You know better than I do how bad things are at the office.

"I admit it's somewhat devastating at the moment, but I can't believe things won't improve."

"Then you're more optimistic than Daddy."

"I hope I am. I thought the old boy was very down in the mouth tonight."

"It isn't like him. That's what worries me. Besides he stated categorically that neither of you was earning a penny because the expenses of running the firm, apart from anything else, are so high and with nothing much coming in."

Q. moved along the bed towards his wife, took her hands and dropped a kiss on each palm.

"M'm, I like the smell of that cream, and you look gorgeous with or without clothes, my love."

"I won't be buying new models any more, either."

Q.'s handsome eyes twinkled at her. His wife was really looking particularly attractive, he thought, even with that greasy little face. She had beautiful features, and those eyes — those dark dramatic eyes — he couldn't resist them. Now he took her in his arms.

"You look like a little girl," he tumbled her blonde hair, and pressed a long kiss on her lips, "I do adore you, Tam. Don't start giving everybody in the house notice and depriving yourself of your comforts — not yet, anyhow. I couldn't bear it. They're not important."

"I agree, but Claire is important. Whatever's left of our money in the long run must be used for her. Do you know Q. in her bath tonight she put up her little fists and beat them on my arm and actually said, Mum, Mum, for the first time. I was *thrilled*."

"You're quite a girl," he said, and kissed her again. "An astonishing girl! All this year I've thought you were a marvellous wife, now you're a marvellous mother. Yet you still look such a child, yourself. But darling, I agree with you — we've both got to give up a lot for Claire and make sure she doesn't suffer."

Tamara nodded. Later, she lay in his arms, enjoying the warmth and security that his love-making always afforded her, but at the same time she felt slightly resentful.

He hadn't yet *mentioned* any necessity to sell his own car.

9

Two years went by.

During this period of time Tamara and Q. were quite happy, and Claire was the great link. They both adored the little girl who as she grew older was as engaging as she was lovely. Both of them devoted as much time as possible to her.

But Mr. Whitfeld was still secretly worried about his daughter and son-in-law. He only hoped that everything at The Little House was as perfect as it appeared.

True, Tamara had carried out her promise to *try* and be less extravagant, and his heart had gone out to her when she came to him one day and told him she had actually saved a few pounds and intended to put them into the Post Office Savings for Claire. He had teased her.

"Jolly good. Not quite a stockbroker's job but might prove even more fruitful in the long run than any stocks or shares."

On the whole Q. spent little on himself and only what was necessary on his family — apart from the moderate drinking, smoking and few luxuries still left to him. But it seemed to Mr. Whitfeld that they were still doing too much entertaining, although he knew they were forced to make a return as they themselves accepted so many invitations.

"Oh well," John Whitfeld said to his sister when they discussed the couple, "I'm sure Q.'s sensible and knows how to tackle my little love of a daughter, and I don't think they're really hitting the high spots like they used to do, so why worry?"

Tamara, however, worried rather more about life than he imagined, and as world tension increased, she took more interest in it and in how it affected her own little world. She thought more about her husband and child, and less about herself. She was almost too busy these days to look back at the past, or think any more about Paul. It was funny she thought, how a lot of hard work could help a human being to concentrate on the present. She began to feel that her feverish life with him had been only a dream — utterly unreal.

As time went on, marriage and motherhood had given Tamara more sense of responsibility, and matured her. She became in many ways a different Tamara. With the exodus of the Norland nanny and the arrival of Eilie, a young Finnish *au pair* girl, Tamara also assumed more responsibility and care for Claire's upbringing. Once Claire said goodbye to babyhood and became a little girl, it was not so easy for Tamara to get away. She had to refuse invitations and stay at home, baby-watching, when Eilie was out. Eilie studied English and attended meetings and lectures with her compatriots. Then there was the problem of running the domestic side of the house and the kitchen. The latter occupied Tamara's mind constantly. She did her own shopping and the ironing with Eilie.

But Panay, the treasured Filipino, had gone. He had wept at the parting, but he needed money and the Marriots could no longer afford him. Anyhow he was shortly returning to his own country. So Tamara had now to put up with Mrs. Taylor — the elderly daily help — who came to The Little House three times a week. Mrs. Taylor was untidy and unpunctual, and often drove Tamara to distraction, but at least she was amiable and could cook a little so was able to leave a few dishes ready for Tamara to warm up for Q.'s dinner.

Obedient to her firm intention to learn to become a good cook herself, Tamara attended a few classes. Aunt Liz, who knew so much about cuisine, was always ready to help and advise.

So Tamara battled on — torn between the occasional wish to go on having a wonderful time without counting the cost, and buckling down to this new sober life.

At times when she was depressed she tried to tell herself her troubles were infinitesimal compared with the gigantic convulsions now shaking Europe — and indeed, the world. As for England there were strikes, inflation, Parliamentary disputes, a general sense of insecurity. So much that was bad, but it was still England, and Tamara and Q. had long since decided not to allow anyone to say a word against their country.

One day at the end of July, the curtain which had dropped between Paul and herself, was suddenly lifted in an unexpected way. It was as though she found herself acting in a play — a fresh scene, and with fresh actors. It had nothing to do with The Little House, or her husband and child.

Q. had to drive up to the Lake District to see one of John Whitfeld's clients to whom he was a trustee. He looked after this old lady's money and did not at the moment want to take the journey, so Q. volunteered to go up to Kendal and return in two days' time.

He wanted Tamara to spend most of her time with her father and aunt, but a telephoned invitation from Q.'s friend, Chris St. John, altered the plans. Chris had arrived in London. When he heard that he had missed Q. he sounded very disappointed. He had wanted to see him, and immediately he heard that Tamara was alone, asked her to dine out with him.

Tamara accepted. She liked Chris and they hadn't seen him for some long time. Eilie was quite capable of taking care of herself and Claire. It wouldn't be the first time, and Tamara had a sudden strong wish to get away from the domestic scene. Chris, as she well remembered when they had seen him in Cannes, was good fun. His prowess as a yachtsman had always endeared him to Q. but he really wasn't like him in other ways.

He was a bit of a playboy. Q. when he first left University had what he called 'been around', but settled down to the sober days of hard work very quickly. Chris had never worked and was too rich, being the only son of a millionaire American father, who loved the English and who had sent Chris to Eton. It was there he had first met Q. Their mutual love of the sea and all the sports had drawn them together. But Tamara remembered Q. saying they were never really close. They were fundamentally different. Chris was good-looking

81

and amusing. He had never married and Q. in a heart-to-heart with Tamara one day had talked of him and said, "I like Chris a lot but too much money has spoiled him. There were always too many girl-friends and too much Bourbon on ice! My old Etonian chum is Americanised. He just takes the odd holiday in Beaulieu. He's got another home in Florida, and a ranch in California."

"It sounds good, and I found him great fun," Tamara had laughed.

She didn't change that opinion when she met him again.

He called for her in a blue Ferrari and drove her from Hampstead to the West End. "Gorgeous car," Tamara murmured, and snuggled down happily, while Chris made all the right remarks about her looking lovelier than ever, and what a break it was for him to find her free to go out with him. Having asked for news of Q. and listened to all that Tamara had to tell him about Claire and life in general, he eventually had to ask about the Arrow.

"That was a peach of a car. I remember admiring it when old Q. first turned up in it when I was living in London before I ever met you, or knew he was going to get married."

Tamara stole a look at him. Then when he turned and smiled down at her, she thought how like schoolboys these Americans were — big, broad, chubby-faced — and this one was rather endearing with his thick reddish curls and clear blue eyes and the sort of light coloured linen suit and flowing tie that the Americans favoured in summer. She anticipated a delightful evening. She only wished Chris wouldn't harp on cars. She had enough of that with Q. Chris was in love with his Ferrari and it made her a trifle guilty to remember that she had just been told by Q. that at long last his Arrow was up for sale. And he would sell it, she knew, not only for the sake of economy, but because of her dislike of speed.

The Ferrari was very luxurious and it was nice being driven in it tonight to the New Berkeley where they were to dine.

Tomorrow Chris was flying back to Florida to visit his parents. He had brought his car over to London and was leaving it in his garage until his return, as he intended to have another session over here before he went back to the South of France.

Dinner was excellent. Tamara enjoyed every one of the dishes he ordered for her — and the expensive wine. But in a while she was frankly bored. Why could she never find someone to go out with who was on her wave-length and could talk about the things that interested *her*? Chris, like Q., had small interest in good music and his favourite author was certainly not Shakespeare. She sighed and wondered if she'd go home early. Then he told her that he intended to take her on to a party to which he had been invited. It was to be held in a penthouse in a block of flats not far from the Albert Hall. It had a wonderful view of the Park, Chris said, and way beyond it. She'd love it. There was a studio there, too. The hostess was an old girl-friend of his, married now to a painter called Laurence Gregg. Francoise used to model for some of the top artists when she was living in Paris. Laurence, her husband, was described by Chris as 'quite a fella' and a successful artist.

"Bit peculiar his paintings, but he sells them. I'm not sure if I like them. Seems to turn the loveliest women into the queerest looking girls. His wife, Francoise, who'd turn any man on — you know — piquante, black hair, blue eyes — is typically French and a beauty, but he did the damnedest thing with her face. It'll probably be hung in the Royal Academy. They say it's bound to be a wow. The critics who've seen it raved, but Laurence did not do her justice. I reckon she doesn't much like it, but she wouldn't tell him so. She's very fond of him."

"And he of her?"

"I reckon so." Chris smiled down at Tamara, "But Laurie's a funny one. I wouldn't say he makes the sort of husband Q. does — all for his one and only. Laurie is rather one for all."

He laughed heartily at his own joke. Tamara joined in.

"Artistic gentlemen are like that," was her gay comment, but she twisted her lips as she remembered Paul.

Chris's remarks about his friends interested Tamara. She was even more interested when she reached the penthouse. The long windows looked over a glittering panorama of London — a fascinating view. By the time they arrived, the party was in full swing. Tamara didn't seem to recognise anybody there. It was certainly a motley crowd. One or two women wore long smart evening skirts — others were in short dresses, and there were the usual members of the younger set, in tattered-looking patched trousers, and a fantastic variety of tops. They rather resembled a lot of raggle-taggle gypsies, Tamara decided, and was suddenly aware that she had never worn those sort of clothes. She was getting older — in her twenties! She grimaced. So many of the girls here tonight seemed to be younger than herself. How awful, she thought, Paul used to call me 'baby'. He wouldn't, any more.

The thought of Paul was with her again — larger than life. This was like one of his studio parties. Not so luxurious, of course, good coffee and cheap eats. Paul had had no money then. But here tonight there was a bar, a waiter, and trays full of smoked salmon sandwiches and every other delicacy. Obviously most of the guests had come to supper. No doubt Chris had also been invited, but had preferred to take her out to dinner and be alone with her for a while.

Then Tamara was introduced to Laurence Gregg. She was immediately impressed. He was not very tall but he looked strong, and had a painter's strong spatulate fingers. She could imagine him drawing one of those thick thumbs across a smear of paint, on the canvas. His eyes were piercing — the eyes of a visionary — clear cool grey with very black pupils. His was an aesthetic face but contradictory. He had a red sensual mouth, and as he took her hand and looked down at her she felt that sensuality flow from him and envelope her like a warm cloud.

"I'm so pleased you could come. Chris told me all about you. You must be Tamara — lovely Russian name!"

"My grandmother was Russian."

"I'm not surprised. You have Slavonic eyes. I'm going to

Moscow before the summer ends. I want to see the Kremlin and do some painting there. But I don't need to look for a beautiful female Muscovite. I've got one here, right now, in my studio."

He held her hand longer than he need and smiled down at her closely. She found herself smiling in return. They exchanged amusing remarks that brought them into close contact almost at once. Funny, Tamara thought, how you need speak only a few words to some man and be immediately drawn into the circle of his understanding, and he into yours.

Laurence took Tamara off immediately, away from the reception-room where the younger ones had started to dance to a beguiling tune from a tape recorder. Tam found herself alone with the painter in a large empty studio. "I want you to see some of my work. I specialise in beautiful women. Will you join the gallery?"

"Oh, of course," she laughed.

But it was all a little fast and furious and she was suddenly conscious of the fact that she was no longer used to this sort of atmosphere. She had become so domesticated. This unconventional exciting sort of life — led by people like Laurence and Francoise Gregg — was on an entirely different plane from the one Tamara had now grown used to.

A little dazed, she followed Laurence around the studio, looking at what he described as 'his gallery'. He pointed out the largest and latest portrait. His wife, he told Tamara, but she didn't like it. She complained that he had given her a mean and hungry look.

"Of course she *is* mean, and always hungry," he added casually, which remark slightly offended Tamara. It was no way for a man to speak about his wife, but perhaps that was the way he saw Francoise. The first portrait he had painted of her had been hung in the Academy, but this, Laurence assured Tamara, was a far better piece of work.

Tamara stared at it. She had been greeted at the door by Francoise and thought her attractive. This was a peculiar likeness of her in all conscience. The colouring was glorious

— outstanding shades of coppery-red and brown and blue brilliant eyes.

Tamara stared at Francoise. The girl on this canvas was curiously vulpine, lips parted showing little pointed teeth, and with that sharp nose and tawny hair.

"I like wolves," Laurence said suddenly, as though he could read Tamara's thoughts.

Halfway round the studio, he stopped and turned to stare with his cold piercing eyes at Tamara. He was intrigued. He had been bored until she arrived. It was not just her beauty that attracted him, although beautiful she was. It was the extraordinary expression of sadness in those huge dark eyes, and the tender curve of her lips. He imagined that any man who kissed Tamara would want, crazily, to kiss again and drown in her tears. He would like to paint her as a suffering madonna.

The colour of her dress was right — that wonderful yellow, with a plunge line just showing the curve of creamy breasts. Her hair was exquisite — golden — almost the same colour as her dress. And how small she was! Laurence felt a strong desire to span her waist with both his big strong hands.

She felt uncomfortable under his steady scrutiny. "Let's go back and watch the dancing," she said. "Of course, I think your paintings are too *marvellous.*"

"And I think you are marvellous, and sad, and intriguing. Also you have made some very intelligent remarks about my work."

"Oh, I'm not sad but I'm *very* intelligent!" Tamara exclaimed with a high-pitched laugh. He recognised the nervous quality in her and wondered what was wrong with this girl. He must find out more about her from Chris.

"I *must* paint you!" he said, "I swear I'll make you as exquisite as you are."

"Not as a little wolf?" she teased him.

"Not as a little wolf — as a little tender lamb, perhaps."

She began to laugh again, but to her astonishment and some dismay, he pulled her into his arms and kissed her with a passion she had never before experienced. It left her stunned. She tried to resist, yet felt herself relaxing, and hating herself for it. She was even frightened, not of Laurence, but because his sudden impertinent, intimate attack upon her, roused instead of angered her. The thought of dear gentle Q. hardly entered her mind — nor the fact that she was a wife and mother. This was how Paul used to behave — at one moment he would be talking about his work, or criticising her because she had said something he didn't like, and in the next instant he would catch hold of her, tangle her hair in his fingers and close her mouth with kisses. Primitive men — Laurence and Paul. And even while Laurence kissed her breath away, Tamara remembered that Chris had told her that Laurence Gregg was a 'great fella', who gave half his income away to young artists who were failures. He was unusual — mixed-up, and terribly attractive, Tamara decided, still dismayed by her own response.

At length Laurence drew his lips away and caught a handful of her hair — so like Paul although there was nothing really of Paul about this brilliant dominant man.

"You'll let me paint you, won't you?" Laurence demanded rather than asked. His face was flushed and eager. "Come to the studio tomorrow, Tamara. I've fallen madly in love with you — do you know that?"

She protested, "Not possible. We've only known each other a few minutes."

He released her altogether, pulled a torn carton of cigarettes from the pocket of his velvet jacket and grinned at her.

"Let me quote you that wonderful line, sweet Tamara — *'Life is made up of moments, and it is for these moments that we give our lives.'* "

"Well, I'm not giving mine — even to a wonderful painter like yourself."

"We'll see about that." His grin widened. He looked, she was beginning to think, rather like a satyr. He was fantastic.

But she had cooled down. Reason returned. There was nothing feverish about her when she spoke to him again.

"I think *I* need a cigarette."

"No — you need me," he said bluntly.

"I think you're really rather detestable." Tamara turned and walked away so quickly that he had to run after her.

"Wait — promise you'll come tomorrow and sit for me."

"No," she said and curiously enough felt on the verge of tears.

For the rest of that evening it was a chaotic party, with everybody high on champagne before it all ended. Tamara refused to give way to any more of Laurence Gregg's attempts to get her alone in his studio again. Neither had she the slightest intention of letting him paint her tomorrow. He had fascinated and roused her. But she was furious because he had the power to wake the sort of feelings she had hoped were dead and buried.

She managed to say good night to Francoise once she had persuaded Chris to take her home. She was quite sure Chris would want to return to the party and stay until it ended. But he said he must leave her at The Little House.

She accepted his cool kiss on her cheek. It was a relief.

"Thanks awfully for taking me to your super party. When Q. comes back you must come and have dinner with us," she said.

"I'd love it once I return from America. I'm glad you enjoyed the party, Tamara. A good fella, Laurence, isn't he?"

"A good painter," she corrected.

She never saw Laurence again.

He tried to contact her on the phone several times and then stopped.

And she stopped remembering him.

IO

Came the morning when Q., putting on his tie, walked into the bedroom where his wife and small daughter were sitting side by side in the big bed. He grinned at them a trifle sheepishly.

"You both look so good I could eat you up," he said. "You make a perfect subject for one of those paintings of Mother and Child — you know the chap who painted it, Tam — the famous what's-his-name —"

Tamara, who had been showing a picture book to Claire, grimaced at her husband.

"By what's-his-name I presume you mean Raphael. His Madonna and Child, or something like that?"

Q. nodded. "I am sure you are right, but I thought the painter's name was Miller or something like that."

"If you mean *Millais*, then you can forget it," said Tamara more coldly. "He isn't the genius Raphael was, I assure you. You can't compare them, and I won't have Claire likened to Millais' *Bubbles*."

"Yes, *Bubbles* — that was the name of the boy. He was blowing bubbles. My mother had a reproduction of it," said Q. and seated himself on the edge of the bed, lifted one of Tam's long hands, and one of Claire's small rosy fists, and pressed a kiss on both, "My two Miss Worlds," he murmured.

Tamara, who always felt vaguely irritated when Q. showed a lack of knowledge either about painting or literature, opened her large beautiful eyes wide, then laughed.. "*Q.!* Honestly, I'm a bit old for that sort of remark, but I'm sure Claire appreciates it. *Me* Miss World indeed, not even *Mrs.* World."

"Claire really is terrific," said Q. on a more solemn note, and eyed his pretty daughter with the respect she deserved. She was a picture with her wonderful peach-bloom skin, those long silky lashes and her beautifully shaped head. Her hair was long, thick and curling — wheaten gold in colour. She thrust out a small hand and looked up at him with one of her ravishing smiles.

"Kiss Clar's hand again," she had shortened her name to Clar.

Q. turned to his wife with some reproach in his gaze. "You can't say she isn't a *bit* like the kid in Millais' painting."

Tamara shrugged.

"Bubbles had golden curls all over his head, and looked soppy. Claire's very intelligent."

Q. grinned. "Oh, well — forget it — what are you going to do today?"

"I was in all day yesterday, as Eilie was out, so I shall make the most of it. Go out somewhere."

"You do that, my love," said Q. gently. "You don't have much of a time these days. D'you know I was delighted old Chris turned up that time and took you out."

Now she gave him one of her wide warm smiles. But she felt guilty, remembering that crazy studio party, and its effect on her.

"Well," she said, "my good time will be lunching at a sandwich bar in the King's Road with an old chum of mine."

"Do I know her?"

"If you want to know, it's a *him*."

Q. who had reached the door, turned back. "The devil it is. Do I know him?"

"No — he works in a book shop. I used to know him in the old days. He 'phoned me up yesterday."

Q. with many office worries on his mind was hardly disturbed by the announcement of Tamara's new date. Vaguely he remembered that there had been a time, three or four years ago, before he married his darling Tammy, that she had run around with a lot of fellows in a pop-group. There had, of course, been that odd composer chap with whom she had the disastrous more serious love affair. He had rescued her from that and he was not by nature a jealous man. He had no reason to doubt that was all over. "Good, ask him round one night," he said. "I must go, darling. See you later. Bye-bye, both of you," and he blew a kiss first to his wife, then to his small daughter. He went out of the room but returned. He had remembered he must give Tamara an important piece of news.

He returned to the bedside. Claire giggled and beat her hand on her book and said, "Daddy, read to me. Daddy's come back."

"Sorry, angel, no time now. I'll read to you tonight."

He handed Tamara a letter that he pulled from his coat pocket. She pushed the heavy silk of her hair back from her forehead and scanned the letter. It was typed, and from the heading she deduced it was from a big car firm in Berkeley Square.

She also deduced that they were making a firm offer to Mr. Quentin Marriot for his Arrow, and suggested that he should accept the offer quickly before prices fell still further. There was not all that demand at the moment for an expensive racing-type car, they warned him.

Tamara drew breath and looked up at her husband. "You're actually going to sell the *Arrow*?" she asked incredulously.

"Yes. I ought to have done it two years ago. You've been so sweet and generous about me not doing so, I'm afraid I let myself be tempted to keep it. But it's been rather disgraceful of me."

Tamara looked up at him again, dewy-eyed, "Oh, darling, but your beloved *Arrow* — "

"I can live without it, and it'll bring us in quite a nice piece of lolly. I can put it in reserve for anything this young woman —" he patted Claire's head, "might need in the near future."

"Oh, what a good father! You really *are* a poppet, Q.!"

"As long as I don't have to part with you, I don't mind about losing anything else," he whispered, and took Tamara in his arms and kissed her more passionately than he had done for some time. She was responsive. They clung together for a moment. Claire beat at them both, obviously bored by this show of affection which didn't include her.

Then Q. recovered his aplomb, rose from the bed and mentioned that he did not intend to let the Arrow go until the end of October. They said the best possible buyer was in Kenya and not returning till the autumn. But he *would* clinch the deal. He needed that money. Everybody today needed capital and good solid cash.

Later that morning, Tamara went off to her lunch date feeling very pleased with Q. Sorry for him, too, because she knew that the loss of the Arrow really meant a sacrifice.

Walking down the King's Road which she had avoided for so long, she inevitably turned her mind to visions of herself moving daily in this same direction to be with Paul. Remembering Laurence Gregg and that strange disturbing night, and the whole atmosphere of that party, she felt close to Paul again.

Suddenly she saw a young man with longish hair, a beard, and horn-rimmed glasses and wearing jeans and a velveteen jacket, striding towards her. Vince Jones. Good old Vince — not much older than Paul but he looked it. Bearded, with drooping moustache — hairy as ever, thought Tamara, and looking as Paul used to say, like one of the Disciples (when he took off his glasses, of course). He had a kindly benevolent face. He gazed seriously upon the world. She recalled that he was almost too serious about his music, and he never bothered about his appearance, except when he used to play with the group, before an audience. Then they all wore glittering silver jackets and trousers, with orange cummerbunds. But Vince had not succeeded like Paul. Tamara had heard that he had given up playing and turned to the book trade. He was, so Tamara was told, working in a book shop in the Charing Cross Road.

Now Vince saw and recognised Tamara. In that booming voice she well remembered, he opened both arms, gathered her into a bear-hug, and said, "Little Tammy, just great! Hiya! Let's have a look at you." He pushed her away and looked her up and down, admiring the slim figure and elegance. She was beautifully dressed, with a chiffon head-scarf over her blonde hair. In the past Vince usually saw her at Paul's studio when she wore jeans, a boy's shirt, or polo-necked sweater like most of the girls around. Beautiful, she always was. Today, Vince decided even more so.

They lunched in a line with a crowd of other young people in the sandwich bar. Everything was displayed. Slithers of cooked meats, a variety of salads, huge bowls of coleslaw, sausages, and sandwiches. Tamara didn't mind the rather bogus Continental food, but she disliked the Instant coffee.

While they ate their choice of cold ham and salad with a roll and butter, Tamara and Vince talked rapidly, absorbed in the subject which was of the greatest importance — themselves. And finally turned to the old days with Paul. Tamara said little about Q. but Vince presumed that Tamara's marriage had been a success, and knew now that she also had an adorable little girl named Claire. She seemed well-off and described her delightful home with enthusiasm. Vince explained that times had not been good for him since his return from South Africa. He said:

"I've taken to the book world. I work in Charing Cross Road and I'm learning a lot, I enjoy the job. The pay's not bad. I share a flat with another fellow — he's a printer, in Fleet Street, so we're in sympathy. But I still dig old Paul. He was my greatest chum and still is."

"Old Faithful!" said Tamara, teasing him. "That used to be his name for you."

Vince gulped more coffee and smiled into her dark velvety eyes. Fascinating, he thought, with that long blonde hair. In the past he had always found Tam rather special and envied Paul.

"Old faithful — I haven't heard that nickname for a long time," he sighed.

"Paul used to say you never betrayed a friend and that you'd never leave a sinking ship."

Vince gave an embarrassed laugh. "I daresay I would if I was offered a fortune. I must say I even get bored handing out books to bookworms, advising females who don't really

93

want to buy a book but come to chat me up. *Etcetera*! I suppose I'm growing old."

"You're *not* old. You're Paul's age. He must only be twenty-seven or twenty-eight, yes?"

"Yes. Time marches on too quickly, Tam."

'It does," she nodded. She no longer smiled. "Still unmarried?" she asked.

"Yep, and likely to remain so."

"What happened to that R.A.D.A. student you used to dig?"

"Oh, Janey! Dear sweet, silly Janey!"

"I thought she was a bit silly but —'

"No buts —" Vince interrupted, grinning. "She *was*! Intelligent about her acting — but stupid over her love affairs. And she wasn't quite as sweet or faithful to me as I'd imagined. She ditched me for one of her fellow students. Funny I never seem to pick a girl I can call faithful!"

"Dear Vince, your trouble is that you're too much of an idealist — too nice. You should try a more masterful approach."

"Hey! You weren't a cynic in the old days!"

"Days that are no more," Tamara said, gave a brief laugh and shrugged her shoulders.

He said, "Tell me, did you rush into marriage just on the rebound from Paul? Or did you really dig this stockbroker guy. He's a partner in your father's firm, isn't he?"

Tamara nodded. She hoped Vince wouldn't ask too many questions. They brought back her feeling of uneasiness. But he continued, "I thought Paul was the guy you really needed in your life."

She felt a stab of pain but answered lightly,

"I needed him at the time, I suppose." Then, quickly, on a different note: "No, that's not true. I *was* terribly in love with him. You were his best friend, Vince. You ought to know. The three of us were so often together. And do remember, please, that I wasn't the one who put an end to the affair with Paul."

94

"True, I told him what a fool he was, at the time."

She bit her lip, and drank more coffee thirstily.

"This girl, Liesel, may have been just that much more attractive."

"Far from it," Vince protested. "She was a good-looker, but nothing like as gorgeous as you. You were great — Paul was lucky. He made a mistake, always grumbling because you came of a wealthy family, and so on. Liesel was cold — frigid almost — curiously so for a Viennese. They're generally warm and friendly. She was sexy, in my opinion, only when she was singing her German love songs, and, of course, with that red hair and white skin and very long legs, she appealed to men. But she couldn't keep Paul. He obviously missed you, my dear. He and Liesel parted six months ago. I will say they did some good work together — recorded one or two of his best songs and that. But she had an offer from America and went over there and stayed."

Tamara felt her heart beats quicken. Paul and all he had meant to her sprang suddenly into focus as though for a long time she had only occasionally taken out a faded print of him which had become almost indiscernible.

Now she knew more about his affair with Liesel. Vince called her 'frigid'. But she obviously had been useful around the place and had done some great entertaining for Paul. Although exacting and mercenary in one way, she had a generous streak, Vince said, and had helped Paul along when he was particularly broke. But Vince didn't think she would ever go back to Paul. Neither did he think Paul would renew the relationship even if she wanted it. In fact, Paul had no particular girl-friend at the moment.

Tamara listened, and learned. She was thinking, I was never frigid or secretive, but perhaps I was too terribly in love, and Paul had really wanted someone like Liesel to battle with, as well as sleep with! Some men are like that. She finished her coffee.

"Do you ever see Paul now?"

"Yes, we had a coffee in here together only the other day."

Tamara looked around. Her eyes were big and haunted. She said, "It was here he first told me he'd just written that song — 'I Loved You Best', then we went back to the studio and he played it for me."

"Sorry, Tammy, a bit tactless of me to have brought you here, perhaps."

She protested, "Oh, for goodness sake, things between Paul and myself have been over years. I've got a husband and a child — remember?"

"Yes, yes, of course," Vince coughed, embarrassed, and walked to the bar to get two more coffees.

He didn't quite know what to make of Tam. He was sensitive to her reactions and sure she had been upset by the conversation. He reproached himself for mentioning Paul's name. Little Tam must have been even more dead-set on Paul than he had thought — yet, remembering several long discussions with Paul, long after the break-up, he was sure Paul had, as far as he was able, cared a lot about Tamara. But he had been afraid of taking entire possession — afraid of being the eventual cause of her leaving home and the sort of environment he could never afford to provide for her. He had as good as said so.

"What have the years done to Paul?" Tamara was now asking. "Is he just the same?"

"In what way — mind, body or both?"

"Both."

"Well, in some ways, he's older. He hasn't grown a beard or anything like that. He looks much the same, I think. I'm not really a great one for noticing details. I'd say he was a bit thinner than when you were around."

"He never used to eat enough or take care of himself," Tamara said in a low voice.

"Oh, I don't think he does too badly. But he's always hard up. I can't say the money's rolling in. It isn't for any of us these days, is it? Inflation has hit us all. At least Paul hasn't had to pay a hefty rent for years. Liesel is making a packet. She kept on the lease of her flat and all the time she's been away she's let Paul live there."

Somehow that made Tamara grit her teeth. She didn't like to think of Paul accepting anything that cost money from Liesel. He was such an odd character. Suddenly Tamara decided it was time she stopped raking the ashes. She had no wish to rekindle the fire, even if she could.

"What actually is Paul doing for money nowadays?" She couldn't stop herself from probing once more.

"Oh, well, he wrote a few songs for a musical that made a hit up in Leeds, last Christmas. It brought him in quite a bit. He also had recorded one or two of the old songs and hit the top in the disc racket recently. As far as I could gather when I saw Paul the other day he was quitting Liesel's place at the end of this month. He has bought the lease of a studio flat in Axhurst Mews, just off Paultons Square. You know he always liked Chelsea."

Tamara nodded. She was glad Paul wasn't going to live forever in that other woman's flat.

She stayed with Vince for an hour. Finally she felt the need to get away. She picked up her shoulder bag. "I must go home, Vince. Thanks awfully for the nosh." (She found it so easy to slip back into the old jargon.) "It's been great, meeting up with you."

He stood up and looked down at her. She was still the fascinating girl Paul used to call his 'Russian Princess', he thought. Difficult to imagine her living a conventional life with her stockbroker husband and a daughter aged three.

"You haven't yet told me a thing about — what's your child's name?" he asked.

"Claire. I'll tell you more about her some other time, Vince. I've got an appointment — I must fly. Please let's not leave it so long before we meet again."

Vince now felt worried. Afraid that the meeting with Tamara hadn't really been a success. Obviously she had not forgotten Paul. Talking about him had upset her. He cursed himself for a fool to have talked so much about the old days.

He stood silent, embarrassed. Tamara, gazing up at Vince's kindly bearded face, had the strangest wish to burst into tears, instead of which she said, "Don't forget to 'phone me, dear Vince. I'd like to give you lunch at my place, or something."

"I'd like that very much. By the way, can I tell Paul I met you?"

"No," she said in a breathless voice. "Please don't. Good-bye and thanks again, Vince. See you!"

Rather blindly, she walked out of the coffee bar into the crowded street.

II

BEFORE TAMARA REACHED home, she experienced a crazy and dangerous desire to turn back and find her way to Axhurst Mews. She wanted crazily — to surprise Paul. She wanted to see him again — if only once more. She argued with her-self. It wouldn't affect her too badly even if she did see him. Long ago — oh, so long — he had become the focus of her existence. Not now. Why not just pay him a visit, out of sheer curiosity. Besides, he might like to see *her*, and hear about her present life. The prospect of this propelled her towards him. It would be interesting, if nothing more, to find out what he thought of her after so long.

Then she dismissed the whole idea as being ridiculous — yes, quite stupid, and even dangerous. Q. darling, kind, devoted Q. would be most upset if he knew. So far as he was concerned, the name 'Paul' meant little these days. Paul was as good as dead to his way of thinking. He was so content with his wife and she gave him every reason to believe she was equally happy with him — and their child. She could not square her conscience and be so disloyal as to make contact with Paul again.

Once back in her delightful familiar home, she heard screams of laughter coming from the back garden. Eilie must be pushing Claire in her swing-seat. Tamara relaxed again and pushed her desire to visit Paul into the background.

Eilie — now a devoted nurse to Claire — came into the hall with Claire to meet her mother. The little girl let go of Eilie's hand and rushed to Tamara.

"Mummee! Mummee! I've been on my swing. It's *soo*per! Come and push me, please, please, Mummee!"

The Finnish girl shook her head and looked at her watch.

"No, no, is time for your tea, Claire. Mummy will push you later, perhaps."

The little girl gripped her mother by the arms and looked up at her with those beautiful grey-gold eyes which were so unusual — Q.'s eyes. Tamara was always glad that their daughter had inherited them.

"Angel!" she murmured and bent and kissed Claire all over her rosy dimpled face.

"I want you to swing me, Mummee, *please!*"

And of course she got her way. Later, while Eilie was giving Claire her tea, Tamara, who never ate anything at this time, had a sudden wish to talk to her husband. It was past four o'clock. Tamara, sitting on the side of the bed, put a telephone call through.

When Q. realised who his caller was, he said with obvious pleasure, "Well — well! Hullo, my love. To what do I owe this unusual attention at this unusual hour? I couldn't believe it was you when the girl said my wife was on the line."

She felt genuinely fond of her husband, and a strange loneliness had made her want to communicate with him.

"I just wanted to talk, Q." she said.

"What about, darling?"

"Nothing much. I just wanted to talk."

"Well, that's very flattering. Carry on," said Q. cheerfully, "But are you sure there's nothing momentous on your mind?"

"No. I told you this morning I was lunching with an old friend, didn't I? A 'he'."

"And am I to suppose that whoever *he* is, he has stunned you into leaving your loving husband and making off to some lovely lonely island with him?"

Q. followed this with a laugh. But Tamara sat silent for a second. Of course Q. was joking. But there was that tiny touch of truth in what he said — what he had meant — that shook Tamara a little. The conversation with Vince, the news of Paul, *had* in its way stunned her. Perhaps Q. had used the right words. Then she, too, broke into a laugh.

"Don't be an old idiot. I haven't the slightest intention of leaving my husband and my child for any lovely lonely island *and* if you want to know, it wasn't even suggested. Vince and I ate some rather ghastly ham, rolls and Instant coffee in a King's Road coffee bar. He's a nice person, Q., and you might like to meet him one day."

"Of course. You must tell me more when I get back, love. I'll try to be early. How's my daughter?"

"Terrific. She's got a 'thing' about being pushed in her swing now."

"Bless the brat."

"I've also had a call from Daddy," added Tamara. "He wants to see me so I shall go round there for lunch tomorrow. Aunt Liz is going out with some ancient chum. I'll have Daddy to myself."

"But I shall be home tomorrow. It's Saturday. Don't you remember, sweetie?"

"Oh, my darling, how *silly* of me. The days go so quickly; Saturday already!"

"Never mind. Go and lunch with Papa. I'll take my daughter out by myself."

"Take Claire out to lunch!" Tamara exclaimed. "She's a bit young."

"Not at all. Anyhow she'll have to get used to being taken out by handsome gentlemen like myself, and driven, if not to a lovely lonely island, to a lovely restaurant; say that one in the Park. It'll amuse her."

"Well, if you're going to get the Arrow out, why not take her for a short drive. You said this morning you wouldn't have it much longer. Enjoy it while you can. She'd be thrilled to be in the car with you."

"It's not much fun in London, darling."

"Okay — I've got a brilliant idea. Take her down to see her godmother. Beaconsfield's not far and now there's that dual carriageway from Shepherd's Bush. You'll enjoy it. Virginia was only saying the other day that she was longing to see her godchild. I'll ring Virginia and fix it for you to lunch with her."

"But must you stay so long with Papa? Can't you join us?"

Tamara explained that her father had mentioned something about turning out a trunk which had belonged to her mother and been stored in the attic for years. He wanted her to go through it and see if there was anything she would like either for herself or for little Claire. He believed there were one or two very good pieces of valuable lace — her mother had adored old lace — and it was now unobtainable. Also some equally valuable ivories which she used to collect. He hadn't thought about it for a long time, but didn't think it really concerned Aunt Liz. Tamara had said she would like to have a look at the treasure-chest and as it might take some little time she agreed to stay after lunch.

Claire went wild with excitement when told that Daddy was going to take her for a long drive to visit her godmother. Virginia was thrilled, although disappointed Tamara would not be with them. And Eilie was pleased because it meant that she could take the afternoon off. It seemed a popular move.

That night Q. came out of the bathroom and, somewhat unusually, was the first in bed. It was not his habit to lie too long in a hot bath. He had intended tonight to finish a thriller which had lately been absorbing him, but when he saw Tamara sitting at her dressing-table brushing her long blonde hair, he was suddenly entranced by her fairness and her grace.

The years that they had been married had not cooled the ardent longing he always felt when he looked at his wife as she was tonight. Still so young, so slim, yet with that charming touch of maturity that motherhood had given her. Her figure was still perfect. Q. experienced a growing excitement when she took off her frilly dressing-gown and stood before him in the transparent 'shortie' which made her look, so he often remarked, more like Claire's teenage sister than her mother.

Q. flung down his paper-back and held out a hand. "Come here, you lovely thing," he said in a low voice.

Halfway to the bed, she stopped. She knew exactly what this meant. Q. wanted to make love to her. She loved him, yet she felt no real response to his passion. Their love-making had, of course, reached that levelling-up common to most people who have been married for some years. The white-hot fervour of early days could not be expected to last. Yet in the past both of them had continued to be lovers, and felt a frank enjoyment and satisfaction in their shared passion.

Why then, Tamara asked herself, experiencing a moment of blind panic, did she suddenly feel she would rather that Q. did *not* make love to her? Was it just that she was over-tired, or just sleepy? There was no real reason why she should be tired. Today had not been particularly exacting, and Q. looked undeniably attractive, holding out his hand with that warm ardour in his handsome eyes. Physically, she knew that the bond between them was good. Mentally, she wasn't sure.

For God's sake, what's wrong with me? she asked herself, and felt disinclined either to step back or move forward. She just felt empty of all feeling. Or was that true? Had the meeting with Vince really shaken her in some insidious, indefinite way? Insidious, yes, not indefinite was the next thought that flashed through her mind. To her dismay she was definitely aware that Paul's image had returned to remind her that *he* had been the only one. *The one she loved the best.*

His song pushed a way back into her consciousness. She hated her own weakness. She put both her hands to her ears as though to shut out the disturbing melody that nobody else must hear, least of all Q.

I am mad, she told herself, I must take a grip of myself. I'm behaving disgracefully. Only Q. and Claire matter. I love them. Anyhow, Paul was cruel to me at the end. I ought to hate him. Oh, I'm round the bend! I ought to be ashamed of myself!

Q. was watching her, a delightful smile on his face. Suddenly his expression changed. He sprang out of bed, took hold of her, and cradled her in his arms.

"Tam, Tam, my love, what's the matter? You've turned quite pale. What's wrong, darling?"

She fought against the hysterical inclination to burst into tears. "Nothing — nothing at all. I just — oh, you know — don't they say 'come over queer' — that's what — I've come over queer. But I'm okay again now. Don't worry."

Shocked and dismayed, he picked her right up in his arms, and carried her to the bed. She was warm, yet when he took one of her hands, it seemed cold, and she was shaking. She looked unlike herself.

"I thought you were going to faint," he said. "Oh, my darling, are you really okay?"

"Yes — quite. Honestly I am. I just felt giddy. It's nothing. I'm sorry."

She broke off and now the tears began to fall — drenching her cheeks. Q. tucked the blankets around her. He switched off the light and began to stroke her hair.

"Ssh! Don't cry, darling — just lie still. Go to sleep, like this, in my arms. You're overtired — that's it. You've done too much. Relax, my poor little thing, and if you don't feel better in a moment I'll ask Dr. Fisher to come and see you."

Tamara clung to him and assured him she did not want Dr. Fisher.

"I'm all right — I'm just being stupid. Overtired, as you say."

He gave a deep sigh and went on caressing her hair. The urge of his own body was forgotten. He wanted to be very tender and comforting. His strange beautiful Tamara! Did he make her as happy as she made him? Sometimes he was forced to admit that even during their most passionate moments he felt that the greater love was on his side. There was just something he would never be able to pinpoint in Tamara's response that left him with an uneasy feeling. But he was not the sort of man to probe too deeply into things, so he had never questioned her. He took it for granted that she was as much in love with him as she could be with any man. That was it. She had a dual personality.

She was two Tamaras — one whom no man could ever wholly possess — the reserved even shy Tamara he had found so sweet when they first met. The other, a warm passionate girl — even a crazy uninhibited one. When they were newly married he was sure she enjoyed their sex-life as much as he did. It was only during the last year or two he had begun to wonder if he had taken too much for granted.

Troubled, even anxious, Q. lay awake this night pondering over his relationship with his wife.

Finally, he turned over and slept and did not wake till morning. He was always a sound sleeper.

Tamara went on thinking, brooding, worrying. She did not want to be the one to put a barrier between Q. and herself. She did not want to go on feeling this craving for the love she had lost. She was aware in all honesty that it was shocking in so far as Q. had done nothing to warrant disloyalty of mind, if not body. Then there was Claire!

There must be thousands of women in the world who would envy her her present position in this house, Tamara continued her anxious thinking, and her possession of such a fine husband and enchanting child. What was wrong with her? She asked herself this question again and again. Why couldn't she control her tendency to think more of herself and not much of others? And wasn't it ironic to be aware, deep down within her, that Paul had never been worth so much as Q.'s little finger.

Not until dawn broke did she hide her face against Q.'s warm back, envying his peace of mind — grateful to him — loving him, in her own way.

But it wasn't the right way, and for his sake alone Tamara bitterly regretted it.

12

ON THAT OCTOBER morning when Tamara was due to go to her father's house for lunch, she was gay and talkative during breakfast. Little Claire — her usual sweet cheerful self — chatted busily while she dipped fingers of brown bread-and-butter into a soft-boiled egg, pausing only to lift her face when Eilie wiped her lips and small sticky chin.

Q., glancing now and then at his wife, felt far less anxious than he had done last night when she had had what she called her 'giddy turn'. This morning she seemed fine, smiling and friendly.

Everything had been organised. Eilie was going to the house of a Finnish friend. Claire was spending the day in Beaconsfield with Virginia and Henry. Q. was pleased about this.

"I reckon I make a good children's nurse," he announced as he finished his plate of cereal. "I've learned a lot lately. Give me some more coffee, Tam darling, then tell me when you'd like us to be back from Beaconsfield."

"Oh, in time for a late tea," was the answer, "I'm sure darling Virginia, much as she loves her god-daughter, won't want her for longer than half the morning, plus a meal."

"Now, let me think," said Q. getting up and looking out of the window, "what's the weather going to be like?"

"Cooler," said Tam, and turned to Eilie. "I should put Claire in her blue trousers and that new white anorak, Eilie."

The *au pair* acknowledged the request and Claire beat upon her plate with her spoon as though giving her approval. She was restrained by her mother.

"Don't be quite so noisy, pet."

Q. laughed and looked fondly at his small daughter. "She's showing how happy she is because she's going to spend the day with her Daddy."

"Not before time. You hardly ever take her out by herself," Tamara reminded him.

"Come off it, darling, I'm never allowed to. You always say you want her, or Eilie must take her somewhere or the other."

"Nonsense, *you're* always too busy."

There developed a typical matrimonial argument, laced with light-hearted reproaches. Then Q. brought the conversation back to serious matters.

"I want to leave here about eleven, darling — it takes a good hour to Beaconsfield, and Virginia said she wanted us down about twelve. *Why* don't you come with us, Tam?"

Tamara gave a little shrug and a faint smile. "Daddy wants me and I decided it might be nice for you to have a day alone with your daughter."

"I shall be thrilled but I'd like her Mum to come, too."

"Well, I can't anyhow, darling, because *I've* promised to lunch with *my* Daddy!"

Q. nodded and lit a cigarette. "Oh, yes, mother's lace in the old trunk. Well — " he touched his daughter's velvety cheek with one long finger and grinned down at Claire, "you and I, my child, will be showing the other drivers on the Great West Road what a super car the Arrow is."

Tamara stopped smiling; "Please don't do anything of the sort," she said sharply, "you promised me you would never speed with Claire as your passenger — you certainly shouldn't."

"Of course I won't," he made haste to assure her, "I was only joking. One's got to keep to a speed limit anyhow on motorways. Honestly, I was just pulling your leg, darling."

"Well, I don't find it funny. You know what you're like when you get going in that car."

He walked round the table and put a hand on Tamara's shoulder, "Darling, you know perfectly well I won't drive fast this morning. I'm quite aware my cargo is precious. Besides, I don't want an accident myself, do I? I'm *not* a dangerous driver under any circumstances. You know that."

Tamara's brow cleared. She felt guilty. Why upset Q.? He was okay as a driver — very much so. It was just her deep-down dislike of fast cars.

She made haste to be especially nice to Q. after breakfast. Eilie led Claire out to her nursery. Tamara took hold of Q.'s arm as they left the dining-room.

"Darling," she said, "I *know* you'll take care of our baby and I'm glad you are having this day alone with her and Virginia and Henry — without your nagging wife."

Q.'s handsome eyes glowed. He laughed. "You're the very opposite of a nagging wife, my darling, I've never heard such a thing!"

"I'm not always as sweet to you as you are to me."

"I haven't noticed it. I think you're marvellous."

God, she thought, did he never wonder at her moods — her uncontrolled emotions? She reminded herself that she ought to be glad that he *didn't* really understand her. It might upset the whole apple-cart. It was good that he believed in his naïve way that she was as much in love with him now as she had been when she first married him.

She was at her most affectionate when she helped Eilie strap little Claire into the seat beside the driver and tucked a small rug across the chubby knees. She knew that Q. liked to drive with a window slightly open on his side, and the October day, though fine now, looked threatening. The good weather was not going to last. Even while they were break-fasting, sudden clouds had billowed over London, and the wind changed. Of course, she remembered now, the B.B.C. weatherman had warned them that rain and wind were on the way.

Q. took his seat at the wheel, gazed at his little girl's flushed excited face, then at his wife's beautiful haunting face. He was never tired of looking at it. He said: "I know you're still worrying about the rain and wet roads but I promise you I'll try and bring the car down to the lowest speed she'll take."

Tamara's heart warmed to him, "Thanks," she said and thought how nice he looked this morning. Because it was much cooler he was wearing his new blue boiler-suit — the latest fashion — ideal for driving. It suited him. The collar was open and tucked in it was a striped yellow scarf. Q. always wore nice clothes, and never looked anything but elegant — even in a boiler-suit. Tamara kissed both passengers, wished them a happy day, and Q. started up the Arrow. He barely touched the accelerator with his foot. The magnificent car moved out on to the road, glistening, powerful, rather gorgeous, Tamara had to admit, despite her dislike of it. And she remembered that he was being terribly good because he had stated categorically that he intended to sell this most treasured possession. If the deal he was now considering came off, the drive in the Arrow down to Beaconsfield today might be his last. Poor old Q. — it would be sad for him! She couldn't really see him in a family car.

After the Arrow disappeared round a bend in the road, Tamara went slowly indoors. She regained her self-control and did some sensible thinking. She loved her husband. Of *course* she did. They were very happy together and tonight she wouldn't wait for him to make love to her, she'd make love to him. She'd show him how grateful she was for all he had done for her.

Eilie departed for her day's outing. Tamara ironed a few of her personal things, hung up four drip-dry shirts for Q., then went off to her father's house.

John Whitfeld was delighted to see her. As the morning

went on she began to feel a good deal more light-hearted.

"All well with you, darling?" her father asked when they were upstairs in the attic.

"All well. Looking forward to opening the treasure-chest," she said lightly.

She spent a happy two hours with her father, sorting through her mother's trunk. They unwrapped the tiers of old lace, so tenderly laid between folds of tissue paper, and the delicately-carved ivories that Nina Whitfeld had collected before she had even met or married Tamara's father.

If Tamara worried that her father might be upset by this delving into the past — for in the early days of his marriage he had loved his beautiful half-Russian wife so much — Tamara soon found that there was no need. Typical of most men, she told herself rather cynically, he did not allow sentiment to control his life. He was more interested in things than people. He spent most of the time, while they unwrapped the treasures, bemoaning the fall of the pound, and telling her how much he would like to go and stay with a bachelor cousin of his in Cannes, but because the exchange with the franc was so bad he did not think it worth while. Then he started to discuss finance in general and to deplore the gloom shadowing the whole country. But Tamara only half listened, so intrigued was she by all she found in her mother's trunk. Poor little mother! Sad that she had died so young. Tamara could just remember how beautiful she used to be — and how fascinating. But it was her grandmother who was the most absorbing memory for Tamara. She was the one Tamara resembled. So often Mummy had spoken of her and told her all about Grandma's dramatic nature — her impulsiveness — her swinging moods. The same nervous reactions from which Tamara so often suffered. Strange thing, heredity, she thought, and sighed.

She sat for some time cross-legged on the floor sifting through the contents of the trunk. A glorious Honiton veil — a magnificent evening skirt made entirely of Brussels lace. What could she do with *these*? Perhaps cover a silk dress, although the lace in parts was a little yellow with age and would have to be cleaned very carefully. As for the ivories, they, too, were yellowing but very beautiful. Most of the ornaments were Oriental. She might get Q. to buy her a corner cupboard with glass doors. She would cover the shelves with dark wine coloured velvet, stand the ivories up on them and have lights fixed so as to show them off.

She had what she called a 'cosy lunch' with her father. They had soup and smoked salmon with brown bread and butter, and one of Mr. Whitfeld's best white wines. They talked about the friends they shared, and finally, of course, about the beloved Claire.

"I reckon my grand-daughter will become a raving beauty," Mr. Whitfeld remarked as he lit his after-lunch cigar.

Tamara smiled. "I'm afraid so."

"Why afraid?"

"Well, I hope she won't be too ravishing. I wouldn't want her to go on the stage, or become a model, or turn out to be Miss World."

"Why not?"

Tamara half shut her eyes. "I don't know. I think I'd just like her to be something quite different; an artist, or writer, or something intellectual."

"You've not done so badly as a beauty," he smiled at her.

"M'm —" she shrugged, "But I don't think I've given enough time to serious thinking."

He laughed. "Well, *well*! Claire is a bit young yet for us to know how she'll develop."

"One thing I *do* know, she is very spoiled."

"So were you," said Mr. Whitfeld and looked at his daughter fondly over the rim of his glasses, "but it hasn't done you much harm."

Yes it has, Tamara thought, everybody's been far too nice to me. I know I'm horribly spoilt.

She rang Virginia's house at two o'clock as arranged, and was glad to hear that all was well down there. Claire had been as good as gold on the drive and just finished a hearty lunch of minced veal and vegetables, followed by ice-cream.

Tamara then had a chat with her daughter, after which Q. came on the line. She told him what a fascinating morning she had had and what glorious things she was bringing home. Then suddenly, with a sudden surge of affection for Q. she added, "I do love you, darling."

"Thank you, darling. I adore you," was his happy answer.

Tamara put down the receiver. She felt in a far better mood when she went to collect a library book and afterwards returned home. It was just before half past four. Claire, she expected, would be back for her tea at five.

Tamara had taken a bus — just to be economical — to her father's house, but he had insisted on paying a taxi to bring her home. "Slump or no slump," he had said, "we're not that broke yet," and he kissed her on both cheeks and pressed a pound-note into her hand, and a box of sweets for Claire. Darling Daddy! He was such a devoted grandpa. And now to prepare tea for her two darlings.

The first shock that greeted Tamara was the sight of a policeman standing outside the front door of the little house busily jotting notes down on a pad. As he heard the taxi, he looked up and came to the gate to meet the passenger.

"Mrs. Marriot?" he asked.

Tamara got out and stared at the policeman blankly. He was young and fair haired. He looked pink-cheeked and embarrassed.

"Yes?"

"Er — good afternoon, Mrs. Marriot, I'm — er — sorry to be here like this and I know I'm going to bring you news you won't want to hear. Could I ask if we could go indoors so you can sit down? I found the front door locked and nobody answered the bell, so I thought I'd hang around a bit in case you came back. I reckoned you might be doing some shopping —" he stopped and cleared his throat, looking at her uneasily.

Tamara turned white. For an instant she felt as though her whole body had frozen, together with her thoughts.

Automatically she paid the driver and her taxi moved off. She turned to the policeman.

"What's happened? Has there been an accident? Is it my husband —" she began and stopped.

He said, "I'd rather you come in with me and sit down, please, Mrs. Marriot."

She tried to reorientate herself. "Yes, of course." She took her key and opened the front door. She was trembling violently now.

The young policeman removed his helmet and sat down. Tamara remained standing, breathing hard and fast. With dark despair she half guessed before he spoke what he was about to tell her.

"There *has* been an accident, hasn't there?" she asked. "My husband — my little girl — an Arrow car — somewhere between Beaconsfield and London —" she broke off. She seemed to find no more words.

"I'm afraid that's right, Mrs. Marriot," the policeman nodded, thoroughly disliking this side of his job.

Tamara dropped her bag on the floor. She did not pick it up. The policeman stooped and laid it on a table. Tamara was conscious of a dreadful sickness in the pit of her stomach.

"They're both dead — that's what you've come to tell me, isn't it?" she asked in a high falsetto voice.

The constable stood up again because she refused to sit down. He was unhappy, but he couldn't beat about the bush. She had got to know. He thought miserably, *these cars — all these reckless drivers — no matter whose fault, the results were all too often the same — agony and death.*

"Is there anybody who could bring you a drop of brandy or something?" he began.

She broke in, "Nobody and I don't want brandy. For God's sake say what you've come to say. I promise not to faint or anything, I'm not that sort of person."

"Please do sit down —" he began again awkwardly.

Now the tension in Tamara broke, ending in hysterical

anger. "For God's sake, stop trying to be polite. All I want to know is the truth and I want to know it *now*!"

So he told her what he could. There wasn't much he could do to soften the blow.

Tamara listened, her eyes huge and full of horror.

Claire dead! It couldn't be true, it *couldn't*!

But it was.

The constable was trying to console her with the news that her husband was unharmed — although in a state of shock. With an effort, she forced herself to concentrate on the facts the man was giving her. *The Arrow had crashed.* As if she hadn't always been afraid that it would. *It was not doing more than sixty miles per hour.* Only? Hadn't she told Q. a thousand times that anyone in a low-lying car like the Arrow might come off worse in an accident and that the only way to drive safely was to drive slowly.

She shivered and closed her eyes. There hadn't been time yet to establish all the details. The gentleman and the little girl, the constable said, had been taken to the nearest hospital — Hillingdon, Uxbridge.

She knew Uxbridge. Virginia went there once a week to push a trolley of library books around the wards. She had told Tamara that it was a hospital with a good reputation. But what good was that to Claire, her heart's darling? Claire was dead.

"The child did not suffer," the policeman went on. "You can be sure of that, Mrs. Marriot. She died instantly. Shall I go on?" he asked, looking anxiously at Tamara's grey-white face.

She nodded.

"From what your husband said, it would seem that he was about to overtake a lorry, when the driver braked suddenly. Unfortunately, the little girl was perched on the luggage shelf behind the front seats, and in that position, she obviously not wearing her safety belt..."

"She could see better from there," Tamara interrupted. "Oh, yes, I know from the bucket seat her little head barely reached above the dashboard. I always said it was a crazy place for a child, but my husband thought he knew best."

Looking even more embarrassed by this hysterical outburst, the constable reiterated that the accident did not appear to be entirely Mr. Marriot's fault.

"The brakes were in perfect condition. Your husband was able to avoid hitting the back of the lorry, but the sudden braking caused the child to somersault — forwards-like. Her head hit the dashboard. She — she never knew about it. The police surgeon was sure of that."

"Oh, God!" Tamara said under her breath. "He must have been mad to let her sit up there. This morning she was safely strapped into the seat beside him. Why not the same on the way home? *Why*?"

"He'll best be able to explain that to you himself, Mrs. Marriot," the man said, looking and feeling distressed for her. "But from what I could gather, the child had been restless — what with not being able to see above the dashboard from that low front seat and she'd been pestering her father for some while to permit her to sit at the back. So I daresay to please her he finally gave in. But for the unfortunate emergency she would have been safe enough."

"But that's exactly what I've tried to tell my husband so many times. There is nearly always an emergency on the road these days." She broke off, hiding her face in her hands, regretting her loss of self-control in front of the constable.

The man was not unfamiliar with the varying effects of shock. And it was certainly not his business to become involved. He pitied the mother. But his sympathies were as much with the poor father. He'd stood there with the child in his arms, unable to grasp the fact that it was useless even to attempt the kiss of life. Death was instantaneous — final.

"I'm very sorry, Mrs. Marriot. Very sorry indeed!" he said. And he scratched his head and twiddled his helmet between his fingers. She was being a little difficult, but he forgave her.

"Am I supposed to say it's God's will?" he heard Mrs. Marriot say in a choked voice.

He hadn't got any glib comments to make about the Creator. He and his wife were, in fact, church-goers, and despite all the terrible things they saw in the way of crime and accident, they both believed sincerely that there was a good God and these terrible things were nothing to do with *Him.* Nevertheless, the constable had to shut his mind to the memory of that lovely little girl lying in her father's arms, her neck broken, and those beautiful sightless eyes wide open. What could he say to her mother now except remind her that at least her husband had been spared. She couldn't say *that* wasn't God's mercy. Tamara listened to him and her hysteria mounted. She laughed.

"Yes, my dear husband is all right I'm sure — not a scratch. He loved the Arrow and he always drove fast but he promised me he'd take care of our child. He *promised.*"

The policeman stood up.

"Mrs. Marriot if you'll come along with me I'll drive you to the hospital to see your husband. Our chaps are making further investigations and perhaps the Chief Officer will be able to tell you more about it all."

Tamara put both hands up and pressed them against her ears. Now the awful surge of feeling against Q. and his love for his car, and the fact that Claire's death might be attributed to a moment of carelessness, died down. Tamara gave a long gasping sigh.

"Sorry, Constable — I let myself go. Of course I must go to my husband. Just let me get my mac, will you? I can see rain is coming. I'll lock up again and come along with you."

"Sure you wouldn't like a cup of hot sweet tea, or a coffee first?"

"No. I want to get to the hospital. She — my little girl — is she there?" Tamara forced the question, her body shaking.

"They'll have taken her to the mortuary, I reckon."

The very word mortuary stunned Tamara. Speechlessly she joined the policeman in his car, and they were on their way to the Great West Road.

13

THE CHRISTMAS AND New Year that followed the death of little Claire were the most desperate and unhappy Tamara had ever known. Nobody in the family wanted the usual celebrations, nor treated December 25th as anything but an ordinary day. The Whitfelds, with Tamara and Q., entertained nobody. The house was tragically quiet. And no one dared say 'Happy New Year'.

John Whitfeld had been deeply shocked by the loss of his little grand-daughter, but he behaved as was expected of a man of his quality. He remained calm and philosophical — perhaps because he had reached an age when he had learned to accept as inevitable the cruel blows that fate chose to deal most human beings during their lifetime. He understood the extreme pain and grief that prevented Tamara from accepting the agonising loss of her small daughter. He insisted that she and his son-in-law should shut up their own house and stay with him and her aunt immediately after the accident.

The Finnish *au-pair* girl, deeply distressed, returned to her native country. In Mr. Whitfeld's opinion it would be bad for Tamara to be alone just now — particularly while Q. was in the City. Besides which, he was a perceptive man and he could see only too plainly, that deep in her heart she half-blamed poor Q. for the accident.

As far as Mr. Whitfeld knew, she had never openly accused him. Q. himself told his father-in-law that she had been quite wonderful since the tragedy — gentle and friendly but un-willing to discuss the affair. John Whitfeld knew that in a sinister sort of manner, she was erecting an impassable barrier between Q. and herself. In all kinds of ways she had changed towards him. Perhaps he knew it. Perhaps not. But Mr. Whitfeld was deeply sorry for his son-in-law. At times, he was even annoyed with Tamara. Things seemed worse be-cause she did not come into the open and tell her husband exactly how she felt.

Once poor little Claire had been laid in her grave and the misery of the burial, all the flowers and the letters of con-dolence, followed, Tamara sank into a kind of apathy. She absented herself from the others. She spoke only when neces-sary, and as far as her father knew, she had lost — at least temporarily — all zest for living, her sense of humour — the many delightful characteristics that had made the old Tamara such an intriguing and attractive person.

Aunt Liz shed her tears in secret and like the stalwart woman she was, did her best to comfort and look after her niece without making it too apparent that she was so doing. She knew her Tamara. The girl was obviously keeping a tight hold of herself for the moment. The time might come when she would break. Aunt Liz grieved but sat back and watched and waited. She had the sense not to preach religion, or say such things as 'Give it time — you'll get over it' or 'Try for Q.'s sake not to be too sad', and all the conventional words of condolence. Least of all did she say, 'Remember you're young — there's plenty of time for you to have another child'. As they drove away from the cemetery, Tamara had made it clear to them all that she was finished with motherhood. "I'll never *never* have another child," she had said and sat in the car like a frozen image.

Looking at the white taut young face, Aunt Liz felt im-mense compassion. But looking also at Q. she pitied him still more. It must be worse for him — the driver of that car — bringing Claire home that fatal day. *He* looked ghastly, Mrs. York thought, and there was a 'little-boy-lost' expression in his eyes that went to her kindly heart. She was so used to the other Q. — the charming cheerful talkative young man, who enjoyed life to the full and had loved his wife and little girl with all his heart. He was in complete control of his feelings. He had great strength of character, Aunt Liz was aware of that, but she could see how badly he was suffering. Only once did she mention this to her niece — that was a month after the funeral — then Tamara turned on her, breaking through her unnatural calm.

"And why shouldn't he be unhappy? After all it was he who — " then she stopped, biting fiercely at her lips, and added, "Oh, don't let's discuss it, *please*!"

Aunt Liz, tactful though she usually was, could not forbear to say, "Tammy darling, forgive me if I just add one thing, because it does worry me. You don't — you *can't* attach all the blame for the accident to poor Q. surely?"

"Please — forgive me but I'd really rather not discuss it," was Tamara's reply.

Aunt Liz then forgot herself so far as to push the matter a bit further. "But, darling, it was proved at the time, wasn't it, that *nobody* was to blame."

Tamara broke in, "But he was driving fast — yes — fast, considering the weather, with Claire at the back — unstrapped. That was *mad*!"

"He only meant to leave her like that for a moment or two."

"A dangerous moment, Aunt Liz. Oh God, I hated that car — *all* racing cars!"

"He made up his mind to sell the Arrow before the accident, dear."

"Only because he found it too expensive to run," said Tamara bitterly.

Aunt Liz felt embarrassed by this unkindness. She also felt that she had unwittingly put a lighted match to a haystack by mentioning the proposed sale.

"Tammy dear, I don't want to pry into your feelings but I do wish you would be more charitable towards poor Q."

Tamara said, bitterly, "When I first saw him at the hospital after the accident, I tried to make him feel he was not altogether to blame. I can't do more."

"Why go on making him feel so guilty?"

Now Tamara swung round. "*You're* sorry for him — so is everyone. Poor Q.! Poor Q.! What about *me*? Poor *me*! Poor Claire, my baby. Yes, I brought her into the world. I adored her. How do you suppose *I* feel? Q. had sworn that he wouldn't let her sit in that car without being well strapped in. If she *had* been wearing the belt, she wouldn't have been killed."

"Tam darling, they said at the inquest that it was a tragic piece of timing. Do try to be kind to Q."

Tamara choked and put her face in her hands.

Elizabeth York felt stricken. This talk with her niece proved what she had feared for so long. The poor girl was no longer the old Tamara; the sweet girl, once so devoted to Q. She had become a hard unhappy woman who had convinced herself that her husband was totally responsible for their child's tragic end. *Poor, poor Q.!*

Mrs. York leaned forward, touched her niece's cheek with her lips and said, "Darling, just try to be less bitter. It won't help."

"Of course not," said Tamara with a laugh that held a note of hysteria, "I must be understanding and say I'm pleased Claire will never know suffering, so I ought to be thankful she's in heaven!"

"No, no, Tammy — don't exaggerate. Just try to believe that it *wasn't* all Q.'s fault. Oh darling, you *mustn't* blame him. It's too unfair, too cruel."

"I feel rather cruel," said Tamara with another hysterical laugh, and then to Aunt Liz's dismay she broke down and wept without restraint. Thankful that there was nobody in the house except themselves at the moment, the older woman did her best to comfort her niece without making things worse. She half believed that it was a good thing that Tamara had broken down. She needed to cry, terrible though it was to hear those heart-rending sobs. Terrible to think too, that she had lost that beautiful child — her ewe lamb — who had meant so much to her. What mother wouldn't feel heart-broken? But Q. was the father. Q. was heart-broken too.

Tamara wanted no comfort. She hugged her aunt, then with the tears pouring down her cheeks, ran away and shut herself up in her bedroom.

Later on, Mrs. York told her brother about it all. Mr. Whitfeld listened, nodding gloomily. "Poor child. Poor Tammy. So like her mother. Emotions always exaggerated — I used to have a time with *her* as you know. Slav blood, and all that — " he sighed heavily. Mrs. York would like to have reminded her brother that Slavs, the world over, were noted for their extreme courage and strength in times of stress. But she dared not voice these thoughts.

She said, "I'm so worried about Tam."

"She didn't like that racing car — never did. I understand that he took the child out of the strap and let her sit on the back ledge. Dangerous, I suppose, but a chance in a million that Q. would have to brake sharply and the poor little girl be thrown on to her head."

"Whatever he did, Tam just can't openly condemn him. It's too *brutal*, John."

Mr. Whitfeld lit a cigar and puffed it in silence for a moment, then he eyed his sister through the pale blue smoke.

"Poor old Q. He's pretty shaken, I can tell that, but have you noticed, Liz, they neither of them talk about the affair. It would be so much better if they did. I don't like this un-natural silence. And they don't seem to want to do anything or go anywhere either. I feel they should take a trip abroad — get right away from England for a bit."

"Well — Q.'s got his job, John, and in these times he can't really desert the office. Besides, if Tamara feels as she does, she won't want to go away with him."

Mr. Whitfeld rubbed the back of his head and pursed his lips. "All very tragic. Tricky situation, too, but don't let's forget it's such a short time since the child died. They'll get over it — both of them — we know what time can do."

Mrs. York shook her head but remained silent. She didn't want to worry her brother with her own secret fears about Tamara's attitude to Q. True, she was quite gentle and even pleasant when they were all together, but the sound of her sobbing just now still rang in Aunt Liz's ears, and caused her much unease. Supposing Tamara never forgave Q., in her heart for what she *thought* he should have done to safeguard Claire? Supposing it was the beginning of the end to their marriage?

That, Aunt Liz mentally decided, was unthinkable. John was right. The two of them would recover their balance in time. Perhaps it would be best if they sold The Little House. She knew there had been talk of it and Tamara had actually said she never wanted to live there again. She couldn't bear the sight of the rooms — especially Claire's nursery — or the garden where the child used to play. Q. would, of course, do anything *she* wanted. Nobody could accuse him of being ungenerous. If she wished it he'd put the house on the market. What a tragedy it all was!

The evenings were proving uncomfortable. Nobody wanted to go out. The family tried to interest themselves in television, or to play bridge. Tam used to love that — but the games fell flat. Nobody enjoyed them.

Tonight Tamara suddenly came into the open and broached the subject of The Little House.

"Do you think it would be a good idea, Q., if we sold it?" she said in a cool voice.,

It was an evening in late January. They had finished dinner, and were drinking coffee in the sitting-room. Aunt Liz looked quickly at her niece. Tamara had put on one of her attractive evening trousersuits and tied her long blonde hair back with a ribbon. The suit was red. There had never been any suggestion of family mourning. Nobody wished it. The one thing on which Tamara had insisted was that her father should remove a large silver-framed photograph of Claire which used to stand on the Queen Anne bureau. She had begged him to take it up to his own bedroom. This had surprised Aunt Liz. Tamara had even put her own framed photograph of Claire in her dressing-table drawer. It seemed that she could not bear to look at anything that reminded her of her little daughter.

However she spoke calmly about the house and Q. with his usual amiability, answered at once, "If you're quite sure you don't want to go back there, darling, of course we'll sell up."

"Well, I *don't want* to live there any more."

"Okay," he said briefly, "perhaps tomorrow you'd pop in and see Mason & Mason. You know — the agents we bought the house from. Remember? You could discuss the price and whether or not they think the place will go quickly. Personally, I think it will. But we must try and decide where we're going first, mustn't we, darling?"

"Nowhere," said Tamara in a cold flat voice.

There was a shocked silence. Her father and aunt exchanged startled glances. Q. clenched his hands, but he spoke quietly again. "We can hardly go *nowhere*, my sweetest. We've got to live *somewhere*."

Her large dark eyes turned now in his direction. They looked enormous and haunted. It made Q. feel sick with despair. He had worried secretly over Tamara's strange behaviour since little Claire died, much more indeed than he had shown. He could never forget the way she had collapsed when she arrived at the hospital and he took her into the mortuary. She had sat staring at the small figure — at Claire's marble face — as beautiful in death as she had been in life. Only the ugly purple bruise on her forehead to illustrate what had happened when she crashed.

Tamara had held on to Q.'s hand, desperately trying to compose herself, not crying, but shivering violently, moaning until one of the nurses took charge of her. After a little time she rallied from the initial shock. Q., too, regained his self-control and had been able to take her home. They travelled in a hired car — very slowly. After reaching The Little

House, Tamara rejected any further attempt on his part to stay close to her — to comfort her. She did not share their bed that night but shut herself in the spare room. She never uttered a word about the Arrow or discussed the reasons for the accident. She merely said that she was 'in a state' and needed to be left absolutely alone. She hoped he'd understand. He had thought that he did, but not as things had turned out since. From that time on, she had drawn away from him until the tension between them became unbearable for Q.

Tamara stood the agony of Claire's funeral well, and survived the wretchedness of the days that followed without breaking down again at least not in public. But she did not return to the bed they used to share. She continued to say that she needed to be alone.

Q. suffered cruelly. He wanted so badly to end their sudden separation. Sometimes he felt a strong desire to force her to come into the open and tell him exactly what she felt about him — what she was trying to hide. He even began to drink more than usual. He was ashamed of it. Almost at once he had the good sense to realise that alcohol could never provide more than temporary oblivion. Finally he cut out drinking altogether.

He knew that he must, before long, find out what Tamara intended to do in the future. Did she want to go on living with him? Sometimes he wondered this in despair. Perhaps not. Perhaps Claire's death had turned her completely against him. That was such a grim thought he did his best to forget it. He kept telling himself that it was just a question of time, then Tamara would relax and be herself again. The Tamara he loved, and who loved him — his own warm-hearted adorable Tamara. She could not go on punishing him. It was hell enough for him to be aware of the part he had played in Claire's death.

The subject of selling The Little House eventually continued to be discussed between the four of them. But they reached no definite conclusion, apart from Tamara announcing that she would certainly put the house into the hands of Mason & Mason tomorrow. Aunt Liz suggested it might be better to wait till February or even March — before selling — when spring was in the air and the bulbs were out in the little walled garden, and the place would look its best. But Tamara sat on this idea.

"No, let's sell it now. I don't want to live there any more."

Q. bit his lip, turned his gaze from her, and muttered, "Okay, just as you wish."

Mr. Whitfeld then suggested that they should for the present remain here in Tam's old home with him and Aunt Liz.

Once again Tamara shook her head.

"Thanks, Daddy darling, but we can't do that. Aunt Liz has quite enough to do to look after *you* without having us here. No — " she turned to Mrs. York, "don't try and persuade me. I mean it. We just must leave here at the end of the month at least. You've both been marvellous to us but we can't go on living with you any longer."

Q. eyed his wife a trifle more uneasily. "But darling, when I told you we must live somewhere, you said *nowhere* — was that what you meant?"

She refused to look at him and lit a cigarette. He noticed unhappily that she was smoking more than he. They were both in a sorry state of nerves. Who could wonder?

Then Tamara stood up. "Oh, don't let's discuss the future tonight. Anyhow why not wait and see what Mason & Mason have to say about the value of The Little House. If Daddy really doesn't mind, we could stay here another week or two, anyhow."

"But of course, darling," said Mr. Whitfeld. "But what on earth do you intend to do even if you get rid of the place quickly? It always means a longish wait before a sale goes through. Couldn't you stay just temporarily in your own house?"

Tamara's cheeks reddened. She walked away towards the door. "No — I don't want to. We'll go to a hotel when we leave you, or even better, I can stay with Virginia or something, and Q. can go to his club until we've decided what to do."

"I thought Q.'d given up his club soon after he married you," said Mr. Whitfeld, coughing. He looked at his daughter with concern. She really was being difficult.

"Oh well, he can easily find some friend to give him a room," said Tamara with indifference.

Silence. None of the four seemed to want to look at the other. Q.'s heart was sinking. He felt as though he could hear the bell of doom — deafening him. At last he said, "Okay, darling, if you want to spend a few weeks with Virginia, I quite understand. I can certainly fix myself up. No difficulty about that. You know my friend, Eric Brotherton, he's always said I could use a room in his flat if ever I was stuck. He's a bachelor and has more space than he needs."

Mr. Whitfeld remained silent. Mrs. York was the one who fastened her gaze upon Tamara's husband and thought how drawn and taut he looked. When she retired that night it was in no happy frame of mind about either of the young people.

Outside Tamara's bedroom, Q. stood for a moment holding on to her fingers. She did not draw them away but she froze inwardly and he knew it. He could *feel* her aversion to any physical display of affection from him. He dropped a kiss on one of the cold slender hands and let them go.

"Sure you're feeling okay, darling?"

"Yes, why not?" She gave an abrupt little laugh.

"And you really do want to sell our nice house?" he asked sadly.

"Don't you?"

He cleared his throat. "Yes, in a vague way, but you — we — were so happy there and — "

"And so was Claire happy there," she broke in, her voice so icy that it stung him. His whole face coloured. He moved away from her.

"Very well, go ahead and see Mason tomorrow. But I just

want you to make quite sure you'll feel better even in new surroundings."

She doubled her hands at her sides. She, too, turned away.

"I'd rather not talk about it any more tonight. You've got to give me time."

"Darling, we both need time," he said gently, "but you must remember that although I haven't said much to you I'm feeling pretty bloody awful about the whole affair. After all I had charge of Claire and — "

She stopped him and swung round, "Don't *please* say any more, and *don't* make excuses. I haven't asked for any, have I?"

"No," he answered unhappily.

Big tears gathered in her eyes. "Oh, go to bed, Q. and let's not open too many wounds. We both might bleed to death," she added in a broken voice.

He ruffled the back of his hair, looking at her with uncomprehending eyes, realising perhaps not for the first time how little he really understood her. He tried to adopt a lighter tone, "That's being a bit over-dramatic, isn't it, darling?"

"Oh, you've always accused me of being too dramatic. I agree," she said, but the tears rolled down her cheeks now, making him feel responsible for her misery. "Do go to bed, Q. and let's try and get some sleep, I don't know about *you*, but I don't sleep at all during the night."

Even that remark had power to hurt him. He couldn't in all conscience state that *he* stayed awake for long. He wasn't that type. True, for the first few days after the accident, he had been inclined to wake up a lot more than usual haunted by the memory of that ghastly moment when Claire had hurtled to her death. But he had always been able to fall asleep again. Lately he had slept less soundly — longing for Tamara to come back to him — and grieved for her. Somehow she made him ashamed of his ability to sleep. For the first time he resented her attitude, and it roused him to unusual anger.

"Good night," he said briefly, and without attempting to kiss her, turned and walked into his own room.

14

THE QUESTION OF where Tamara and Q. were to live in the future could not be laid aside permanently. It had to be revived. Following that unhappy night, Q. had had little chance to indulge in an intimate talk with his wife. The senior partner of his firm asked him to take a quick journey down to Geneva, where lived a certain Monsieur Bonner — a Swiss client who was unable to get over to London easily. He was an invalid. He urgently needed an interview with one of the partners in Whitfelds. Before the present recession he had had a considerable sum of money tied up in English stocks and shares. M. Bonner liked Q, so, it was Q. who was chosen to deal with him again. He had been invited to spend the night with the Swiss in his villa on Lac Lamont.

Q. telephoned from the office to ask Tamara if it would be all right with her, and could have sworn when he heard her reply that she sounded relieved because he was going away. She spoke in a friendly enough fashion and told him the change might do him good. Q. quick to respond when she was gentle with him said, "Wish I could take you with me, darling."

"I'm afraid I've got too much to do here even to think about it just now," she said quickly.

So quiet, so polite. Nothing really to upset Q. Yet upset he was, for he had to face up to the certainty that he was not just being ultra-sensitive or over-critical. Tamara just didn't love him any more. He hardly dared wonder why.

Just before he left his father-in-law's house — Tamara had dutifully packed an overnight bag for him, and the taxi came to take him to the Cromwell Road Terminal — Q. made an abortive attempt to get closer to his wife.

He put his arms around her, and despite the fact that she held herself taut, and was obviously hostile to the embrace, he said, "Tam, dearest, do you realise that this is the first time we shall have been apart for even a couple of days since we got married?"

"Yes."

"Tam, *Tam* darling," he said huskily, 'try not to hate me. You know I'd give the world to put back the clock, but I can't. Nobody ever can. I wish to God I hadn't taken Claire out of that safety-strap but she seemed so hot and restless and — "

Now Tamara pulled away from him. He saw a blind look in her eyes that gave him a fresh sense of despair.

"Don't go on repeating yourself, Q. Q. — *please* don't. I don't want to discuss it. You know I don't."

Q. was usually a tactful man, sensible of his wife's needs — knowing that when she was in a 'mood' she was capable of sinking to the depths, but as quickly, soaring up to the heights. But his customary caution deserted him suddenly. He caught hold of her wrists and pulled her nearer him. His face was hot. He was shaking.

"Tam, *don't* please let me go away knowing that you feel so badly about me. I should never have taken off her safety-strap, and oh God, *God*! I know it." He broke off, turning away from Tamara, and covered his face with his hands.

Tamara felt sick. She had a suffocating feeling that everything was crowding down on her and that her head was going to burst. The sight of Q.'s anguish only magnified her own pain. She had meant to keep calm. She was perfectly well aware that she hadn't been behaving magnanimously to Q. no matter what mistake he had made. Her personal shattering grief seemed to close every channel that could admit tolerance, or compassion for Q. But in this moment, Q.'s unexpected breakdown deeply distressed her. So far she had avoided discussing the details of Claire's death. She had put a concrete wall between Q. and herself. Now it had cracked and she broke with it. He had always seemed so strong, so cool and self-assured. She saw that he was actually trying in this moment to hold back his tears. She was suddenly ashamed of the fact that she had been so anxious to lay the entire blame at his door.

Now when he was about to leave her, she could not bear to look at him and remain aloof and insensible to his grief. She flung herself at him. They put their arms around each other. She felt his cheek, wet with tears, against her own.

"Try to forgive me. Try," he begged in a hoarse voice which she hardly recognised. "Please don't go on hating me, Tam."

"I won't — I won't, Q."

"Oh, Tammy, but you *do* hate me, don't you? You've shown it."

"I'm sorry," she said, and she, too, was crying, her face hidden against his shoulder.

"Claire's death will be on my conscience until the end of my days."

Now suddenly she found pity enough to make her defend him.

"Don't Q. You yourself said that at the inquest the Coroner didn't put the blame on you — at least hardly any — "

"The little bit was enough," he said bitterly.

Embarrassed by his own emotional outburst, he pulled a handkerchief from his pocket and wiped his face.

"I must go. I've got to catch my plane. I don't want to leave you, darling, but I've got to."

"It's best. When you come back we'll try not to talk about it — ever again. It can't do any good."

Q. blew his nose forlornly. Taking one of Tamara's hands, he put it against his lips. "I'll say 'au revoir' then, darling. While I'm away please do anything *you* want. Make any arrangements. Just tell me now that you don't want to leave me or anything ghastly like that."

"I don't want to leave you, Q." She spoke with her back to him, finding it difficult to reorientate her emotions.

"I'm not sure I believe you," he said with a twisted smile, "but thanks for being so nice. I rather dreaded flying to Geneva feeling I was completely in the dog-house."

Now Tamara turned round to him and tried to produce an answering smile, but it wasn't much of one and she knew it.

After Q. had gone she knew also that for a dozen reasons she could never love him in the same warm gay way she used to do in the past. She could like and admire him, perhaps. She could and would pity him. She could even visualise starting life with him in a new home, and hope that in time the whole terrible affair would recede into the mists of the past. But nothing more. And it didn't really seem enough for either of them.

She felt deadly tired. She must try, she told herself, not to brood. But what motive had she for living without her child? Especially as the death of Claire had divided them instead of bringing them closer together. Was it very dreadful of her? Was she just utterly self-centred and cruel? Other women had lost children, taken the blow with courage, and comforted and supported their husbands. Why should *she* be so beastly? How perverse life could be. In a queer way (she hadn't realised it until today) she despised the weakness that used to make Q. say 'yes' to anything she asked him for. Now she dreaded the future. They had kissed with kindness, with love of a kind just now. But it was not the love it used to be. She supposed Q. would come back from Geneva full of hope because she had softened to him this morning. He would expect her to 'cheer up' (that was what he would say in his schoolboy way), and hope she'd be all brave and gay again. He would let her choose a new car; start to entertain again, or even — God forbid — suggest that they should have another child.

This was the last thing she wanted, and because of it she felt that life with Q. would be full of difficulties. How could she put the whole disaster behind her? Could she ever accept him as her lover as well as her husband again? What she had always needed — hoped for — right from the beginning, was absolute love between them. The deep, driving passion she had felt for Paul. But she had never really known it with Q.

He had always been second-best, even though she had deceived herself into thinking otherwise.

Once Q. had gone to Geneva, she found herself wondering what Paul would have said about this disaster. Perhaps he would have understood her reactions to her husband after her child's death. Perhaps he would have despised her for being so unforgiving.

Desolately Tamara walked round her father's elegant house. But she could only see Paul's dusty studio in her mind's eye. Shabby or not it had held all the beauty and warmth and ecstasy of the world for her. They had so much in common, shared so many things. They had made marvellous love — listened to his music — sung their duets — and laughed. Oh, God, she thought, I have never laughed enough in my life with Q. Once someone said love means laughter. It *does*. I can't forget those days and nights with Paul. I'm utterly disloyal to Q. — even to the memory of my dead child. Sometimes I feel I want to die.

But she went on living, recalling those hours of companionship with Paul. Paul who had never been as good, as generous to her as Q. — never as unselfish. Quite the reverse. Paul used to give her orders. *She* obeyed. They had had arguments, vital debates, especially when the studio was full of friends, who joined in discussions on so many things. Tamara had adored the exchange of ideas. She was a good conversationalist and had a quick wit. It had appealed to Paul, too and generally Tamara held her own. Only once could she remember that she had allowed herself to be talked down. Afterwards, when they were alone Paul had been rough with her.

"You shouldn't have given way in that argument about divorce, Tamara. It infuriated me. All those 'yes, dears' and you doing the silly 'little me' act. *You* ought to know best. I prefer it when you stick to your guns. Sometimes I feel you're fundamentally weak."

She had repudiated this indignantly. Then he had added that courage, both physical and mental, were the things he most admired in either man or woman. She must always act with courage, he would say, stick to her own convictions.

What then would he think of her today? Would he have expected her to accept Claire's death more bravely? He was not like Q. — not a practical business man whose hobbies were in the sporting field. He was all artist, with that touch of genius which so often made him difficult, even intractable, yet so attractive, and never, never boring.

She could hardly bear to go on thinking all these things while Q. flew to Geneva. She reached a point when she realised she must not be so egotistic.

But over one thing she would never change her mind. She would not return to The Little House. When Q. returned from Switzerland she would try to face up to life — and her marriage — more realistically.

She went up to her bedroom to sort out a few shirts she wanted to wash and iron for Q. She had to think of these things now. There was no Eilie to help. Poor Eilie! Tamara had received one or two very sad letters from Helsinki since she returned home, expressing her great grief over the loss of little Claire. She had been quite devoted to her charge. Tamara would never forget the Finnish girl. She decided that after she had attended to Q.'s laundry she would write a letter to Eilie and give her various items of news. The girl had loved London *and* The Little House.

For the rest of that morning she was busy, then she joined Aunt Liz and they did some shopping. She made a great effort to be more normal and to think of all the things she'd say and do to make poor Q. happier — even if she kept to her own bed for a bit longer.

Then the telephone bell rang. She answered and heard Vince Jones's voice. It was the first time he had contacted her since their meeting in the King's Road.

"Tam, can I come and see you?"

She thought a second. Did she want to see Vince again? That last meeting, bringing all the old stories up about Paul, had torn her apart. Wouldn't it be foolish to repeat it?

"I must see you, Tam," Vince spoke again, "I've been trying to get you for ages, but there was no reply from your home number. I just guessed you might be at your father's house, so I looked it up in the directory."

The urgency in his voice was undeniable.

"What gives, Vince?"

"It's about Paul," Vince answered.

Now Tamara caught her breath and felt the colour rush to her face. "Don't tell me something has happened to *him*. I couldn't take it. I've had enough."

Vince questioned, "What do you mean — had enough? What's happened to you?"

"Of course, you don't know."

"Tell me."

She found it difficult but surprised herself by the fact that she was able to answer that question calmly. A little while ago she couldn't have done so.

"My child — Claire — there was an accident. She died."

"Oh, my God, Tam, how *ghastly*!" Vince's voice was shocked.

"Don't sympathise with me. Don't talk about it. Just tell me what's happened to Paul?"

"He's a very sick man, Tam. I've just come from his pad. I went to see him yesterday and stayed for the night. He had nobody with him and I felt he needed me. But so far he absolutely refuses to see anybody else."

Tamara felt suddenly sick. "Stop beating around the bush. I've got to know about Paul."

"He isn't actually dying now, Tam, but he will — it's leukaemia — that's what they've discovered. He can't live for long — I mean not many more months."

Tamara's fingers tightened convulsively around the receiver. She shut her eyes and then she spoke again in a dull flat voice. "Paul is dying. My God! Leukaemia! That's cancer of the blood, isn't it? I knew he had been in hospital with some kind of blood trouble before we ever met. But how did he get *leukaemia*?"

Vince did not answer her question, but said, "I may be making a mistake by involving you, but you convinced me when we met that day that you hadn't forgotten how much you two used to mean to each other. I just thought somehow you might like to go and see him."

Tamara was silent. She felt that she could almost hear the beating of her own heart — quick, painful throbs.

She asked, hoarsely:

"Where are you, Vince?"

"In a call-box — there's one on the corner of the Mews leading into Paultons Square. You remember I told you Paul had a studio flat in Axhurst Mews? Well, he had asked me to buy a special score he needed for his work — he's working like a maniac still. He has been too tired and weak even to walk down the King's Road. I thought he looked worse than usual today but he didn't seem to want me to stay, so I had a sort of brainstorm when I came out of the flat and decided to ring *you*. Ever since he was told he had this ghastly thing he has shut himself away from all his old friends. I don't know whether it's because he actually feels too exhausted to talk or entertain, or that the medical report hit him so badly he no longer wants to face the old gang, or a party. He hasn't got a girl-friend these days, and he won't let me bring anyone I know with me when I go there. So he's always alone. It's bad for him. It's what drove me to ring you, Tam. I know you're married and obviously can't stay with him but I somehow felt in my bones you could be *the* one to help him."

"If I can do anything you know I will. But he may not want to see me. Remember he sent me away, Vince. I didn't leave him."

"Yes — and he may tell you to go away again, but I honestly don't think he will, once he sees you. You always meant more to him than any of the others. I know Paul well. There were a lot of factors that made him break with you, and it was not because he didn't care for you any more. I'd swear to that. You know, Tam — he thought you would do better for yourself if you married a fellow in your own set. He used to say so. You must remember."

"Don't let's go into that," Tamara said tersely. "I'll meet you at the Mews at once. Please be at the corner of the Square on the left, then you can take me on to Axhurst Mews. I'm not sure where that is."

"Okay. I'm terribly relieved, Tam. I've really been uptight about poor old Paul lately, and if he sees you — "

Suddenly Tamara broke in with an hysterical laugh. "*If*, Vince — but he may open the door, see me, then shut the door again. Okay! I'll risk it."

She dressed with feverish haste. It was a cold bleak January day. She put on slacks and her short ocelot coat with the brown leather belt. Paul used to like her in that. She had never got rid of it. She had always preferred it to the expensive mink jacket her father gave her before her marriage to Q. It was queer, she thought, as she tied a chiffon scarf around her head, but she had absolutely no compunction about going to Paul. Her whole mind was concentrated on the thought that he had just received his death sentence. Still in his twenties, surely not ready for death. *Oh God!* What an unspeakable thing to have happened. Why couldn't medical science find a cure for this illness? In all her dealings with Paul she had never once connected him with the possibility of an early end. He had been so alive, so full of mental and physical energy. She used to tease him about being thin, but he was never ill. He never put on weight. He had seemed able to turn night into day and to work at his music until the early hours of the morning, yet have strength enough left to begin again the next day. She used to be glad, too, because he could fling himself down and fall asleep like a child, and be swiftly renewed. At times she would fall asleep beside him. He would laugh at her and rejoice because they shared this tremendous capacity for filling every hour with the joy of living.

In a taxi, driving to Paultons Square, Tamara closed her eyes tightly and clung to her shoulder-bag as though to an anchor. She needed strength now. Q. — her marriage — her dead child — everything that had happened over the last four years faded into the background. She was the old Tamara who had belonged body and soul to Paul.

She found Vince on the corner waiting for her. He wore his old shabby leather coat with its bedraggled fur-trimming. His rather long hair was blowing in the sharp north-east wind. He looked like a hippy. She didn't care. She needed his friendship, his strength. He, too, loved Paul. She paid the taxi and rushed up to Vince.

"Thank you for 'phoning me. Here I am."

He gripped her hand. "Thanks for coming. But I wonder if I've done the right thing after all. You've got a husband and — " he stopped and shrugged his shoulders. "Well, Tam, I've always been close to Paul. I felt I must do something to help him, and you seemed sort of the answer to it all. But *you* don't look too good. Are you okay? Should I have 'phoned you?"

"Yes. What would I have done if I had heard about Paul casually from somebody else? Oh, Vince, is he really so bad?"

"They say so. He's under a very decent doctor who lives at World's End — a Dr. Finch — a Guy's man. I had a word with him the other day. He told me everything possible had been done. Poor old Paul — his daily found him in the studio one morning stretched on the floor — in a dead faint. Christmas it was. They took him to hospital and he had a month's treatment there, sort of changed his blood entirely. And he is on pills, of course. Not even in bed. They tell him to rest but he goes on with his work. He's trying to finish a special song to fit into a T.V. musical, and as it is commissioned he never flags — you know him! He puts everything out of his mind but his work, when he's interested. I expect you'll get a shock when you see him, though. He's a shadow of the old Paul."

They started to walk up the Square. Tamara held on to Vince's arm.

136

She looked with tragic eyes up at Vince's kindly bearded face. "I'm not shockable any more, Vince. The day my child died I think I reached rock-bottom. Nothing mattered any more, but now I know Paul matters still — just as much as ever."

"By the way, it was tough for you, Tam, losing your little girl. What about your husband?"

Now for the first time, Tamara spoke in Q.'s defence. "It's all been dreadful for him, but it — the accident — wasn't his fault. But of course you don't know the facts. I'll tell you about it."

"Don't if you'd rather not. You've got enough on your plate."

"No, I'd like to tell you."

Briefly she outlined the details of Claire's tragic death. "Don't be sorry for me, Vince, just take me to Paul. But I'll tell you something straightaway. Whether you think me mad or not, if Paul wants me — if he's really so ill — so much in need of someone to take care of him — I shall be quite ruthless where Q. is concerned. I shall just move in with Paul. Q. can do what he likes, and nothing that he or my father, or my aunt, or anybody else in the *world* says, will change my mind."

"Oh, God," muttered Vince, "I *knew* I ought never to have 'phoned you. I didn't think you'd take it quite like this."

"I'm probably jumping my fences," Tamara said with a brief laugh. "He may not even want to see me for five *minutes*, let alone stay with him."

Vince looked and felt awkward. "Okay, well, here we are. I'll leave you at the door. I honestly don't think I want to come in with you. You'd best work out your own problems, darling. But you've got my address, and if you haven't, Paul has, let me know what you think about him, and what gives today."

For a moment Tamara was speechless. There was a lump in her throat. There was something so kindly and decent about Vince. In the old days she had called him her big shaggy dog — waiting to have his head patted. Now her eyes filled with tears. She put out a hand and touched his cheek.

"You really are a darling. You care about other people and that's more than a lot do."

He kissed her forehead and gave an embarrassed laugh. "Nonsense. Come on now. It's only up the top of the Square, then we turn right."

He left her at the front door of the Regency house in which Paul lived. His flat was on the first floor. The main door wasn't locked, Vince said. She could just turn the handle, and walk up Paul's private staircase. She'd see a black-painted door. Paul occupied the two upstairs floors. Once at the top, she'd see he had a thirty-foot long room with two windows which he had turned into an attractive studio.

Tamara listened to all this attentively.

Outside Paul's own door, which had a brass knocker, shaped like a lion's head, Tamara stood for a full moment, aware of her heart's frantic beating. A host of doubts crowded down on her. Supposing both she and Vince *had* been too hasty? She put a hand up to her neck, drawing the collar of the ocelot coat closer around her. Other disturbing thoughts flitted through her mind. Supposing he still cared for Liesel — Liesel — the girl he had gone to when he left her, Tamara? Or if there were some other girl? Vince said Paul did not live with anybody but somebody might exist who was, secretly, his girl-friend. If so, it would make her look so stupid — coming here, uninvited. Almost Tamara turned and rushed down that staircase again, then she stayed still. She thought, *I must see him. I must — whatever he says or does.*

There was a push-bell by the door, with a card over it. *PAUL PRYCE.* Very smart. Different from the old days when he had been less affluent, and the place he lived in was often dirty, even squalid. This was an expensive flat. He certainly wasn't poor any more.

Now, courage returning, she pressed the bell and used the knocker. There was a dry sensation in her throat. She listened

138

acutely. Silence reigned. *Was he in?* Vince said he was bound to be. But he might have gone out.

Tamara banged the knocker again, and pressed the bell twice. He must surely hear if he was at home. He wasn't playing his piano or his guitar. Not a sound came from the flat.

Suddenly she heard footsteps. She clasped her shoulder-bag desperately as she had done in the taxi, in a sort of panic.

The steps were slow. It wasn't the old Paul who, especially during the winter, used to tear down his staircase two at a time, fling open the main door and yell at her, "*Come in angel,* for God's sake, and shut the door. It's freezing. You're letting in all the cold." Then he would take her arm and pull her upstairs. No question of a long passionate kiss. He would rush to the piano, smile at her with his brilliant eyes, and tell her to listen while he played his latest song. And how she had loved it! Loved being ordered about by him. Loved being the first privileged person to hear his latest composition. The kisses would come after.

Suddenly while Tamara waited and worried, she heard the letter box being thrust open and Paul's voice through the slit. It *was* Paul's voice. "Who's there? I don't want to see anybody at the moment. I'm in the middle of my work."

A gasp from Tamara. She began to shake from head to foot, but she answered his question, "It's me, Paul — Tamara — " she broke off, her throat dry.

She had a moment's ghastly fear that he would just leave her standing outside and go up his staircase again. But he flung open the door and stood facing her.

"What in the name of all that's holy are *you* doing here?" he asked. She thought that his voice had changed. It was on a lower key and hoarse.

"I've come to see you," she said wildly.

"What for?"

"Paul, please ask me to come in. I *must* talk to you."

He opened his mouth as though to speak but shut it again. He looked dazed, she thought, thoroughly taken aback. Now her whole mind was concentrated on his appearance. Vince had warned her that she might find him changed. Yes, he was horribly thin. His dark blue pullover seemed to hang on him. His face was so white and his eyes so sunken, he had aged alarmingly, she thought. He always stooped but now his shoulders seemed more bent than ever. He was not shaved and his chin had a bluish look. His hair was as dark and thick as ever, a little longer and perhaps less curly. His eyes upset her most. Once they were brilliant and eager, now almost dull and sad — the eyes of a much older man. He wore horn-rims. He peered at her through them as though the light hurt him.

"Well?" His voice was harsh. "What's brought *you* here, my dear? And who gave you my address?"

"I just — found it."

He shook his head. "Somebody must have told you. Vince — blast him."

"What's it matter," she said, helplessly. "Paul — are you going to keep me standing out here? I know we haven't met for a long long time but I would like to sit down somewhere and talk to you."

Silence. She felt a kind of despair. He didn't seem the least pleased to see her. On the contrary, at any moment he might ask her to go away again. He had never been over-polite. There had always been that rather rough ruthless streak in him, and he had been unpredictable — yet such a fascinating lover. Perhaps that was why she had been so madly in love with him. But what was the use of remembering what used to be? And his very next words brought her right down to earth.

"I thought you were a married woman, living it up in style."

She winced, "I am married," she managed to answer. "So what?"

He thrust both hands into his pockets and jerked his head to and fro. A mannerism she recognised. She used to tell him he tossed his head like an impatient pony. With a politeness that she knew to be insincere, he questioned her again, "All happy and cosy, I hope!" He spoke in the old half-teasing, half-sneering voice.

The colour drained from her face. "Is that all you've got to say?"

"Oh, for God's sake — why have you landed up on my doorstep anyhow? I thought you and I were washed up. I told you I didn't want to see you any more."

Her face burned.

"You're being very unkind and very rude," she said indignantly. "I *know* we were washed up. But it was years ago, and of your choosing, not mine. It can't stop me from coming to see you years after — just as a friend," she ended lamely.

For a second Paul jingled some loose coins in one of his pockets. He stared at her through his glasses. God, he thought, he'd almost forgotten how beautiful she was. *Those eyes* — well, Tamara's dark, velvety eyes had always eaten him up. And that ocelot jacket — he remembered that. To say nothing of her slimness and grace. She certainly hadn't changed much, in spite of the years. Lost a bit of weight, perhaps — grown a bit older, of course. A few lines around those magnificent eyes. The long fair hair was as gorgeous, as appealing, as ever.

He spoke again, "Don't I have to congratulate you on having a child as well as a husband? Someone saw it in the papers and told me. Three or four years ago, wasn't it?"

It was her turn to keep silent. She broke out in a perspiration. She was shivering. When she answered Paul it was in an almost inaudible voice, "Yes. My little girl was three. She was killed in an accident just before Christmas."

For a moment there flashed through her mind the recollection of that small grave in the cemetery at Haslemere. They had laid her to rest beside her grandmother. For a long time Tamara could not even bear the idea of visiting her small daughter's grave but lately she had been persuaded by Q. to go with him and lay fresh beautiful flowers on the green, pathetic mound. But it had upset her so much that Q. had told her he would go alone in future, and that she must let more time elapse — wait until she was more stoic, then visit Claire's little grave.

That has always been the trouble with me, Tamara thought bitterly, full of self-reproach, I have never been stoic enough. I'm being just as much of a coward today. Seeing Paul — knowing what's wrong with him — it's unbearable.

Thinking over the grim news she had given him, Paul stopped staring at her and shuffled his feet.

"I'm terribly sorry —" he began.

She turned and started to walk away. He hurried after her, "No — don't go. I'd like to talk to you, Tam. Come along," he said.

15

TAMARA WAS SO confused that she never quite knew how she got up those stairs and reached Paul's studio. Her eyes were half-blinded by tears. She saw nothing of the beauty of Paul's new home for quite a time after she was led into it. Gently he put her down on to a curved sofa in front of an electric convector which was sending out an agreeable heat. She needed it. She felt ice-cold. She leaned forward and hid her face in her hands. It had never been her intention to let herself go in this way or get involved in an emotional scene with Paul. She had resolved to put all her grief and bitterness aside and to concentrate on his tragedy. But somehow just having to tell him that Claire was dead had shaken her to pieces. She was amazed and touched by his sudden switch from sarcasm and hostility to this extreme tenderness.

So like him, she thought, swinging from one mood to another. In the old days she had found it disturbing. But she needed his kindness desperately in this hour. Paul seated himself beside her. She began to cry. She felt his arm go around her and heard his voice unusually gentle and comforting.

"Poor darling! What a ghastly thing! Don't cry, please. *Please*, don't cry. Or cry if you want to and let me help. I was beastly just now. I ought to have known better. It was the sight of you standing there — so unexpected — I admit it shook me. But I never dreamed — Vince didn't tell me — about your child. It must have been frightful for you."

As though it was the most natural thing in the world, she turned to him and was gathered wholly into his arms. Not even in Q's arms had she cried like this. She sobbed uncontrollably, her body shaking. Paul stroked her hair, and kept saying, "No — no — don't — don't cry like that, you kill me!"

Then through the fog of her wild grief she heard that word — *kill* — and remembered what was happening to *him*, and why she had come here in the first place. She buried her face against Paul's shoulder, and in a small, hoarse voice made her apology.

"Sorry, Paul. I'm afraid I just lost control. Everything seemed to crowd down on me. It's all been a bit much, you see!"

"Sure! I know what it means to feel things cracking you up. I've often wished I could cry. It's a sort of relief, isn't it?"

She drew away. She couldn't have cared less that her face must be ugly and blotched after the violent weeping. She looked up at Paul, her eyes tragic — *his* tragedy that she had put second to her own. She could not think sensibly.

"Can I use your bathroom?" she whispered.

"Of course. I'll show you."

She shut herself in the bathroom, took off her coat, then ran cold water into the basin and sluiced her face. She grew calmer, but still felt sick with herself and terrified for him. She was shocked by his appearance. In his arms just now she had felt the sharpness of his shoulder-blades, the pallor of his thin face. Vince was right, Paul was desperately ill.

Claire was dead, Paul, whom she had once loved more than anything in the world, was going to die. The double blow paralysed all other thought. She was aware that she had no right to compare the two tragedies. Paul was no longer the mainspring of her life. She had married Q. and given birth to Claire. How could she possibly wipe out the memory of those years — that existence which had nothing to do with Paul? She looked in the mirror and wiped her disfigured face with a towel. Vaguely she began to notice the luxury of this room, the soft expensive towels, the jade green bath and mirrored walls. He had certainly raised his standard of living. Of course he had made money. He must have decided to spend it, and change his whole life after his success in America.

In the studio Paul walked slowly to a pinewood corner cupboard in which he kept his drinks. He poured out a stiff brandy and soda for Tamara. Like her, he was undergoing a somewhat confused analysis of his feelings.

At first when he had seen her on the doorstep, he had resented her coming. Only one thought had entered his head. To make her go away again — quickly. But once he had heard her curt announcement of her three-year-old daughter's accidental death, he had undergone a complete reversal of feeling, and when he had sat beside her in the studio and felt her scalding tears against his neck, he knew that he still loved her. The years between had not killed the old, overwhelming passion he had felt for her. His climb to success had been exhilarating. He had enjoyed life in America. But never had these things — and certainly not the other girls in his life — obliterated his memories of Tamara, and of those crazy studio days when they had been lovers.

When Tamara joined him, he looked at her critically, and with a strange feeling of pity. How young she still looked and how vulnerable. Being a wife and mother had not spoiled her. She had tidied that long fair hair which had always excited him, and made up her face. She was still the girl of his dreams.

She came slowly towards him. Like a boy, she thrust both hands into her pockets and gave a shamefaced smile.

"Sorry I was so stupid —" she began.

He interrupted, "Sit down by the fire and sink this." He held out the drink he had poured for her.

"What is it?"

"Brandy."

"At this hour of the morning?"

"You need it," he said briefly.

Obediently she took the glass. They sat down on the sofa, side by side. She asked, "Aren't you going to have one with me?"

"I don't need it."

"I rather think I do!" she admitted with a faint smile.

He looked at the hand holding the glass. She had always had exquisite fingers — slender, tipped with rose-pink varnished nails. The same old colour, he thought — the same hair-do — but no, she had a slight fringe now. That was new. It suited her. She used to favour the colours he liked. She hadn't changed. The burnt orange of her polo-necked pullover with black velveteen slacks was stunning.

She sipped some more of the brandy, grateful for the warmth and stimulus. Her brain was clearing. She looked up into Paul's eyes — dark, unfathomable. So like her own everyone used to tell her. Now she came straight to the point.

"I want you to know that I know about *you*, Paul!"

He scowled. The old Paul, she thought. He always scowled when he heard something he didn't particularly want to hear. She said, "Don't be cross. Vince just mentioned it."

"*Why*? How can my state of health affect *you*?"

She flushed, "I think he thought I ought to know —" she paused and swallowed.

He said, "My state of health is my affair — not Vince's — neither is it yours."

Tamara set down her glass. How like him to be so difficult. "Vince knew perfectly well that it affects both of us," she exclaimed. "You've had a rotten report from some specialist. Vince knows that and he is your dearest friend, and naturally, it hit him. Well — whatever you think, it hit me too when I heard. I can't believe even now that it's true."

Paul got up and walked to one of the long windows. He stared out. It had begun to snow — a few greyish flakes were whirling down from a stormy sky.

"Glad the central heating is working again," he said with studied nonchalance, "it went wrong the other day. This is rather a big room but it's pretty warm in here now, isn't it?"

She switched her thoughts to the temperature. "Very warm, and your room is lovely." She looked around her, trying to turn her attention to the décor, the fine golden rugs on the polished floor — the beautiful olive-green curtains, and the new baby-grand. The lid was covered with sheet music. Paul had always wanted a glamorous studio. He had it now.

"A change from the old pad," said Paul with a dry laugh.

Now her eyes beseeched him, "Tell me about yourself, *please* Paul."

"Tell me about *yourself*," he laughed. She knew that maddening teasing laugh.

She took another sip of the cognac. "Oh — don't fob me off all the time," she said, suddenly angry.

"Why not?"

"I've just got to hear about *you*, Paul."

"Why?"

"Because it *affects* me. You must know it does."

"I know nothing of the sort. I haven't set eyes on you for years. Remember — you're a stranger to me. I don't confide in strangers." His smile was sarcastic now.

Her eyelids smarted. She wanted to hit out at him. "Oh, you haven't changed, have you? I really *do* feel I'm back with you again," she exclaimed, and put her glass down on the table so clumsily that it shattered. He saw that she had cut her finger. It was bleeding. He said:

"For God's sake, go and wash your hands. There's plaster in the cupboard over the basin, and do stop being so hysterical."

She ran out of the studio, hating him — loving him — she didn't know which. Most of all she hated herself for losing her control. Why, *why* was he able to wield this power over her? She attended to the finger. It was only a superficial cut, and soon she returned to the studio.

"I'd better go," she said, miserably.

"Sit down. I want to play you my new song," he said unexpectedly and started to walk towards the piano.

"No," she said. "No, not now, please. I don't want to hear it."

He lifted an eyebrow. "I don't seem to remember you ever saying that before. When we were together and I wanted to play you my latest, you couldn't wait."

Her splendid eyes flashed at him. "Oh, stop being so sarcastic. You were so nice just now — so kind to me."

"Just now I felt sort of sad for you," he said, shrugging. "It's plain you don't want me here. I'll put on my coat."

Suddenly Paul's expression changed. "Sit down again, Tam. I want you to stay. Honestly."

Her gaze levelled with his. Her heart beats slowed down, and the colour returned to her cheeks. "You were always difficult. I never did know what you wanted, did I? And in the end —"

"In the end," he broke in, "you found out. I just didn't intend to go on playing the poor boy to the rich girl and letting you waste your life and time on me."

"That's mad. You know there was a — a terrific bond between us. I was perfectly happy so long as I was with you. It didn't worry me because you hadn't a sou, and all that nonsense. I would never have left you. *You* told *me* to clear out!"

"Okay, I did. And you married a nice rich stockbroker.

When I came back from America I met one or two people who knew you and I asked how you were and they told me you were flourishing. Of course I had no idea about you losing your little girl," he added on a lower key. "That was tough."

She ignored this. She didn't wish to discuss Claire. She said, "Well — I had no news of you till I met Vince, and that was quite by accident the other day. For a long time I was unhappy, I admit it. Then I accepted the fact that you didn't want to have any more to do with me. So, as you said — I got married. You had Liesel, and went over to America and that was final for me. I don't suppose you ever gave me a thought and I —" she stopped, clenching her fingers convulsively, at a loss for further words.

He gave her a long enquiring look. "Well — did *you* remember *me*?"

She bent her head, "Yes", she said in a whisper, "yes, I did."

"Even when you got married?"

She flushed. "No — I was — happy with Q. in a way. He was wonderful to me. I needed him. But my marriage only worked at intervals. I know I shouldn't say so, but I want to be honest. I never really forgot you, Paul, or *us,*" she added in a whisper.

He stared at her. His breathing was uneven.

"And I bloody well never forgot *you,*" he said roughly, and turned back to the window and stared out again. "I needed Liesel at the time," he said, "but it didn't work. Nothing is working for me at the moment."

"Don't say that, Paul. Don't let's argue any more. It'll get us nowhere."

He smiled. "Why worry, my darling? The only place I'm likely to get to quite soon is the crematorium."

She gasped, "Paul. *Paul!*" and stumbled to the sofa, sat down, and began to sob bitterly.

It was the second time she had cried like this today — first for her child — now for Paul. She was crushed by the conviction that she loved him as much now as she had ever done — maybe more.

He came across to her and taking her arms lifted her bodily up. He looked down into that beautiful face so ravaged by grief, so drenched in tears. He shook her gently.

"Stop it, Tam, darling. Please! I understand why you wept for your poor little girl, but why shed one tear for me? I'm nothing to you any more really and not worth your love. I've got leukaemia — okay — but I don't want to be pitied, and I can't stand scenes — *you* know that. I never could. So for my sake get a grip on yourself. I don't feel too good — your fantastic loyalty to me — to our old affair — is marvellous and I thank you. But I don't feel too good."

That made her stop crying at once. She was ashamed of her weakness. She put an arm around his thin frame. He held on to her. She gave a long shuddering sigh and closed her eyes. Perhaps it was the sight of those long dark lashes sweeping against her cheeks, childish, wet with tears, that finally went to Paul's heart. His normal dislike of sympathy and his secret terror of death, were exchanged for the old crazy passion he had felt for her years ago. He clasped her around the waist and began to kiss her, her lips, her hair, her long, slender throat. She returned the kisses and they clung together like two frightened children, afraid to let go, afraid to be left alone, afraid of so many things. Children who found themselves plunged into the darkness.

For a long time they did not speak. Then it was Tamara's turn to be strong. She knew she must comfort Paul — he needed her support so much more than she needed his. It was as though all the six years they had been parted they had both been waiting for this revival of their love — for this sad, sweet reunion. They were still wildly in love. They were made for each other, and they were in a closed little world into which no one else must be admitted.

Tamara felt his lips moving across every inch of her face and throat. His heart pounding against her — her heart beat to the same tune. But very soon, she felt his thin body

149

trembling and was shocked into remembering that he was a very sick man, and that this emotional scene could not be good for him. She was filled with remorse. It was essential he should conserve every ounce of strength, of energy, that remained.

So quickly she drew away from him. She took both his hands and led him back to the sofa. "Darling, sit down. Sit down, *please*. You must." Her voice was hoarse and urgent. He made no protest. He did not even argue when she put her arms under his knees, lifted his legs and helped him to lie down. He leaned his head against a cushion. He was pale and breathless, it terrified her.

"I'm going to get *you* a spot of brandy this time," she said.

"I don't want it," he whispered, "I don't drink much these days. But I never did, did I?"

"No, but you need a stimulant. You gave me a brandy and I drank it to please you. Remember?"

He shook his head, but she found the bottle, knelt down beside him and lifted a glass to his lips.

"Please — just a sip, please, Paul darling."

He gave her that heart-breaking smile again. When he smiled like that, staring up at her, with his dark, haunted eyes full of love — no longer of bitterness — how tragically young he looked. She longed to take his head between her hands and smooth the dark, untidy hair. It had grown long — much longer than usual. He sipped the brandy and shut his eyes again.

"Don't leave me, Tam. Stay a bit longer," he said drowsily.

Her heart suddenly sang. It was as though Q., her husband, had never existed or was part of another life. Only Paul and the present mattered. "I'll never leave you again," she said.

He didn't answer. He had felt so giddy just now. He remembered what his doctor had told him. He was to go easy — very easy. The stress of the last hour had been too much.

Damned red corpuscles, he thought bitterly, *where are you, blast you?*

For a time he rested, eyes still shut, holding on to Tamara's hand. She crouched by him — she watched over him like a mother would stay beside her sick child (just as she had watched Claire when she wasn't well — her poor little Claire).

It was a long time before Paul opened his eyes and spoke to Tamara again. His return to reality was triggered off by the sound of the telephone-bell.

"Answer it for me, Tam," he whispered. "It doesn't matter who it is — just tell them I'm not here."

She walked to the white telephone that stood on a Queen Anne bureau at the far end of the room. She lifted the receiver and said "Hello!" A girl's voice answered, "Who's that?"

"A friend of Paul Pryce's," was Tamara's answer.

"Is he there?"

"No, I'm afraid he's out. When he comes in, I'll tell him you called if you'll just give me your name." Tamara took up pad and pencil.

"Liesel," said the girl on the other end of the wire, "just say Liesel."

Silence. Tamara was conscious of the most ridiculous suffocating jealousy. Liesel — the girl he had lived with after *she* had gone out of his life. But hadn't Vince said that Liesel was no longer in touch with Paul?

Then Liesel, herself, enlightened Tamara. "Tell him I'm back from the States and staying with Maria Minitti — he'll know where *she* lives and he can phone me there. I have an exciting piece of news for him concerning one of his songs."

"I'll tell him," said Tamara and put down the receiver.

She went back to the sofa and sat down. How ill Paul looked. More so than when she had first arrived. The skin seemed stretched across the fine bones of his face. Such an attractive face despite his illness; nothing could alter the moulding of those high cheek-bones, those wonderful eyes. She met his enquiring glance. "That was Liesel."

His brow creased in the old familiar scowl. "Hell! Is *she* back?"

When Tamara gave him the message, he shrugged. "I shan't 'phone her. Her friend Maria's an Italian with rather a nice voice. The group used to use her sometimes when Liesel wasn't available. I thought she'd gone back to Florence, but then I've not seen Liesel for some time, and had no news of that crowd. I'm out of it and intend to stay out."

Tamara gave a short sharp sigh of relief. If he didn't want even to telephone Liesel, that was *that*. There was no foundation for jealousy. Paul's next remark confirmed it. "Liesel used to be a charmer, but before we broke up she started on the drugs. It didn't do her much harm at the time, but I suspected she'd soon be on the hard stuff. We started to quarrel, so I quit. I want to write songs — not fight with drugged females."

Tamara sat silent. Her hands moved restlessly in her lap. She didn't really want to hear any more about Liesel — or any other girl who might have figured in Paul's life.

What a tragedy it had been — those years of separation. A waste of all the time they could have spent together. He had not stopped loving her — at least that was now a fact. She had known it beyond doubt when they stood in each other's arms sharing their mutual grief and despair. For her, Paul's death could only mean the absolute end of loving — this time he would leave *her* and forever.

She walked to the window and looked out over Paultons Square. The snowfall had been light. Now she could see a blue patch in the sky, and there was even a hint of sunlight. She remembered vaguely that she had heard on her radio that today would start badly but clear before tonight. Her mind was still so confused and her emotions so heightened that she could not begin to think what to do next. Of course, everything, she reflected, depended so much on what Paul wanted. When she turned back to him, the speech she had prepared died on her lips. He was lying still with his eyes tight shut. For a moment she had a ghastly fear that his heart had stopped beating, but when she knelt down and put her face close to his, she could feel his breath coming quite regularly. He had fallen into a sleep of sheer exhaustion. She stood up and sighed. She was stabbed suddenly by the memory of one of her aunts — younger than Aunt Liz —who had died of leukaemia. Tamara had gone with her father to visit Aunt Joan at the clinic where she eventually died. Now Tamara was face to face again with the same dread enemy. Aunt Joan had had constant blood-transfusions. All the same treatment that Paul was receiving. At the end she had developed septicaemia. She had died quickly. That was what Tamara hoped might happen to Paul. That he would sink into a coma and would never realise he was dying.

Tamara could only suppose that at the best he would have a few more weeks, or perhaps months, to live. His doctor would certainly not allow him to go on living here alone in his flat much longer.

Sick with misery Tamara stared intently down at Paul. He seemed so peaceful now. It was unbelievable to her that anyone still so young, and talented, could have set foot on that long dark road that led to total oblivion. Even today, sick man though he was, she had felt the passion of Paul's kiss, and the strength of his arms about her. He had become like the old Paul. He was the same wonderful, unpredictable lover — loving her — close to her at times — harsh and critical at others.

While Paul slept, her thoughts turned at last to the man she had married. Poor Q.! At this moment in Geneva, talking business with his Swiss client. Poor Q. — the man who had filled the void in her life after Paul went out of it. The four years as his wife had taught her that she could always rely on him, always find him agreeable, polite and kind. He had loved her no matter how difficult or selfish she had been. He bore no resemblance to Paul. Gentle, amiable Q.! She genuinely admired his excellent character and had been grateful for his unstinted devotion. She knew that she had had no right to resent what she called his 'schoolboy' attitude to life. Still — regrettable that it might be — Paul was the one who mattered most.

The glamorous honeymoon with Q. in Cannes had been great — but left no deep mark on her. Neither had the early days spent with him in their flat on the Embankment. Admittedly she had enjoyed The Little House. She had danced on, believing she was happy — that she would never meet Paul again. Today her life with Q. seemed like an extraordinary dream. But the birth and death of Claire, and the accident in the Arrow — these things had left their mark and, rightly or wrongly, she had been near to hating her husband from that time onwards. When he had embraced her so tenderly just before leaving for the airport, she had resolved that once he returned, she would try to make him happy — whatever her personal feelings. She had wanted to begin again on the old friendly footing. She had even come near to believing she could soon accept him as lover as well as husband.

Now everything had changed. Time stood still. It was as though she had been struck by a lightning flash which had split her entire life in two. She was back with Paul. He was going to die, so until then, she would not leave him. No matter what he or anybody else said — *she would not.*

A tumult of emotion shattered Tamara while she sat there beside the sleeping man. She tried to consider Q. She did not want to hurt him any more. He didn't deserve to lose both his wife and child. People would say justifiably that she was mad, and even bad. Yet Paul had been her first lover and she had never really got him out of her system. Her thoughts turned wildly round and round. If she left Q. even for a brief time, her father, and Aunt Liz, too, would be horrified. Even the faithful Virginia might turn on her if she acted so badly, particularly now, so soon after Claire's death. But abandon Paul — no — not now — on that point Tamara remained inflexible.

154

When Paul woke up he found her huddled in the chair beside him. He put out a hand and took one of hers.

"Tam — dear, dearest Tam — I thought I'd been dreaming, but you are here. Tammy, my darling, you really *are* here with me again."

At once she was kneeling beside him, her arms around his neck, her cheek pressed to his. "I'll never leave you again, Paul. I've come back. You won't banish me this time, will you, darling?"

He hugged her close and laced his fingers through the heavy strands of her blonde hair. He whispered,

"I must have been out of my tiny mind ever to make you leave me. But whatever you think, I swear I didn't really want to lose you. You can ask Vince. You were used to having everything, although I knew you didn't care about the money all that much, and I know you wanted to be with me, but I still felt it would be wrong of me to *let* you live with me openly, or even marry me. Your father would have been dead against it. I made a mistake, but I did what I thought okay at the time."

He touched her cheek with his forefinger.

"You were always an odd, intense sort of girl. You haven't changed."

She laughed, near to tears.

"I loved you so much. I still do."

"But Q. was a good chap, and it was your scene — that super life you led with him. You must admit it."

"In a way," Tamara said grudgingly. "But, oh, Paul, Paul!" She broke off, sobbing. He took her in his arms again. He felt wretched — for her — for himself — even for her husband — yet he knew he still loved and wanted this girl — for the short time that was left to him.

Her beauty, her quick wit, her chic — all the things that had first attracted him, were no less attractive to him now, after six years of separation. Liesel had been a stop-gap — never a serious love. Paul thought bitterly, Q. will have her when I've gone. Why should I send her away again?

"Tamara," he said aloud, "I still love you — more than — er perhaps — but are we being crazy? I've only got a few months to live. I've very little strength and I sleep a lot. I'd be a poor companion and lover, wouldn't I?"

She clung to him. "I don't care. It isn't that I want to sleep with you. You know that. I want just to be with you. Call me your sister if you like — your girl-friend — anything — but I can't leave you again."

Paul gave one of his quick unexpected smiles. "Might I ask, Tamara, baby, what you'll do — how you think you'll enjoy living with me as I am now, and you a respectable married girl?"

His sarcasm hurt her as it always used to do. "Oh, shut up, Paul. You know I don't care whether I'm married or not. Q. will understand, anyhow."

"Good for Q."

"You want to quarrel with me?" she asked the question furiously.

He held up a hand. "Cool it, Tammy. We used to like our quarrels. You know what you're asking for. Why let yourself into it?"

"Because I love you more than anything. Don't you understand yet? I know the time may be limited and you may hurt me again and again, but I'd be much more badly hurt if you shut the door on me. I couldn't take it." Her voice cracked. "Please, Paul, let me stay."

He pushed her away. He looked white and tired, and when he spoke again it was quietly and even kindly. "Try to be practical, Tammy, for once in your life. You're crazy, and I'd be even more crazy to let you come here. Oh, God —" he broke off, coughing, breathless.

She was full of remorse then. "I'll go if you really want history to repeat itself. But you need me. You know it."

"Okay. I need you all right, but what the hell will your husband say if you do stay with me?"

"Do you *want* me to?"

"I want to die in peace."

156

That shook her. She saw the immense weariness on his face, and at once was all contrition. She put an arm around him. "Darling, darling, you're not fit for this sort of argument. I feel awful. Instead of helping you, I'm making things worse."

He said quite gently, "No, love, it's all my fault. I've asked for a row, but it's just because I know how much I do want you back. I can't go on saying I don't. Look, I've written a song I'd like you to hear. It's all about us — listen to it, will you?"

"You aren't fit —" she began in deep distress. But he reached the piano, sat down on the stool and ran his fingers over the keys. His tragic eyes devastated her but she watched him, listened to him with her heart beating in time, in tune to that song. And mixed up with her misery was a fierce joy because she knew now that he loved her more than he had done when they first discovered each other.

He couldn't sing properly. He crooned the words in a husky voice.

> Last night I went again to our hotel
> Where once we stayed and always loved so well.
> They gave me the same room — the same key
> But nothing seemed at all the same to me.
>
> You took the magic from me when you left
> I felt so crushed and lonely, so bereft.
> How gay we were, how crazy, you and I!
> But I want you still — oh, come back, yesterday!
>
> Why did our love and laughter have to end?
> How long does it take a broken heart to mend?
> I turned away and I left our room again
> Nothing was there but the memory of my pain.
>
> But I want you still — oh, come back, yesterday!
> Just once again, just once — you need not stay.

At the end of the song he turned to her. "It'll just be called 'Come Back, Yesterday'."

She walked to the piano and placed her hands on his shoulders.

"That was beautiful — marvellous! Oh, Paul darling, now I know how you feel, I'll stay — you can ask for anything and I'll say yes — yes — all the time. Oh, darling — it's a glorious song. I want to cry?"

"Don't," he said and turned and looked up at her with a tenderness she had never before seen in his eyes.

"I won't cry. I'm so happy, Paul — let's be happy together again."

He gave a long sigh. She read capitulation in it and his next words confirmed her belief. "You can stay, but I make reservations."

"Tell me something first. You have these blood-transfusions, don't you, Paul?"

"Yes — all too often. I go to hospital when necessary. It's a bore."

"It *could* save your life. Don't despise it. What about antibiotics? Are they of no use?"

"None."

I must see his doctor, Tamara thought. I'm not his wife but I must find out exactly how things stand with him and how long he has got. I'll ask Vince to help me.

She stayed with Paul for an hour. She must go home, then come back. She had decided upon that. She must pack a suitcase and tell them all that she had to be away for a while. She must talk to Q. again. God, how utterly terrible, Q. — poor Q. — had been forgotten.

Paul looked at her. He seemed to read her thoughts. "Tam — you're not going to stay here tonight."

"Oh yes I am —" she began, but he broke in.

"Oh, no, you're not!"

"Why?"

"You were always a great girl for saying *why*! Don't argue. I'm not quite the same Paul you once knew. All these discussions are pointless! I'm too bloody tired to argue with anybody, anyhow."

Now the tears sprang to her eyes. "Then I won't argue, darling, but just tell me I can come back later — to stay."

He closed his eyes, "No — not stay. I'm so tired, Tammy, let me have my way. Be here during the day, yes — sleep here, no! You're married to Quentin Whats-his-name. It wouldn't be fair on him."

She bit into her lower lip. The tears came blinding down her cheeks now. "Oh, Paul, you're a better person than I am. I haven't given poor Q. much thought. My only excuse is that I feel so dazed. My mind is still chaotic."

He twisted the wedding ring around her finger. "I understand. I only wish I felt better. I'd enjoy a good fight with you. Do you remember sometimes years ago at the end of a violent argument we hardly knew whether we loved or hated each other. But whatever we agree now — no sleeping here for you. I repeat — come and stay all day if you want, but of course if you tell your husband and he doesn't have a nervous breakdown. You know him. I don't. I can't imagine what he'll say. I presume you told him we were lovers."

She flushed. "Yes, I did. He didn't mind all that. All men these days don't expect their wives to have led absolutely celibate lives before marriage. He knew I'd be faithful to my marriage vows, and I have been. I *will* be. In a sense you and I can't be lovers now in the full meaning of the word."

"No," Paul nodded. Seated on the sofa again, he felt exhausted. He looked up at Tamara and caught her hand and kissed it. "I want you to stay. I want our Yesterday to come back. I'll give up battling with you, darling. Just wait till Vince comes for night-watch, then come back tomorrow."

She drew a deep breath. Her eyes shone. "I'll do what you ask. Yes, anything you say. Do you know you haven't had anything to eat since I arrived. You've been too busy sleeping or arguing with me — I'll go and cook an omelette for you. Would you eat it?"

He gave her that disarming grin which even now when he was ill and gaunt, made him look like a young boy.

"Might! Try me and see. Anyhow, I want to go to the bathroom. No — don't help me. Leave me alone. You're not a hospital nurse, lover. And I certainly haven't reached the state when I need to be helped to the loo. I still go for short walks. Vince takes me out at night. You've no idea how terrific he's been. He knows I don't want to leave my home and go into some grim hospital ward — or nursing home. They do their best but if I've got to die, I'd like to do it in my own studio. I want my piano till the end. But I *am* hungry, Tammy, and after I've eaten your omelette — if it doesn't finish me off, I'll play to you again."

Fighting against her emotions, Tamara grinned back at him.

"Okay. See you!" She disappeared into the kitchen, and did her crying there.

16

THAT NIGHT A long unhappy telephone conversation took place between Tamara and Virginia.

Prior to Q.'s Geneva trip, Tamara's father had arranged to take her and Aunt Liz out to dinner — just for a change. He had told them, smiling, it was especially to get Liz away from thinking up menus and buying food. But Tamara couldn't face a restaurant meal after her soul-searing reunion with Paul. She excused herself on the grounds that she had developed one of her bad headaches. They both said how sorry they were to go out without her and offered to stay in, but she had bundled them off.

She needed to be alone tonight. She had a lot of thinking to do. Also she wanted to see what her best and most helpful friend had to say about the new crisis.

Tamara had left Paul in Vince's hands. The omelette had been eaten and enjoyed. The new song had been played again. It had broken Tamara's heart, listening to his music. He played with such feeling. She couldn't bear to look at his back — a little bent and so thin, oh, so thin!

She had wept silently all the way home to her father's house. Vince seemed delighted that she and Paul had been reunited. He told Tamara, when he saw her to the door, how relieved he was that she had decided to stay with Paul all day, things being as they were. He would have given up a week's work — but Paul had been dead against it and refused the offer. He disliked being treated as an invalid, and accepted Vince at night only because he hated the long, dark often sleepless nights alone. The time would come, he knew, when he would have to have both day and night nursing. Only then would he be forced into a clinic. When Tamara discussed it with Vince he said: "Okay — until then, you and I'll do day and night nursing between us" — These had been his farewell words to Tamara.

Once home, Tamara made no mention of Paul to her father and aunt. She went straight to her room and telephoned to Virginia, not without a niggling little feeling that her friend, much as Virginia loved her, was not going to approve what she was doing. She undressed, put on a warm dressing-gown and sat on the edge of her bed. She felt truly exhausted after the events of the day.

Virginia's husband answered the call. "Hullo — oh, it's you, Tamara! How are you, my dear? Virginia and I've only just been talking about you. We've had a bit of trouble over the sale of that field — you remember there was trouble with the farmer — but she'll tell you. Tell me first how *you* are."

"All right, thank you, Henry."

"It's been a bit nippy today, hasn't it —" he began, but Tamara cut in.

"Henry dear, can I please speak to Virginia quickly, as it's rather urgent."

"Of course. Hold on, my dear. Virginia is just here."

Tamara liked Henry. He was a delightful person and was obviously making Virginia very happy. But she just couldn't cope with small talk at the moment. She was a bundle of nerves. Virginia took over.

"I gather something's wrong. Just wait a moment and I'll shut the door. I'm in Henry's study. He's just gone upstairs, so you can talk freely, darling. What's happened?"

Tamara blurted out the whole story. She left out nothing. She had always been able to confide in Virginia. This evening she felt more than ever in need of moral support. She would get it, she knew, whether Virginia liked the idea of Tamara's leaving home in order to nurse her former boyfriend, or not. If she didn't agree, she would at least avoid the sort of prejudiced criticism which many so-called friends might have levelled at her.

Virginia listened without comment until Tamara finished her story. Whatever her opinion, she knew she could not go cold on her friend. It was all so tragic. Now, more than ever, Tamara needed understanding. Virginia — better than anyone else — knew well that Paul had always been first with her friend and that her marriage to Q. had been second-best.

"You can't think what it did to me," Tamara said in a voice of despair, "seeing him so changed physically, if not mentally — it killed me, Virginia. His mind is just as alert as ever but he's obviously a very sick man. He sleeps a lot. He just closes his eyes, and goes off holding on to my hand. Oh, Virginia, I can't leave him alone all day with no one to look after him. Vince has a job. He can only be with Paul from six p.m. till the morning. You remember Vince? I used to tell you about him. He's got a heart of gold. He was always terribly nice to me and devoted to Paul. They have so much in common. Not only their interest in music but they get on in heaps of ways. He's being most helpful to Paul just now."

"Yes, I remember you telling me about Vince."

"I can't *not* go back, Virginia. I must look after Paul. I wanted to pack my bag and move in for as long as he lives, but Paul said I mustn't. I know you never thought he was worth all the love I felt for him but he's really a wonderful person. He wouldn't hear of me moving in. He thought of Q. I'm hopeless. I didn't give poor Q. a thought when I first offered to look after Paul. What must you think of me, Virginia?"

Now Virginia's answer was warm and reassuring. "Nothing you could ever do would alter my feelings for you. You know that, darling. Obviously people who had no idea of what happened between you and Paul would be highly critical if you just walked out like that on poor Q.! But I know."

"Poor Q." repeated Tamara with a touch of bitterness, "That's how *I'm* beginning to think about him now. Honestly, Virginia, nobody is sorrier than I am that I've turned out to be such a poor wife."

"Don't start flogging yourself, Tam darling. You did your best. It's all been a sad mistake — leave it at that. You never should have married him of course, but you did seem to be in love at the time — at least we all thought so."

"I was — I *was* in my way, but I couldn't help remembering Paul from time to time and missing him. That was the trouble."

"Even on your wedding day," Virginia reminded her gently, "but what use looking back? You've got to stick to Q. whatever happens. Paul was quite right — and I do admire him for what he said. You've got to be brave and honest with Q. and tell him that you want to be free to stay with Paul all day until he goes into hospital for good."

Now Virginia heard a gulp the other end. She knew that Tamara was crying. The next outpouring from her was a jumble of words — full of self-reproach, self-pity — and more than anything, her undying love for Paul Pryce. There must have been something about Paul that had got right into her blood — never to be eradicated, thought Virginia with deep compassion. The poor little thing's in an awful state. What a tangle! And even if she did go and look after Paul for the few weeks or months that were left to him it might prove more of a strain on her than she imagined. It couldn't be very nice to have to watch the man you love die by inches.

Tamara spoke again. "Do you think it awful of me? Would I be doing something quite unforgivable?"

"If you just walked out and deserted Q. *and* your father and aunt — yes. But that's not really at the back of your mind is it? You're too kind-hearted for that, Tammy. You wouldn't want to deal such a blow to Q. on top of all he's been through recently."

Silence from Tamara, then she said in a steadier voice, "No, you're right. I wouldn't. I just want to do what I can for Paul while he is so ill. It can't last long. The doctors have told him he's probably got less than six months to live."

"Quite frankly, six months is a long time. It will be pretty hellish for Q."

"I've got to go to Paul. *I've got to.*" Tamara's voice rose. "I'll go down on my knees and beg Q. to forgive me and understand, but I've got to go. It would drive me mad if I didn't. I couldn't bear just to arrive there and find him all alone, struggling to fend for himself, and write more music, and growing weaker and weaker, and so on. He *needs* me, Virginia."

"Is there no one else to help him? Has his affair with this other girl finished?"

"Yes. And he has no relatives alive, only an old cousin miles away and he doesn't much care for her."

"Then, darling, you've just got to be strong and tell Q. *all* you've told me, and hope he'll be heroic enough to say 'Go ahead'."

Silence. A long deep sigh from Tamara. "I dread it. I *don't* want to hurt him any more."

"To be frank, as I always am with you darling, you've really been pretty hard on him so far."

"Over the accident you mean."

"Yes."

"I know." Another deep sigh from Tamara. "I've been facing up to my wretched behaviour and I think I have been ghastly. Cruel, too. I felt so crazy after poor little Claire died. Can't you understand?"

"Darling, it hit me hard too, although I was only her god-mother. We were all bowled over. I do understand. It was a terrible thing to have happened to you, but you've got to face up to things and stop blaming Q., or you *will* be unforgivable."

"I admit it. I'll do as you say, Virginia. I'll tell Q. every-thing when he comes back, and try to let him down lightly. I won't be horrid about Claire ever again — I'll just ask him not — not to mind if I help Paul till he dies."

"And if he says he won't allow it — that he doesn't want his wife to spend all day, every day, with a former boy-friend — what then?"

"I'd still go," said Tamara, in a low voice.

Virginia told her husband afterwards that that was the point at which she, herself, felt desperately sorry for Tamara. She realised how deeply Tamara must always have loved Paul, and spending the next difficult months with him could hardly prove romantic. She was virtually to act as a sick nurse, and as far as Virginia could remember, and from all she had heard, Paul had never been patient or loving and giving. Most of the giving had been on Tamara's side — even when they were sworn lovers.

Henry Randall put an arm around his wife's shoulders — his tall beautiful Virginia whom he loved more than ever as time went by.

"It sounds grim. A pity Tamara ever met Vince and got in touch with her composer again. They don't seem to have had a really happy relationship in the past. From what you've told me he didn't treat her very well. Funny how girls hang on to that sort of man — there's poor old Q. Marriot — one of the best — and she prefers this other fellow."

"It's awful, but you've got to know Tamara really to understand her, Henry. And don't forget that Paul isn't altogether self-absorbed because his initial reason for ending their affair was that he did not think he was good enough for her and couldn't even afford to marry her. He wasn't a success at that time, and he had nothing to offer, and quite rightly, he thought she ought to look for a better man."

Henry Randall shook his head and looked for his pipe. "Well, well, how will it all end?"

"I just don't know. I've no idea how Q. will take the idea of Tam nursing Paul, but I *can* imagine what her father and aunt will have to say. They'll blow up."

Henry shook his head again, "It's beyond me, my dear. I'm sure you'll give her the best possible advice." And now Henry Randall came towards his wife and put both arms around her. "Thank God for you. You're such a calm sweet responsible person, and I adore you."

Virginia, bright-eyed, laid her cheek against her husband's. "And I love you, and I'm very lucky,' she whispered, "because we're so right for each other. And because we're right, it makes me all the sorrier for less fortunate wives. For someone like Tamara who seems to have made a mess of her life."

Henry walked back to the fireplace and the solace of his pipe. "Funny little thing, Tamara, I'm very fond of her as you know, but I don't always approve of her attitude to life."

Virginia stood beside him and spread her long fingers to the fire. "I think I'll go up to town and see Tam as soon as possible, if you can spare me, Henry."

"I'll drive you up, my dear. Actually I've an invitation which I meant to tell you about, from my old Chief, Bill Shawness, you remember, the General? I'd like to have a chat with him one day."

"Then I'll phone Tam and fix it. I don't think she can possibly go to Paul because she said she'd wait and talk to

Q. who is only flying back from Geneva early in the morning. She promised me she wouldn't run off until it was all buttoned up between Q. and herself."

The Colonel looked at his wife out of the corners of his eyes and gave her a humorous smile. "You know, my love, I don't really understand any woman in the world but you. You're so reliable. Most women are unpredictable, and Tamara is a little startling, you must agree."

"She's a mixed-up kid and always has been, Henry. But honestly, one can't be surprised if she's a bit round the bend just at the moment, what with the death of poor little Claire when Q. was driving the car, and now Tam having to face Paul's imminent death. God knows what *I* mightn't have done in the circumstances."

"You aren't the sort of woman who would ever find herself in such circumstances, darling," said Henry drily.

"Perhaps you're right. When I lost my poor Robert, I thought I'd never marry again. Then you came along."

"We've been lucky," said Henry, and looking at her with deep love in his eyes, he pressed the tobacco down into the bowl of his pipe and lit it. His pipe — his panacea for any moment of trouble.

"Yes," said Virginia softly, "we've been very lucky."

17

Q. ARRIVED BACK at his father-in-law's house in the early evening, his aircraft having been delayed because of fog.

He had had a somewhat difficult session with his client. He was tired and had been sleeping unusually badly for him. It was always a dreary business hanging around airports, waiting for visibility to improve, added to which he had a lot on his mind — his wife in particular. Despite the fact that Tamara had given him an affectionate send-off, and he hoped and believed that things were going to be better between them, the thought of her troubled him. He loved her so much. She was so young and immature for her age, and so vulnerable. Her gaiety, her brilliance — all that made her so enchanting — were badly clouded because of the loss of their child. Q. himself, strong-minded and far less emotional, had been devastated and although he made many attempts to forget, he couldn't help from time to time remembering that Tamara had blamed *him*. The very idea haunted him still. Once she told him in a moment of irritation that he had no imagination. Perhaps he hadn't. He could put unhappiness behind him so much more easily than Tamara. Not that deep down he ever forgot the shattering blow fate had dealt him that day when he saw the small body of his lovely child lying still — for ever still — in the car.

However, when he let himself into the house this evening, he thought only of Tamara. As he opened the door he saw her standing there in the hall. He put down his case and seized her in his arms.

"Tam — my darling, at last I've made it. Sorry I'm so late. Oh, it's good to see you!"

She made no answer but stood still while he kissed her, her lips only moving faintly under his, then she tried to draw away and said, "Let's go up to our room. Beastly old fog! I'm surprised you're here already Q. We all thought you mightn't be back until after dinner."

"Let me look at you," he said, and felt more emotional than usual. But that beautiful young body which he loved so much was cool and unresponsive, so he let her go, and walked upstairs with her, chatting as though nothing was wrong. The lights were on in her bedroom. It was warm and inviting and he thought how inviting *she* looked, wearing her damson-coloured caftan — a new purchase he admired. It was made of soft cashmere and there were little black lace frills at the neck and wrists. It was essentially French and elegant and suited her.

He threw off his coat and turned towards her — smiling and rubbing his hands together. "Phew! London's chilly, but it's colder still in Geneva."

She drew breath and seated herself on the edge of the big bed, biting hard at her lips. She wished to God Q. didn't look so happy and so pleased to see her. The remembrance of Paul was a knife in her heart, yet she didn't want that knife to cut Q. to pieces. *She didn't!*

He seemed not to notice that anything was wrong with her. He went into his dressing-room, telling her that he would wash and put on a dressing gown. He called out to her as he changed, telling her about last night in Geneva, and the excellent dinner he and his client had had in a hotel on the lake (she didn't catch the name), and how firmly he had refused to eat anything on the aircraft because he knew dear Liz would have a welcome-home dinner ready, and he wanted to preserve his appetite. And what had *she*, Tamara, been doing? She must tell him everything. Dad was having a bath was he? Well, he'd see the old man later, and he wouldn't disturb Liz at her favourite pastime of cooking specialities. He'd run down and get a couple of sherries and bring them up here to drink in their warm attractive room. He appeared in his comfortable Jaeger dressing gown, his fair hair smoothly brushed. Tamara thought he looked pale and quite tired, but still so happy, Tamara's determination to tell him the truth tonight wavered. Perhaps they would both be better able to face a possible 'scene' tomorrow morning.

When Q. returned with a small tray bearing two glasses of sherry and a packet of cashew-nuts, he placed them on the bedside table, then sat down on the bed beside Tamara and put an arm around her shoulders.

For the first time since Claire had died, he dared to act the lover as well as the husband. He leaned closer to her. She could see the warmth of passion in his eyes, and a feeling of absolute despair gripped her. God, oh *dear God*, she thought, why must he be like this, *now* of all times? It's going to make things worse for both of us. What can I do?

But Q. was lost now — on fire with the old desire for his wife. He leaned back against the pillows and pulled her down beside him. He began to cover her face with kisses.

"Darling, my darling!" he kept whispering, "I love you so much."

She was dumb with misery. In that moment it was not only that she was unwilling to accept Q. as a lover, nor even that she found his kisses and caresses repugnant. In a curious way she felt a new tenderness for him — a very real compassion — and a wish not to hurt him more than was necessary. When she had seen him emerge from his dressing-room looking like a big overgrown schoolboy, wearing that rather shy look of passion that had once attracted her, she had felt this tenderness — this disinclination to be cruel to him. Yet cruel she must be — as well as true to herself — to all that was concerned with Paul — or she would fall into an abyss and sink completely. Paul had looked better when she left him. She was sure he had been glad of her company. But would she be able to go to him tomorrow? Supposing Q. refused to allow it? Without his permission she would be helpless. She knew Paul. He might be weak in some ways but he was strong in others and he had shown her that he was quite determined not to accept her offer without Q.'s approval.

At last she could no longer bear to lie still and feel Q.'s lips, hungry and demanding, upon hers. Gasping, she pushed him back from her. She looked up at him. His face was flushed and ardent. Poor darling, she thought and felt utterly wretched. After Claire's death she had been sure she could never make love to Q. again. Yet she shrank in this hour from wiping that look of happiness from his face.

Breathlessly she said, "No more now, please Q. darling. *Please* not now — !"

"I want you so badly, darling."

"Not now, please. It's the wrong time. Dad will be calling

you to have a drink with him at any moment. Let's calm down."

Q. controlled himself and gave a slightly nervous apologetic laugh. "Sorry, Tam, even after the years we've been married, you see you can still seduce your husband. But I understand. You needn't say any more. I'm a tactless fellow. Sit up, darling, and let's enjoy our sherry. You're quite right. It's not a good time for me to lose my head. Actually I can hear your father's voice this very moment."

He handed Tamara her glass. She sat up, gave him a crooked smile and sipped the drink. He raised his glass and said, "We've all the time in the world, haven't we, darling? We won't rush it. Here's to you, my lovely!"

She managed to return the toast. And after that, Mr. Whitfeld without realising it, saved the whole situation by banging on the door and calling again.

"Q! Was that you I heard just now? Everything okay, my boy?"

"Come in," said Q. and greeted his father-in-law with a cool serenity that won Tamara's admiration. She wished she could be as well-controlled. .

The crisis was over. An hour later they were all sitting at dinner — they started with prawn cocktail, and the sauce Aunt Liz made so well, while everyone listened to Q.'s news from Geneva. He told them about the Swiss client and his finances — and the awful fall of the pound alongside the Swiss franc, Tamara, having made up her face, looked flushed and glamorous and tried to avoid continual meaning glances from her husband's eyes. She forced herself to chat with deceptive brightness in order to cover her inner depression.

She had to remain calm and listen to the general conversation, then they watched television which as a rule Tamara enjoyed. But tonight her thoughts winged remorselessly to Paul's studio. She was not a coward but she was fearful of what lay in front of her — of having tomorrow to tell Q. the facts — to ask so much from him. Now and then

171

she wished feverishly that she could die with Paul and so end all this misery.

Then the telephone bell rang.

"I'll answer it," said Tamara as her father half-rose.

He gave her his affectionate smile and sat down again. "Do — sure to be for you, duckie."

"Why not for me?" asked Q. grinning. "Tamara little knows how many girl-friends I might have locked away in London. Any one of them could be ringing to welcome me back from Geneva."

The laughter that followed was not shared by Tamara. Q.'s joke was lost on her. Hurriedly she shut the door and answered the call in the hall

"Hullo, Tamara here!"

"It's Vince. You know!"

Her heart jumped. "Yes, I know. Is it about Paul? Is he worse?"

"Not exactly, but I thought you ought to know what happened this evening"

Tamara felt her whole body go cold. "What happened, Vince? Tell me."

"Well, I went round there as I always do, and he seemed very exhausted and on edge — you know!"

"Yes. I'm afraid he's worried because I oughtn't to spend what time is left with him. But I shall, Vince. Don't try and stop me. Paul wants me to make sure my husband gives his permission. Perhaps he won't. But I shall go to Paul — nothing is going to alter that decision."

A moment's silence, then Vince said, "Make quite sure, Tammy. It's a pretty big thing you're going to ask the man, you know."

"Yes, yes," she agreed impatiently, "but leave it to me, *please*. I shan't change my mind. All I shall do is what Paul asked me to do — to be honest with Q. and open about it. Why have you rung, Vince? It can't be only to talk things over."

"No. Paul's appearance worried me a bit. He was worse,

I thought. Didn't even want to listen to his favourite concert. Said his head ached so abominably."

"When did he last see his doctor?"

"Oh, he pops in about every other day. He's a conscientious sort of medicine-man."

"Do you really think Paul's worse?"

"I hate to say so but he looks bad tonight."

"Then is he *worse*? Ought you to send for Dr. Finch?"

"I phoned him after Paul went to bed."

In her present emotional state, Tamara had little control over the tears that sprang into her eyes. "You're so good Vince. There never was such a friend. What did the doctor say?"

"He's coming in the morning but doesn't think I've any reason to suppose Paul's in danger. He might even improve if he has a good night. He has been working hard you know. When I suggested he would have to go into a clinic — "

Tamara interrupted, "Oh, Vince, did he say yes?"

"No, he didn't, but he did say it might be necessary sooner than we think. Everything depends on the results of his next test. He's due for one at the hospital at the end of this week. He might have to have another blood-transfusion."

"Is that all? Did you ring me to tell me that?"

"Yes, I wanted to warn you that whatever decision you come to when you've spoken to your husband, and of course before you turn up here tomorrow — you must realise you won't be with Paul for long. You've *got* to consider that point, Tammy. It might be for such a short while so ought you to upset things at home? See what I mean?"

She answered without hesitation, "I know it's very selfish of me but I'm afraid I must give Paul all I can for as long as he needs me. I just pray that Q. will understand."

Whatever Vince thought about that, he said nothing. He bade her good night, adding a few words of advice. "Take care of your health, Tam. You've been through a hell of a lot lately. I know you're young and strong and all that —

but just take care. Don't lose sleep and go off your food and so on, or you'll be no use to Paul, or anybody else."

"Thanks, Vince, you're a darling. Good night."

"Wait a minute — supposing your husband cuts up rough and — ?"

"He won't. He isn't like that. Anyhow, I'll be at the studio first thing tomorrow," she interrupted

Vince rang off. Tamara ran up to her own room before she rejoined the family. She was afraid her father and aunt might see that she had been upset. Her mascara was smudged.

When she got back to the drawing-room it was only to stay for a while, then told them she wanted an early night

Q. stood up. He laid a half-smoked cigar on an ashtray. "I'll go up with you, darling. I've got a lot of sleep to make up. I wasn't in bed till the early hours."

She nodded. It was as well he should join her. Why postpone the inevitably unhappy scene between them? Somehow the news Vince had just given her had strengthened her resolve to go through with this thing. Paul was gradually sinking. She was all the more determined to tell Q. that she would be going to Paul first thing tomorrow.

18

WHEN Q. CLOSED the bedroom door after them, Tamara didn't wait long before she began to unburden her tormented mind and heart. He noticed that she was shivering, switched on the electric fire, and sat on the edge of the bed, opening his arms to her.

"Poor little thing, you look frozen! It *was* a bit draughty downstairs this evening. I never did think much of Dad's central heating, did you? Come over here — let me warm you, darling."

Tamara set her teeth and deliberately pushed a small velvet covered chair nearer the bed so that she could sit facing Q. She ignored the outstretched arms.

"I'm all right, but I must talk to you, Q. I wouldn't sleep a wink if I didn't. I'd feel so guilty."

His expression changed. He stared at her, his brows drawn. "Guilty," he repeated. "Over what? What's wrong, Tammy?"

"Everything," she whispered.

Now the first definite sensation of alarm seized Q. He hadn't the slightest idea why Tamara had used the word 'guilty'. He had known, of course, that since Claire died she had become withdrawn from him. He had not felt close to her or even really happy in her company. Things seemed no better now between them, so long after the tragedy. But her affectionate goodbye to him before he flew to Geneva had led him to believe that he might receive a different welcome, so he now felt not only alarm, but distress. It took a lot to depress Q. but he really felt it was going to be too much if she was still to hold him entirely responsible for Claire's death. He was well aware of the effect that tragic death had had on Tamara. He grieved for her and for himself in silence — and if he felt she had been unnecessarily hard on him, he had put it down to Tamara's highly emotional state.

Tamara, hands locked so tightly that they hurt, began to make her confession, and as she did so she wished that there was a wall between them so that she need not see the expression on Q.'s face. She understood now why Catholics creep into the shadow of a confessional and never face their priest. They just tell him their problems and wait for advice and absolution.

She talked to Q. for a long time without interruption. She hated the way the light died out of his eyes, and hated herself for being the cause, but she could not draw back. She told Q. everything from start to finish.

"I'm desperately sorry if this is a shock to you Q. I really am terribly, terribly sorry to upset you because you've been so good to me. As you knew when we first got married, I'd had this affair with Paul and I — " she stopped and for a second hid her face in her hands.

Q. spoke with difficulty, "Oh, hell, darling — honestly — it *is* a shock. It really is."

She uncovered her face. "Of course it must be. But do you *understand*? Do you?"

"Not altogether. You were in love with this boy before we met. I do know that. But I thought that affair was absolutely over — er — I thought you fell in love with me," he ended awkwardly. Q. had never been good at dealing with emotional scenes.

Tamara continued to clench her fists, feverishly locking and unlocking her fingers. "I did. I did, Q. I *was* in love with you."

He winced. 'I *was*.' It was in the past. She wasn't mincing matters. But it was all so unexpected that Q. was momentarily nonplussed. His little world seemed to be crumbling around him. He felt like a man trying to find his way home through a city that had been destroyed by an earthquake. He heard Tamara's voice again.

"I do *still* love you in my way, Q. Not perhaps as much as you love me. You're such a much better person than I am, so loyal and reliable — all those things I'm not. I don't deny I've been too impulsive and sort of crazy, from time to time. I'm so ashamed, I don't know what to do, but I can't help myself over this affair. When I saw Paul again yesterday and heard they only gave him a few months (if that) to live, my old feeling for him sort of came back. I was lost. I used to be so terribly in love with him. Forgive me but I was, and I want to be honest about it now. You *do* understand, don't you?"

He shrugged. "I understand your wish to be honest and that you thought Paul was the love of your life before you met me. But it just never entered my head that it was how you still felt."

"I didn't, until I knew he was dying," she whispered. "You'll never forgive me. I see that."

Now for the first time Q. hit back.

"I didn't know you were asking for forgiveness. I thought you merely wanted me to understand why you intend to dedicate yourself to this boy for the duration of his life. Isn't that it?"

"Yes," she said, "yes, that's it, but I'm so fond of you still, I don't want you to hate me and put me right out of your life."

"Aren't you putting me out of yours?"

"No, no — only for a short time," she said desperately.

"You want it all ways," Q. said more harshly than he had ever spoken to her.

She remained silent — her whole body trembling, her thoughts confused.

Q. walked to the fireplace. He stared at a framed photograph of Claire which stood on the mantelpiece. After her death Tamara had refused to allow this to be on show. But a week ago she had suddenly found it possible to put it back in its place. A head and shoulders study of Claire — such a beautiful little race, such fair lovely curly hair, and *his* eyes. He agreed that she had inherited them from him. They were like his mother's too. Now it seemed that a terrible weight crushed his whole soul. He swung round and looked with unusual bitterness at the girl who sat there in her chair. Tamara's attitude of despair did not for the moment move him. He said,

"I'm quite sure you've hated me since Claire died. You put that tag about the safety-strap on me and never untied it. I tried to understand you, but well, if you believe I deserve to lose your love completely — it seems to be the end for us, doesn't it?"

Terror seized her. She sprang up and rushed to him, clutching both his arms. "*Don't* say such things. I know I've behaved badly. I meant to make it all up to you once you came home. And I swear to you that I wouldn't have dreamt of going back to Paul if he hadn't been so ill. You know what leukaemia is — cancer of the blood. He's almost at the end." She broke off, and released her grip of Q. He had become a stranger to her, this bitter angry man. Not at all the Q. she knew so well. And of course she'd brought it on herself.

In despair, Tamara turned and walked away from him.

"You're wrong on several counts. First, I do *not* hate you. It was a fatal accident and I realise it was not all your fault. I've been hateful about it, and I understand why you can't understand or forgive me."

Q.'s face reddened with sudden anger. "Don't go on talking about understanding and forgiveness. What does it matter? You're still in love with this wretched boy and you want to stay with him until he dies. Well, go to him, my dear, I'm certainly not going to try and stop you."

"But I don't want to break up our marriage," she cried. "And you can't pretend it's exactly a *love* affair. I don't intend to *sleep* with Paul. How can I? He's dying. If he'd been well and things were normal, I'd never have considered going back to him at all. I'm sure I wouldn't. I've never once even thought of leaving you, Q."

"You just want to leave me now until he dies — is that it?"

"Yes — just to be away during the day. *You're* in the office all day, anyhow, aren't you?"

"Hardly looking after some girl I was once in love with," he said sarcastically. "Surely if the boot had been on the other foot, *you* wouldn't have been very pleased with me, would you?"

"No, perhaps, I wouldn't, but I would try to understand."

"You keep using that word," he said wearily. "Perhaps I'm not very tolerant, but I'd have found it all easier to accept if you'd come and told me you just wanted to go and see him now and then. But to stay at his place all day — even if I'm not at home — and at weekends, too — it's a bit different. Can't you see that?"

She shook her head. "Vince takes over at night. I'll come home every evening."

Q. stared at his wife. His face was pale and sullen now. He had known about her infatuation for Paul Pryce, but he had never asked her for details, and she hadn't volunteered them. They *had* been lovers — yes, he had presumed that and wiped it off the record. The girl he married — gay adorable Tamara who had flown to Cannes with him — had seemed absolutely his.

Tamara sat down in her chair again. She leaned her head back against the cushions and closed her eyes. He stared at her. The light from her bedside lamp showed up the tiny lines under her large beautiful eyes. He had never noticed them before.

Christ, thought Q., *now I've lost both my child — and my wife.*

Yet was he possibly exaggerating the whole affair? Wasn't it just his pride that was bitterly hurt, knowing that she still cared so deeply for the other fellow. After all she only wanted to be a sort of nurse to him. But it was scarcely a pleasant pill for *him*, her husband, to swallow.

Gradually Q. tried to see things more in perspective. The plain facts grew plainer, easier to take without such acute jealousy. The other chap was dying. Her visits couldn't be very pleasant or glamorous. He could see that, so why go into such 'a thing' about it.

Q. drew a hand across his eyes. God, what a mix-up! He had been a bit too savage with Tam, he thought. He began to relent. The sight of her sitting there looking so lost, so vulnerable — softened his heart. He was about to move towards her when she opened her eyes and spoke to him.

"You know, Q.," she said, "I repeat — I don't want to break up our marriage — if you can find it possible to allow me these few weeks of freedom. You must realise there couldn't be grounds for divorce even if you want one. Paul can never be any woman's lover again. But if you feel absolutely fed up with me, I won't come back at all, and if you want a separation or something — " she broke off hopelessly.

That finished Q. He walked to her and took both her hands in his. He said, "Hell no, I don't want a separation. There's no question of it or of me supposing I'd have any cause to take such a step. But try to see things from my point of view. I've been pretty upset since the accident in that damned Arrow. I'm afraid I haven't been at all myself any more than you have been the same, my dear. It's broken us both up. Only I hoped you'd got over my part in it and forgiven *me*. Now I owe you an apology for being so unkind to you *and* the wretched boy. I'm not incapable of feeling sorry for anyone as young as he is, and as talented, to be dying of an incurable disease. It's tough. And I *do* understand why you want to help him. Go ahead, Tam. I know how soft-hearted you are. Who am I to try and stop you from making his last days happier. Go ahead, but for God's sake don't let it take you from me for good and all."

Now he put his arms around her and drew her against him and stroked her hair so gently that she burst into tears and put her own arms around his neck. They sat like that together. He went on stroking her hair. He realised, with some bitterness, that he had never loved her more. She looked up at him at last, her face wet and ravaged.

"I don't deserve this. I don't, and I'm sorry for the way I behaved when our baby died. Oh, Q., you've been terrific. You've taken such a weight off my mind. I won't leave you for ever, I *swear* I won't. I don't want to — please believe me, will you?"

He had never found it more difficult to answer, and for an instant she was cold with fear that he might, despite his sudden display of kindness, change his mind. In a curious way she had never felt closer to him. Even the thought of Paul could not wipe out her admiration for the man she had married.

"Promise me you understand why I want to help him," she begged yet again.

Q. nodded. "Yes — you're only human, my dear. It's just that at first I didn't quite realise you were still so fond of this boy. But — " Q. gave an ironic laugh, "they say a woman's first love remains her best."

That somehow hit Tamara between the eyes, although she knew he hadn't meant to be unkind. Shame smote her again. What he had said was so near the truth.

It seemed possible that she could feel the old crazy love for Paul but love Q. as well. It was an accepted fact that a man could be in love with two women at the same time. A woman could surely feel likewise?

She took Q.'s right hand and laid it against her wet cheek. The tears were flowing again and she couldn't stop them. She whispered, "I'm so sorry, Q. It's awful of me. But you can be sure what I feel for Paul is like the love of a sister — even a mother. He needs me. He's all alone. Vince can never be with him during the day, and anyhow Vince can't do any nursing, and I can if necessary. I know you may think I'm a spoiled helpless brat, but I'm not. The real *me*, isn't."

That made Q. smile. He heaved a deep sigh.

"My darling Tam, those who love you like to spoil you, and I think I, more than anybody, know how kind and generous you are, fundamentally. By no means always a 'spoiled brat', as you call it. Let's get this clear between us. You want to help Paul until he dies. Okay, you go along and do it darling I'll be here when you want me — when you come home again for good."

Overwhelmed, Tamara found no words with which to thank him. She hid her face in her hands again. But he drew them away and pulled her up on to his lap. He held her as he used to hold Claire when she cried. He caressed her very gently.

"Don't darling, *don't* upset yourself any more. You've been through enough. You know I'm rather stupid, and I'm not always good at what you call 'understanding'. When I was in Geneva I built up a lot of nonsense about our finding each other again, once I got home, and — "

Here Tamara broke in. "It *wasn't* nonsense, I think you were sweet to want us to get close to each other again. I suppose losing Claire in that car accident with all its implications sent me a bit off my head. Don't ever be sorry for anything *you've* done, because you're the best person I've even known in this life and I shall come back to you if you want me, Q. I swear I will."

They went on discussing the immediate future for a moment, then Q. said, "All very fine for me being a tolerant husband, my love, but what are we going to tell your father and Liz?"

"Yes, that is a problem," Tamara said.

She left him and walked through to the bathroom, rinsed her face with cold water, then returned looking much calmer.

He made no attempt to touch or kiss her again. He lit a much needed cigarette and lit one for her, putting it between her willing lips. Now they sat and discussed the future like friends.

Tamara had made a plan. She would telephone Virginia first thing in the morning. Virginia, her friend, who knew all about things and was always so helpful. Virginia would back her up if she told Daddy and Aunt Liz that Virginia wasn't well and she, Tamara, was going away to stay with her for a while.

"And what about the nights when Vince takes over?" Q. asked. "Dad and Liz may accept the story that you're in Beaconsfield, but if you don't come back here — where will you actually go?"

"When Vince takes over I'll leave Paul to him," was Tamara's reply. "I can't come home every night if they think I'm at Beaconsfield, so I'll have to make other arrangements even if I tell a few lies. Better than hurting them with the truth. It *would* be best for me to stay away altogether until it's all over, wouldn't it?" she asked Q. anxiously.

His heart sank but he nodded. "Perhaps, but where will you go? It's all very complicated."

She hesitated, then answered, "I can't ask anybody who

knows us to put me up, because it must be hush-hush. It's essential I lie low and do nothing to rouse suspicion. Virginia will back me up."

Q.'s spirits lifted again. At least Tamara convinced him that she had no intention of making a permanent break from him. Then she had a sudden brainwave. He listened ot her, dubious but not sure it was a bad plan. She had just remembered the existence of Old Nanny as they called her in the family. She had looked after Tamara during her childhood in Haslemere. Once Tamara had grown up, Nanny, then in her late forties, took another job with a family in Putney. She had stayed with them for a long time and even after the children went to boarding school. Lady Morden, her employer, was a wealthy woman, and she had kept Nanny on as a housekeeper until she retired as an old-age pensioner. The Mordens showed their gratitude by buying the lease of a little flat for her in Putney, not far from them. Tamara visited her regularly during the following years. Q. himself remembered driving her there. They had taken Claire, who was still a baby, to see the old nurse who was crippled with arthritis and could rarely go out.

"But she adores me," Tamara ended, "and Lady Morden and her husband have gone to South Africa for good and all, so I'm rather the star in Nan's life. She'd put me up any time — of that I'm certain. I know she has a tiny spare room. Putney isn't far from Chelsea. It would be ideal for me."

At first Q. was doubtful if this was a good idea. "Wouldn't you be terribly bored living with an ageing Nanny? After all it might be a long time before the poor fellow dies."

"I don't think so — don't worry about me being bored. After a full day's work looking after him, plus shopping and cooking, etcetera, I'll be pretty tired. I shall want to go to bed, and I'll have my old Nanny to rock me to sleep," she ended with an attempt to laugh.

Q. looked at her forlorn face with pity. "Poor Tam, who ever thought all this would happen to you? But for the

moment let's agree you stay with Nanny — that is if she ha
her spare room free."

"I know it is. I actually had a letter from her yesterday
telling me she was alone. Some friend left her so she'l
welcome me. So many of Nan's friends older than hersel
have died. Yes, she'll be absolutely delighted if I sugges
staying with her. Some time during tomorrow I'll take a tax
to Putney and fix it all up. And I can tell her the truth –
she's as safe as a house with confidences."

"But she won't be on the 'phone. I shan't even be able t
'phone you."

"But there *is* a 'phone. Her flat's on the ground floor an
there's a public call-box for the use of all the residents ju
outside her door in the hall. You can always 'phone me afte
nine p.m. Q., and of course, I'll have to ring father an
Aunt Liz now and again. I shall do that from Paul's fla
They won't hear any pips so they won't wonder where I ar
— even guess I'm still in town, and not with Virginia"

Q. suddenly felt a blinding pain in his head. He realise
that he was deadly tired. All he had gone through this evenin
had hit him badly.

He stood up. "Forgive me if I push off to my bed, Tar
I'm a bit exhausted," he said.

She ran to him and hugged him. "Thank you, *darling* (
Thank you, for everything. I'll never *never* forget all yo
kindness to me tonight. I don't suppose one husband in
thousand would be as decent as you've been over this affair.

"Get to bed and get some sleep," he said gruffly. "Goo
night, my dear."

He walked out of the room.

19

It was a harassed, conscience-stricken Tamara who rang the doorbell at Paul's flat that following morning.

She had a lot on her mind — almost more than she could tolerate. First and foremost, her anguish at the thought of Paul's approaching death, and her remorse because she had hurt the husband who was treating her with such fantastic generosity. There had only been that small outburst of bitterness and reproach when first she had made her confession.

She had left home before ten o'clock and taken a taxi out to Putney where, as expected, she received a heart-warming reception from her old nurse. True to the old woman's nature — humane, understanding of other people, and preferring to give, rather than receive — old Nanny had drawn Tamara into her arms and told her she could stay with her as long as she liked.

"I won't ask questions. Don't want to know anything, dearie — my little Tammy — so just leave your suitcase here and I'll have a nice cup of coffee waiting for you when you come back tonight. Any old time. I watch my T.V. till it ends. Oh, it will be good to have you here, dear."

Tamara had left the old woman standing there leaning on her stick, looking at her with deep devotion. She felt almost guilty for using Nanny's home as a 'hideaway'. To her she was still 'my little Tammy' — it was just what she used to call her. Tamara was very moved. She had appreciated that welcome, following a difficult goodbye to her father and aunt. She hated lying — especially to Daddy who looked at her with such trust in his kind wise eyes. And Aunt Liz was a shrewd woman. Perhaps she didn't altogether believe Tam's story about Virginia's illness, and her niece's reason for so suddenly rushing away. She said, "Your poor Virginia, I must ring her up. What's the matter with her?"

Hastily Tamara answered her that Virginia was in bed,

and no telephoning allowed, but she — Tamara — would 'phone Aunt Liz later this evening. Tamara could see there were likely to be more awkward moments before this crisis came to an end.

Daddy, of course, swallowed the story and went off to the office with his son-in-law quite happily. His last words were, "Don't stay down there too long, pet. We shall miss you."

As for poor Q. — she was afraid he looked as though he hadn't slept all night. She had a horrible uneasy feeling that he was far more upset by what she was doing than she imagined.

But now in this critical moment when Paul opened the front door to her, she forgot about her family. She was conscious only of him — and his need for her. He looked desperately ill this morning. His dressing gown was too big for his frail body. His eyes were large and red-rimmed, his face was colourless.

She walked in, holding out both hands. "Paul, my darling, darling Paul!"

If he had meant to say anything gay or flippant in return he made it obvious that this morning he was glad to see her.

"Tammy, baby! Bless you for coming. You're terribly early, but it's terrific to see you. I didn't have a very good night. I lay awake wondering if your husband would allow you to come."

"I'm here and I shall stay with you all day long." She caressed his hair and put her lips against his neck, that poor thin neck. "Nothing would have kept me away."

"What did Quentin. — Q. — as you call him, have to say?" Paul asked as he shut the front door and they moved together into the flat.

"Well, I told him the facts and he was remarkably understanding. He gave full permission. He understands the situation."

They walked up to the studio. The central heating was full on. There was an electric fire burning at the end of the room near the piano. It was hot in there. But Paul's fingers holding on to hers were cold. She drew him towards the sofa and looked anxiously at him.

"Sit down. I'll make you some coffee, darling. Have you had breakfast?"

'Sort of. My daily came very early this morning and gave me a cup, but I wouldn't let her stay after ten. I had an idea you'd be here early, you strange, lovely, wonderful creature."

He pulled off her scarf and eased her gently out of the scarlet leather jacket she was wearing. He looked long into her eyes — those dark fantastic eyes. Whatever doubts Paul had entertained previously about reintroducing Tamara into his life, especially now that she was a married woman, ceased to trouble him. For the first time, during the long night, he had felt deeply dejected. He had sunk into melancholy that had taken away even his desire to get up and play his piano. A thing he sometimes did when insomnia defeated him. He was badly in need of an uplift to his spirits and Tamara's presence gave it to him this morning.

They stayed close on the sofa, talking. Tamara recounted some of the dialogue between Q. and herself. Paul hunched his shoulders and shook his head. "He really sounds one hell of a guy."

"That's nostalgic — that word 'guy'. You always used it. Do you remember I called you a phoney American and you were furious?"

He smiled: "And you were always so gorgeous. Now you're even more so. No other girl to touch you. I ought to know."

"I'm far from gorgeous at the moment," she said. "I look a fright. I've done nothing but cry lately. My eyelids are swollen."

"I don't notice it," he gave a short laugh. "I want to bellow myself but I don't. Let's make a pact that neither of us will cry any more — *neither of us*. Hear me?"

"Okay. Not a tear — not a sob."

"We'll forget why you're here, we'll be very gay. We'll have lots of music. I swear I'll write a super new song before I die, and it will be full of hope as well as love. You know — sort of Noel Coward's *Bitter Sweet* — '*I'll see you again, When Spring breaks through again,*' — how does it go on?"

She whispered, " '*Time may lie heavy between, But what has been, is past forgetting.*'

"Dead right. I never forgot what went between us, Tam."

"Nor did I, but don't go on," she whispered, clenching her hands with the effort to be jocular and brave. "Don't finish that song," she added, "I don't like the last line."

"You mean — 'Just the echo of a sigh — goodbye.' "

"Yes."

He ran his fingers through his thick dark hair. "My dear darling. Goodbyes between lovers go on all the time."

"Okay, but I'm not going to say goodbye right now."

"And I should never have said it to you six years ago. I was misguided. I took it for granted that you were so rich and rare and living in such exalted heights compared to my lowly studio life, I had no right to keep you."

She squeezed the hand she was holding. "You were a fool — mad — any horrid word you like to put. You should have known money and position didn't matter to me. I loved *you* — loved *you*!

"Now you're quoting me instead of Coward," Paul sniggered. But his smile speedily changed to a look of intense love as he looked into her eyes. "But you were the one who loved me best — yes, *yes*, that was a sort of premonition on my part — writing those words."

"I've heard it quite often over the radio," she said in a low voice. "Even driving back from Cannes after my honeymoon I suddenly heard it. It upset me terribly."

"Poor little Tam — and poor old bridegroom! I'm afraid I've got a lot to answer for."

"Oh, don't let's talk about the past! Let's think only of today. I want to be practical now."

"Okay," he said. "What gives?"

She gave him a little hug, kissed him and sprang to her

feet. Before she could speak again, he added, "You're wearing the colour that suits you so well. You look divine in that suit. The scarlet jacket with your black slacks — you sure are cute, honey."

"And you're still my phoney American," she laughed, shutting her mind to inner misery. "You're looking mighty smooth in that seducer's dressing gown, darling. I love the deep blue satin with the black collar and cuffs—you're pretty cute, too."

"I'm no seducer," he echoed the word grimly, "Wish I had the strength to earn that word, lover."

Tamara tossed her head. "Now, now, no seduction necessary."

He seemed to have difficulty in getting on to his feet which she was quick to notice. She gently but firmly pushed him back against the cushions.

"Stay where you are, Paul darling. I want you to have all the rest you can. That's why I'm here. I want to wait on you hand and foot."

"And what do you think you're going to do now?"

"Go shopping. Tell me what you'd like most for lunch. I'm quite a good cook. You won't want one of my omelettes again. What about a grill? A nice steak?"

He scowled. "My digestion's not too good at the moment. Maybe a bit of fish."

"Anything you fancy."

"The price of fish is escalating, so Vince tells me. You'll find my wallet on my dressing chest. Take a fiver and buy anything you want. I'm not the Paul you used to know, my darling. I've got more cash. You know I still make a royalty out of *your* song. The group plays it and Des Curtis sings it—you remember Des? In the group?"

"Yes, I remember him. How are they all?"

"Split up."

"Did Liesel ring again?" Tamara tried to ask the question casually.

Paul's dark eyes — so lack lustre and weary, half-shut. He

gave his mocking smile. "No, she hasn't and I don't want to see her."

"But once you did live with her. Didn't you really care much about her?"

"Darling," Paul said, "I'll only get depressed if I start talking about Liesel. I used to have a guilt complex about her. She was very good to me after you went away — or if you want it — *after I sent you away* — then I found I couldn't go on with it. Your memory kept popping up — yes it did, you know. Anyhow Liesel went to America on a job and I suggested we should make a complete break. *And* I hear she has a new boy-friend."

A sigh from Tamara. "It may be nasty of me but I'm glad about that."

"And I'm glad you're here with me now. Dear God, I'm glad," Paul said.

She wanted to run to him but dared not. It was quite obvious that he had lost ground even during the short time since she had last seen him. Vince had been positive that he would deteriorate slowly. She wondered if there was anything else that could be draining the life out of Paul.

"When does the doctor next come to see you?"

"Oh — old Finch — today, as a matter of fact. He usually turns up in the middle of my lunch. They all do."

She nodded. She was glad. She would take the opportunity of talking to the doctor, herself. If he bluntly asked why she was so concerned, she'd just tell him that she was an old friend and he had nobody else. He wouldn't want a watertight explanation. Doctors were far too busy these days to enquire into the personal lives of their patients.

"Well, if you don't think Dr. Finch will turn up just yet I'll go now and buy you a nice Dover sole. I won't be long."

He leaned back, shutting his eyes. He was worried — yes, a bit more worried than usual about himself this morning. He had never felt quite so weak. Of course he knew he was going to die. *But he didn't want to die.* The thought was absolute agony now that Tamara was his again. He must say goodbye for ever to the love of his life — this wonderful girl who had been the inspiration behind most of his best work, and who had returned to him in such a miraculous way.

How strange and ironic fate had been to bring her back into his life years after she had gone out of it, and at a time when he could be with her only for a brief while.

Tamara fetched his wallet. He took out a five pound note and handed it to her. She searched the kitchen for a shopping basket and found one. After this she put on her coat and scarf. Paul looked at her and grinned, "Quite the little housewife — Mum looking after her little boy."

"I feel quite Mum-like towards you," she said with forced gaiety. "And now while Mum's out, don't try and do anything stupid."

Suddenly his mood changed. He glowered at her, "And don't you be too bossy. I hate being bossed. Added to which you're no ward-sister and this isn't a clinic."

She swung the shopping basket to and fro and glowered back at him. "*When* you've finished."

With great difficulty he got on to his feet and started to walk towards the piano. "As long as I'm alive I shall do what I want. All you females try and impose your will on others. *You* always know best! You're as bad as the rest!"

It was impossible for Tamara to feel hurt — she knew perfectly well that he didn't say such things because he really thought her 'bossy', but because he dreaded the very idea that he wasn't able to *do* the things he used to do. She stood still while he lumbered towards the piano stool. Just before he reached it, he looked as though he might fall. She ran to support him. He pulled away and turned on her, snarling.

"For God's sake leave me alone, Tam, or you can go back to your extremely tolerant husband, and leave me to do exactly what *I* want."

Now she walked away from him — feeling as though he had hit her. Her face changed from red to white. The same old Paul, she thought. The remembrance of former days in his old studio — of fights they used to have from time to time — of the occasions when he behaved like a spoiled and rather unpleasant child — ran through her mind. He had the power to upset her. She used to run out of the studio declaring that everything was over between them. He'd run after her, pick her up in his arms and carry her back to the divan, and force her down on it. The struggle would end in tears, and passion, and that magnetic force of feeling which so often overwhelmed them in those early days.

God, she thought, it couldn't be the same now. If she was to be of any help at all, she *must* humour him.

"Sorry, my fault. I'll be back soon — " she began to apologise. But already he had turned his back on her, opened the piano lid and struck a few chords. As he ran his fingers up and down the keys, she thought with dismay, it sounded discordant rather than harmonious. But she decided to leave him, she turned towards the door. Then Paul swung round on the stool and faced her, "Oh, Tam, my own Tammy, I don't care whether you're married to the other guy or not, you're *my* Tammy! But I'm no good to you — never was. I always acted bloody when I felt like it and I don't know why you stuck to me so long, or why you've come back."

"Because I love you. I loved you then, and I love you now!" she cried and dropped her basket and ran to him. Kneeling by the piano stool, she put both arms around his waist and laid her head against his knees. "I *am* your love, and you are mine. You know I'm being unfaithful in my mind if not my body to poor Q. but I loved you first, I loved you best — oh — didn't I?"

He pulled off her scarf and ruffled the fair gleaming hair. Bright as the sun, he used to call it, and like satin to touch He felt the warmth of her cheek against his hand and her feverish kisses against his fingers. But when she lifted her face to him her eyes were dry and desolate. She was not going to cry.

"This isn't the way to make you better," she said. "Let me go to the shops, darling. I shan't try to boss you again."

"Hell, I don't care if you do. I don't care about anything as long as you stay with me until I have to go away."

"I'll be with you even then, for as often as they allow it."

Now it was Paul's eyes that glittered with tears. "Go on then, darling, get the fish and forgive me if I am bad-tempered from time to time. I blew old Vince's head off the other night for nothing at all. Don't know why."

"You were always pretty temperamental," Tamara tried to laugh. She stood up, pushing the hair back from her flushed face. "Keep warm, my darling. It's freezing today, and *don't* try to play your piano if it is too much of a strain."

"Bossing again," he grinned back at her but this time they looked at each other with deep love and yearning, and with complete communication.

It was only when she was outside in the raw cold January day, Tamara had to make a considerable effort to walk away from Axhurst Mews. When she reached the King's Road, she fumbled for a face-tissue. Only now did she want to cry.

She bought two good Dover soles for lunch. She paid more for them than she thought they were worth but she was determined to halve the cost of meals for as long as she was with Paul. And of course she wouldn't mention the price of anything he wanted, and Paul — being as vague about money matters as he was — probably wouldn't even look at his change when she gave it to him.

She also bought rolls and fresh butter. She hadn't liked the small messy piece she found in his fridge. Finally she made her way to a shop down the King's Road where she knew she could buy excellent Continental coffee. Paul had always liked good coffee and she knew how to make it. The shopping ended with a bag of fruit and a bottle of grape-juice. Paul had already made it known that he had not touched wine or spirits since he fell ill. During their discussions he had made it plain that he intended to do what he wanted for as long as he lived. But alcohol he had never craved for, when he was well.

What, she asked herself, as she climbed the stairs with her

loaded basket, would I feel if I were told that I had only a short time to live?

Most dying people seemed to extract some kind of extra spiritual strength when their bodies began to fail. Vaguely Tamara remembered a discussion she had once had with Paul in the old days, about God and Christianity. He called himself an agnostic. She believed in God but was not a church goer. Everybody had their own sort of faith. Aunt Liz went to Divine Service regularly — Daddy didn't. Tamara rather ashamedly admitted that she, herself, only walked into a church for a wedding, a christening, or a funeral.

However, whatever Paul imagined was in store for him — she was positive he had never led a really bad life, nor was he a bad man. To live clean and be kind to others — wasn't that some sort of religion, he had asked her — and all one needed?

Tamara wanted with all her might — now more than ever — to believe in God — in a future meeting with Paul to which she could look forward.

She was encouraged by a new strange belief this morning, that she was on the verge of something big and beautiful. Death could be both these things, she decided, and she was privileged to be allowed to see Paul through the rest of his life. She wasn't going to moan about it or ever again let him see her cry.

She made lunch with Paul a big success. He ate everything she cooked for him, and he complimented her on the delicate sauce she made for the sole. He enjoyed the iced grapefruit with mint she provided as a starter. Then he said he would like to sleep for an hour. He told her she could lie down in his bedroom. He preferred the soft deep sofa in the studio, and it was warmer there.

But Tamara couldn't sleep. She wasn't really tired. She lay down and pressed her face against his pillow. It held the familiar faint odour of Paul's hair. She lay quietly like that, wide awake, while Paul slept. She could picture him, his thick black lashes fanning his high cheek-bones, his thin pale face in repose, lips slightly parted, both arms flung up above his head like a child. He always used to sleep that way, and the memory of it touched her heart.

She must have slept eventually, because her mind was only alerted when Paul knocked on the wall between their two rooms. In a flash she was up and in the studio, at his side. She was astonished to find that it was nearly four o'clock. The studio was full of shadows. She looked anxiously down at Paul who was still stretched out on the sofa under his rug. He seemed well enough. A little more colour in his cheeks. Black thick hair tousled, making him look untidy and young. He gave a sleepy smile and held out his arms.

"Hello, lover, did you drop off? I did."

"Yes, I had some rest," she said.

"How wonderful it was, knowing that when I knocked, *you* would hear and come to me."

She lay down full length beside him, and pulled the soft cashmere rug more closely around his meagre body. She laid an arm across his waist and put her lips against his cheek. It was too cold for her liking.

"Oh, my darling, you haven't kept the rug over you!" she said. "You're quite cold. You should have kept warm."

"Who's being bossy again? I did keep the rug over me. I'm always cold these days. So what?"

"Well, thank goodness you have an electric blanket on your bed. I noticed it."

"I hate the thing. Old-fashioned hot-waterbottles are much more comforting."

"Let me stand in for the hot-waterbottle," Tamara gave a laugh and drew him closer to her. For quite a while he stayed motionless, eyes shut. It seemed that her proximity and the way she held him was soothing enough, for he drifted into sleep again. This time she stayed very much awake, not daring to move — her whole being suffused with a yearning tnederness that she had never known before, nor imagined herself capable of feeling — except towards Claire.

Yes, she had felt like this when Claire, then a baby, was ever ill or cried a lot. She used only to fall asleep if her mother took her into bed with her and cuddled and rocked her.

Now Tamara was able to think of her child without bitter resentment against the fate that had taken her away. And at last without deep resentment against Q. She could even think of him in this hour and be sorry for the wrong she was doing him. Wrong it must be — even though her present association with Paul was innocent. There was nothing sexual about this kind of embrace — only deep, tender love. Paul had become her child, and because of it she remembered her little girl with the same anguish and tenderness.

It was quite dark before Paul opened his eyes again. They were disturbed by the sound of the door-bell. Immediately Tamara sprang off the sofa. Paul sat up, glancing at his wrist-watch.

"Oh God, we've forgotten Finch. He was supposed to have come this morning. I bet this is him now."

"I'll open the door." Tamara closed the studio door behind her and ran downstairs. She hoped she could talk privately to Paul's medical adviser before he examined his patient. He proved to be a short, nice-looking man with strong glasses, and very grey hair. She was glad he wasn't young. He looked somehow experienced and fatherly. She took an immediate liking to him.

"I don't think we've met, Miss — er — " he began. She broke in, "I'm Tamara Marriot — a very old friend of Paul's. I'm looking after him. He needs looking after, doesn't he, Doctor, and he doesn't want to go into hospital until he has to."

In the glare from a fluorescent ceiling light, Dr. Finch — busy overworked man with a huge practice — eyed this young woman with some surprise. He hadn't expected to find her with Paul. Beautiful girl — he admired the grace of her figure and that long silky hair.

He said, "Hullo, glad you can be with my patient. He does

need watching. That nice bearded fellow, Vince, who sleeps here at night — he said he'd get on to me if Paul got worse. But I didn't like Paul being alone all day. I saw him the day before yesterday, and I wasn't really very satisfied. But he kicked so hard against coming into the clinic, I gave way."

Tamara nodded. "Paul does seem rather miserable in a way but he slept all night, Vince said, and was no worse than yesterday. Anyhow I shall be staying with him all day now until he's forced to go to the clinic."

Dr. Finch was too diplomatic to enquire further into this somewhat extraordinary arrangement, but he did ask Tamara if she had had any previous experience of illness or nursing.

"No," was her answer, "but I can use my common sense. I will make sure he only eats the right things and has plenty of fluids — and keeps warm. What worries me is that he seems so terribly cold. And the studio is almost unbearably hot. What do you think, Dr. Finch?"

"People with his trouble generally feel the cold. What I'm concerned about is whether or not he ought to have another transfusion. He had a blood-test two days ago. They said it wasn't necessary, but we know there can always be a sudden change."

Tamara turned her face away from the strong light. She felt suddenly sick with fear, but she spoke calmly. "I understand. Do please come up and see him. If you don't find him too bad, I know he'd prefer to stay in his studio a bit longer. He's writing some music for a new special show and there's one particular song he wants to finish."

"I assure you we won't take him away unless we have to. There aren't enough beds these days, my dear," Dr. Finch said regretfully. "Incidentally, will you tell me your name again?"

"Mrs. Marriot — "

Dr. Finch cocked an eyebrow. *Mrs.*, he had long since deduced that young Paul liked pretty girls and why not, but this lovely creature with her magnificent dark eyes — was she a widow — or — ? Oh, well . . it was not his business. Finch reverted to the thought of his patient

During the examination, Tamara waited in the kitchen trying to interest herself in preparing supper trays. But it was her turn to feel cold — ice-cold with nerves and the dread that Paul might have to be removed from her at once — and from all he liked most. The kitchen clock told her it was nearing five. She bestirred herself to switch on the kettle. The doctor had looked as though he needed a cup of tea. A real biting wind was blowing this late afternoon. She had had a taste of it when she went shopping.

To her utter relief, Dr. Finch told her that he found no great change in Paul's condition. He refused the tea because he was in a hurry. He had many more visits to make. Outside the studio, as he put on his coat, he cautioned Tamara to worry not so much about Paul being cold as too hot. This might mean fever.

"You may or may not know much about leukaemia, but there is always a chance at this stage that he could develop septicaemia. I haven't time to explain it all to you now, but I will, if I see you tomorrow. Take his temperature and let me know if you're worried. Sorry I was detained this morning. Will you be here tomorrow, Mrs. Marriot?"

"Yes," she said, "I'll be here"

Outside the studio door again, she was relieved to hear the sound of music. Paul was playing the piano. She had always adored his touch. This was a soft haunting melody — his latest composition. It held her full attention.

Once with him, she switched on the big shaded lamp that stood on the piano, and pushed an electric fire surreptitiously nearer his back. He was still wearing only his thin dressing gown.

He stopped playing, turned his head and looked up at her with that boyish grin that used in the past to make her feel so happy, especially after he had been in a 'mood'. He could be so ready to start an argument. But he wasn't in a 'mood' tonight, and she hoped he was feeling relaxed and content because *she* was with him. When he handed her a piece of paper with some verses scribbled on it, he told her to sing them. She forced herself to joke, and comply.

"You know I've never had a voice," she declared.

But he reminded her that she could croon quite well. He used to be amused by this. He had played this new song over and over again, and she knew the words now — 'Come Back, Yesterday'. Trite ordinary words, perhaps, but this evening the song was like a knife in her heart.

She could hardly whisper the last verse,

> *I turned away and I left our room again*
> *Nothing was left but the memory of my pain*
>
> *But I want you still — oh, come back, Yesterday!*
> *Just once again, just once — you need not stay.*

Terrified that Paul might see the expression on her face, she stood behind him and uttered a few breathless words of congratulation.

"Darling, each time I hear it I feel the magic. I feel so privileged — so lucky to be the first to hear it. I know it will soon be heard on every radio. All over the world perhaps and — " she couldn't go on. She ended with an excuse that she must pop into the kitchen and look at the dish she had made for supper. Vince was never able to come and take over much before seven, but she had promised to stay and eat with the two boys before going on to Nanny. It would be like old times and she would have to be very cheerful or go to pieces — and *that* would not be good for Paul.

When Vince arrived that night, he glanced from Paul to Tamara and thought that the girl looked worse than her patient. There was little colour in her face. Her eyes were deeply under-shadowed, and Vince, being a man with imagination and sensibility, understood what a strain it all must be for her.

The supper was appreciated. Paul seemed a little brighter

and even though he showed signs of increasing weakness, Vince was better pleased with him than he had been last night. Obviously Tamara's presence was having effect.

After she left — Vince put her into a taxi to take her to Putney — Paul retreated into the shadows of his own private misery. Vince was worried but said nothing.

Paul put his music away, turned out the lamps, and said: "I'm off to my bed. I've got indigestion. I suppose I shouldn't have eaten all that food. Dear little Tamara — she took such trouble with it. Vince, am I being a criminal, letting her stay away from her husband and family just to look after me? I've no right and it must be hard on *him*. Tamara said he's a very tolerant guy but I wonder if *I'd* take it if my wife dashed off to the bedside of an old boyfriend just because he was about to turn up his toes."

That macabre jest was too much even for Vince. He snarled at this man whom he loved like a brother. "Oh, shut up for Christ's sake! Get lost, Paully."

"Sorry," said Paul, grinned and dragged himself more slowly than usual towards the studio door. "I was just wondering what you thought of this arrangement with Tam."

"Don't let's analyse it. It's been arranged. Let's leave it at that. She wants to do it and you want her. We three had a great time together — you and Tam and I this evening. Leave it at that," Vince repeated.

Paul went to his bedroom. Under his pillow he found a crumpled face-tissue. He knew who had put it there. Tamara had lain here this afternoon. He put the tissue to his nostrils and caught the faint perfume of the scent she used — *Calandre* — intriguing, unforgettable. I can even recognise it after these long years, he thought, and was stricken by the memory of the passionate moments they had shared in the past. Even more was he hit by the picture of her lying beside him on the divan earlier today. Of the utter peace and beauty of that hour. Her softness and warmth against his starved body.

Leave it at that, Vince had kept saying. But suddenly Paul shed all effort to be courageous about his approaching end. He doubled his hands — still clenching Tamara's pathetic little paper handkerchief and beat them against the wall. He cried into the pillow.

"I don't want to die. *I don't want to die!* I want to go on living and loving Tamara, and having her love me. I don't want her to go back to her husband. And I won't die. I'm too young — Tamara needs *me* — " he broke off, the sobs racking his thin frame. Vince suddenly heard the *cri-de-coeur* but knew that Paul would not like him to go in there and try to offer consolation. Vince needed a strong drink, and poured himself out one and while he drank it, he stared at Paul's piano with bitterness in his heart.

Why had it got to happen? *In God's name, why?*

20

TOWARDS THE END of February, snow fell over London. One morning, when Tamara left her old nurse's flat, she felt more than usually miserable. The snowflakes, falling so gently, were somehow soothing. She walked instead of taking a taxi to Paul's flat.

She was rather relieved to get away from dear old Nanny's endless endearments, and cautions, and words of sympathy. Tamara's nerves were frayed. She had had a bad month since she left home and started to live with Nanny. A whole month since she had turned herself into a nurse, cook, bottle-washer — all the things — for the man she loved.

It had not been easy. Perhaps more difficult than she had expected. Each day brought problems. Paul was a difficult patient and as his state of health deteriorated, he grew more irritable. At times he held on to her hands with adoration, thanking her for all that she did for him. At other times he resented her being in the studio, and as he put it, 'trying to organise his life'. She told Vince one night, that she tried hard never to let Paul think she was nagging or interfering, but the black moods persisted. She found them very trying. Dr. Finch had asked her to do her best to stop Paul from taking too many sleeping pills, or working too hard — if at all. He strongly advocated rest and moderation. For if he did not follow this advice, his condition would worsen, and *if* he ended with septicaemia — it would be the end indeed.

On his good days Paul and Tamara had music together. Then he seemed better, and quite happy and was a wonderful companion. At these times Tamara was deliriously happy too, and had doubts as to whether he was really going to die. She prayed passionately for a miracle to save him. Otherwise if the collapse came, and an ambulance arrived to take him to the clinic, it would mean the end of all his hopes and dreams as a composer. The curtain would come down.

When he felt particularly bad, he would lose control and storm at Tamara, tell her roughly to get out of his sight.

"I'm sure your husband would welcome you. He can't like being a grass-widower. I ought never to have let you come. I bet your poor Q. needs you more than I do — go and ring him up, I don't care. I don't want you hanging around waiting to watch me pass out."

Against those sort of gibes, Tamara had learned to steel herself. But she dreaded the scenes and could hardly bear to see the haunting misery on Paul's young face. He seemed to her to grow more emaciated and white as his energy drained from him. And, of course, she knew Dr. Finch was rapidly reaching the point when he would insist on Paul going to the clinic.

One of the hard lessons Tamara had had to learn was to avoid reproaching or arguing with Paul. She had to accept his tantrums in silence. Once, when she tried to make him swallow a dose of medicine, he pushed her away and staggered to the piano stool. The liquid spilled on the carpet. He laughed, "Stop trying to pour filthy stuff like that down my throat, Tammy. It won't make me any better."

She cleaned the carpet and removed the spoon. She said nothing, but waited passively until the storm in Paul's brain passed and he beckoned her to him, held on to her and begged her forgiveness.

"I'm a bastard. I don't know what I'm doing or saying. Hold on to me, darling. Hold on."

She pressed his head against her breast. She was almost at breaking point herself.

"You're looking worn out," Dr. Finch said on his last visit, "and believe me, my dear, he'd be better in the clinic now. You're not really used to nurse's work and you take it all too much to heart. A lot of emotional scenes are bad for both of you. If you're not careful, I'll soon have you as a patient as well as Paul."

She smiled. "I won't break down. I'm really very strong. He says he doesn't need me but I know he does, and it's just his way — with all this tension building up. You know, he always ends by telling me he wouldn't last a day and night without me being here."

Finch touched her cheek with his forefinger. He looked at her with great kindness. "You're full of courage, and he's lucky to have that sort of love given with such generosity."

His praise made her eyelids sting but she never cried these days. She began to understand why it was said that grief can be too deep for tears. It helped her to know beyond doubt, that no one could do more for Paul than she did. And especially to be able to tell herself that he truly loved her now.

When he had strength enough to play to her he would make her sing 'Come Back, Yesterday' again and again. Vince heard it several times and each time put his thumbs up and declared that this song was bound to be a world-shaker. But he and Tamara exchanged troubled glances once

Paul stopped playing — staggered back to the divan, and almost immediately fell asleep.

Vince would carry him into his bedroom, and Tamara would go back to Putney, feeling desperately sad and alone. But before leaving him every night she telephoned Q. She had promised to do this and never failed.

Strange, she felt, there was still room in her heart for Q. Sometimes she thought, if she could cry at all these days, it would be as much for him as for Paul. Every time they spoke, Q. told her he was fine — perfectly okay — and busy because he'd taken up a new hobby. He and Tam's father now played Backgammon every night, and sometimes Q. went along to Crockford's to play in a tournament. Twice he had got through to the semi-finals. He seemed pleased and told Tamara he'd have to teach her the game when she came home. Dad and Aunt Liz were fine, too, and still believed she was in Beaconsfield with Virginia. They had, in turn, spoken to her regularly over the phone. She was at least thankful they never suspected she was in town. She hated the lies and deception but they seemed necessary. She could not bear to upset the old darlings by telling them exactly what she was doing. They would not have understood. Why hurt them?

Last night Q. had said he hoped Tamara was looking after herself and not working too hard and was not too uncomfortable in Nan's flat. He ended with a polite enquiry about Paul. "Is the poor boy worse or is there a chance for him?"

She answered, "No chance at all."

Q. sympathised, "Sorry, darling, it must be hellish for you."

With a confusion of feelings she thanked him. Told him to go on allowing Daddy and Aunt Liz to think she was looking after Virginia.

"Goodbye for now, darling. Take care of yourself," he said.

"You're teribly nice to me, Q.," she said. "Oh, I'm so grateful to you. You know I am — don't you?"

"I know," was his reply and that ended the conservation.

This sort of thing upset her for hours afterwards. She was torn in two. She knew she was still so much loved and wanted by Q. How could she help feeling guilty, even mean to him? Yet she knew she was not doing any harm.

She began to feel exhausted, mentally and physically, wondering when Dr. Finch would insist on taking Paul away. But Paul never went to that much-dreaded clinic. His end was sudden, and came late one night, four weeks after Tamara left her family.

To her lasting regret she was not with him. Vince, who was on duty thought he heard a cry coming from Paul. He rushed into the bedroom. The lamp was lit. He was lying on the rug beside the bed, arms outstretched, eyes wide open. Vince's heart lurched. Oh God, he thought, Paul must have felt very bad and tried to get to me, then passed out. Vince knelt down, frantically trying to hear Paul's heart-beat. But long before Dr. Finch answered Vince's call, Vince faced the tragic certainty that the end of Paul had come at last.

21

IT WAS OLD Nanny who stayed up with Tamara after Vince had broken the news to her. She did not leave her for the rest of that grey desolate dawn.

And to old Nanny, Tamara poured out the whole tragic story. How she had answered the telephone outside Nanny's flat — the old woman had not heard it because she slept heavily — and Vince had told her to ring for a taxi and come at once. This, she had done leaving a note behind her, and once at the studio she found the doctor already there.

He told them there was nothing more he could do for Paul. He had suffered a massive coronary. His over-fatigued heart had suddenly failed. The Doctor said it was mercy. The young man might well have had to face a more lingering death. The coronary had not been expected but it did not surprise him. Paul had been ill for a long time, trying to lead a normal life — always fighting — crazily fighting — against his strength.

Tamara looked her last on Paul's much-loved face and found it very beautiful in death. Like a tragic mask — yet, in a way, it was the face of a youth. That seemed to her the saddest thing of all.

For the last time she kissed those cold clever fingers which once had power to extract such wonderful music from those piano keys. But now the studio held no more interest for her. Paul was no longer there. Once his body had been removed by ambulance to the mortuary, she let Vince take her back to Putney.

She wondered how she ever got through the rest of that night or the terrible awakening in the morning. Old Nanny kept saying things like "It's for the best, my pet", or "You must try now to think of your poor husband, and always remember you did do all you could for the poor young man." And being religious, Nanny also assured Tamara that she and Paul would meet again. That was the only time she extracted the faintest smile from Tamara, who said, "Let's stop talking about it, Nanny dear. But surely Christ said that in heaven there would be no marriage or giving in marriage? After all it *would* be a mix up, wouldn't it, if a widow married again and had to pass through the pearly gates and choose which husband she wanted to be with. I'm afraid I don't believe I'll see either Q. or Paul again once I die."

Nanny was a little confused by that, but soon had other things to think about. Cups of tea during the rest of the night, then breakfast, which Tamara barely touched. She fell asleep again and did not wake till mid-morning.

While she dressed, Tamara faced a bleak future. She felt

that something inside her own heart had died with Paul. And it was strange on this cold empty day after Paul's death, she found herself thinking, not only of him, but of Claire, her lost child. Maybe, she thought, if Nan is right and people do meet in heaven, Paul will find darling Claire and tell her all about me.

She called Virginia before she left the Putney flat. Virginia was distressed for her friend, but she took the news with her usual calm. Platitudes such as *'it was all for the best'* were always an anathema to Virginia, but she told Tamara firmly that she must go home now and do her best to put this tragedy out of mind and be kind to Q.

"I'll get Henry to drive me up at once, and we'll collect you from Nanny's and take you home. You'd like me to be with you, wouldn't you, and it'll seem right — as they think you've been staying with me."

For an instant Tamara hesitated. It wasn't altogether what she wanted, yet she felt there was no fight left in her, no strength — and she couldn't face a cheerful Aunt Liz who knew nothing. She put herself into Virginia's hands.

"Yes, it would be super. Do come and fetch me, please, Virginia."

"While you settle in, I can stay on for the rest of the day. Darling Henry has business friends to see this afternoon, and he can go to Crockford's tonight. You know he loves his backgammon tournaments, and he can always find a game at the club. I particularly want to be with you when Q. gets back from the City. It might help."

"Thank you, it will."

"After all," Virginia went on, "I shall just say something like Henry is bringing me to town to see a specialist. I haven't been feeling myself and he wants me to stay at a hotel for a night or two, and have a thorough check-up, which will account for us driving you back today. I can also apologise for having kept you with us for so long. They must think it odd. I'll say I have no domestic help just now and you've been so wonderful to me."

"For God's sake, Virginia, I've been the reverse of wonderful. But it would be super if you could stop any possible questioning. You aren't really in need of a check-up, are you?"

"I've just got one or two problems, and I'm going to set Henry's mind at rest."

"But why?" demanded Tamara anxiously.

Then she was told. There was nothing really wrong. Virginia was going to have a baby in six months' time. Henry wanted her to see a good gynaecologist. She wanted to know exactly how to deal with her impending motherhood.

"But isn't it *super*," she exclaimed — more excited than Tamara had ever known her. "You know how much I love children. I've always wanted one and — " Virginia suddenly stopped. She hadn't meant to tell anybody about the baby yet. Was it the wrong time to tell poor unhappy Tamara? Then she decided that it might take her mind off her tragedy, and Virginia was relieved to find Tamara was indeed thrilled by the news.

"I am so happy for you, darling. It's terrific. Isn't Henry pleased?"

"He certainly is. He's been clucking round me like an old hen, if you can call a man a hen!" Virginia laughed. "I have to keep telling him I don't need all this tender care, and that thousands of women have babies every day all over the world and come to no harm."

"Oh, please may I be godmother?" Tamara asked on an impulse.

"Certainly you may be, darling Tamara," she said.

Inevitably both girls fell to thinking of Claire and the sudden juxtaposition of their relationship. Virginia felt a little embarrassed but Tamara put things right by saying 'she hoped it would be a boy'. Somehow after this Tamara felt better. She must reorientate herself. She would take Dr. Finch's advice. He had begged her to accept Paul's death as a merciful release. It was just that she could not yet believe that she would never see Paul again, and when she thought

208

of his last composition she shivered. Yesterday — this word was too nostalgic and painful. *Yesterday* — their Yesterday could never come back. So she must stop remembering the past and look ahead. She owed so much to Q. Virginia was right — she *must* try to communicate with poor Q. again.

Later that morning when Henry deposited Virginia and Tamara at Eaton Terrace, they were received with delight by Aunt Liz.

"You've been away so long — dear Q. will be so happy you're back, dear," she said as she kissed Tamara.

After which the three of them sat together drinking coffee, and the first few moments of her return, which Tamara had so dreaded, passed quite happily.

Virginia talked about Henry. Tamara listened to her and to Aunt Liz and said as little as she could. She still felt dazed and somehow unreal.

All kinds of things were said that embarrassed Tamara. Aunt Liz, for instance, asking Virginia anxiously if 'she was all right' — because she was supposed to have been ill, and that was why Tamara had gone away to help Virginia. Now, of course, Aunt Liz wanted to know what was wrong with dear Virginia.

The two girls exchanged glances. Virginia said quickly that she had wonderful news for Mrs. York. Aunt Liz then heard about Virginia's pregnancy, and was enchanted, and so the whole conversation became domestic and bright and so cheerful, that Tamara began to wonder how things could be like this, while her beloved Paul lay dead.

Virginia did not stay long. She was due to join her husband.

"Can I come back later for the rest of the day — until just before dinner?" she asked Mrs. York. "Henry is meeting a business friend this afternoon, and I know they won't want me there."

"I don't think your Henry will ever want to be without you, dear," was Aunt Liz's comment.

Then Tamara was quick to say, "Please do come back, Virginia darling." She still needed Virginia's moral support when her father returned. Q. knew all about things, but Daddy was ignorant of the whole matter.

The meeting with her father was unexpectedly easy. He was the first to arrive back from the City, and was so pleased to see his much-loved daughter again that he did not bother his head about the whys and wherefores of her strange absence from home. And he was glad to see the lovely grave-eyed Virginia. He had always been sure that her friendship was a fine thing for Tamara. And when he, too, learned the truth about Virginia's 'illness', he insisted upon opening a bottle of champagne and drinking a toast to the son or daughter of the future.

Tamara thought — it's all gone off well! Thank goodness Daddy isn't going to worry about me at all.

And now, there was nothing left but the reunion with Q.

He arrived just before dinner, apologising because he had been held up at the office. Virginia thought he looked extremely tired and was far from being his normal cheerful self. But she could not fail to see the light that came back into his eyes when he saw his wife sitting there by the fire, cigarette in one hand and a goblet of champagne in the other.

She smiled at him and he bent and dropped a light kiss on her hair. "It's wonderful to find you home again," he whispered, but he felt bewildered. What had in fact dragged Tamara away from Paul's studio?

The conversation remained general until Virginia rose to leave and asked Q. brightly if she could have a word with him alone. She had some stocks and shares she wanted to sell, she said, and could she consult him for a moment? *Of course*, was his answer.

Once alone with him in the study she told him everything. "I realise that you knew about Tamara not really being at home with Henry and me. I hope you'll forgive me for backing her up, but I thought it was best to do so, once she had been honest with you."

Q.'s face coloured. He lit a cigarette with fingers that were not quite steady.

"Of course I'm glad you've helped her. You always were a good friend. And I don't think you need make any more excuses or imagine that I shall be in the least rough with her. Good God, don't I realise all that she has been going through!"

Virginia sighed. "Dear Q.! You're such a nice person, Tam is very different — from either you or me. She has a sort of crazy streak, Q. — a dramatic sort of nature. On the whole I think she's behaved very well. She had a shock when she heard about Paul's fatal illness, but she *didn't* want to deceive or hurt you — I know that!"

"I know it too." He nodded, swallowed some cigarette smoke and coughed, then went on, "You can feel quite happy about her, Virginia, I'll look after her. And I'll be very tactful. I'm sorry the poor boy died so suddenly. It must have been a horrid shock for Tam, and of course, she said he was quite well-known in his set, as a composer. I suppose there's to be a theatrical sort of funeral, and that'll be the next thing for Tam to worry about."

"No, there's to be no funeral. Paul left his body to the hospital, so Vince told Tam. One can do that, you know. His old group may suggest a Memorial Service later on, but that's not definite. I think as time passes, Tam will get over this completely, so don't worry."

His stern face flushed again, but relaxed as he looked at Tamara's friend.

"I hope so, Virginia dear. She means much to me and she does need to be looked after. Claire's death came properly between us, and *she* just hasn't recovered from it. That makes two disasters on her plate and she's a bundle of nerves."

"She'll get over it, even if she never forgets. By the way, she's agreed to be godmother to my baby when he or she arrives."

"Splendid," he said, and now he looked and felt more cheerful. "And Virginia — bless you for everything." He stood up and touched her cheek with his lips. "Henry's a lucky man," he added.

"And Tamara's more than lucky — you're one in a hundred."

"Not at all. On the contrary. I'm not nearly sensitive enough, and I've paid far too much attention to fast cars, sport, and business. Yes, I know where I've failed her. Tamara never really found a soul-mate in me."

Virginia, practical as ever, said she didn't really think there were such things as 'soul-mates'. It was merely that some couples had a lot in common, but even then there was a stile here and there to get over, and a few faults one had to learn to live with. Married couples had to accept each other's failing. "No one's perfect," she went on. "You and Tam are no exception — neither are Henry and I. We had a dispute over something quite infantile the other night — it's so often like that — not a big issue."

"You're right," Q. agreed.

After Virginia left, he went up to his dressing-room to wash and change a grimy City shirt, and felt better. Virginia somehow had the power of making people feel better. Also he was very relieved that Tamara had come home. The tragic end of the young composer would, he hoped, mean that *he*, Q., would stand a chance of establishing a new relationship with Tamara.

Virginia had told him it would be best if he tried to avoid all reference to Paul when he was alone with Tamara later on.

It was she who lifted her face to be kissed when he came to her bedside to say good night. He bent down and touched her cheeks with gentle lips.

"Poor little darling, you've had one hell of a time. What about a sleeping pill?"

"I don't need one, I'm half asleep now. Q. please forgive me — " He interrupted, "Forget it, darling, I love you, and I always will, and I don't want to have any discussion about what has passed. Let's look to the future."

She looked up at him, her brilliant eyes swimming wild tears. "It *has* been hell, Q."

"Try to forget it," he repeated. "Fate has decided it should all end this way — just keep cool and believe as I do — it was for the best."

"You don't hate me?" she asked and the tears rolled slowly down her cheeks as she looked up at Q.'s kindly face.

"You know I don't. I repeat — I'll always love you. Goodnight, my love, I'm not staying to hear another word. Sleep well. We'll have breakfast together and talk then."

"Yes — I'd like that," she said.

Somehow those words were very comforting to Q.

But that night he did not get to sleep for a long while, and when he managed to do so he kept waking up, and wondering if all was well with Tamara. From time to time he even got up and looked beneath her door. He could see that the light was still on in her room. Miserable and confused though he felt over the whole situation, a sudden trifling worry entered his thoughts. Seeing that white line of light he remembered that just before she left home, a draught from the hall had troubled her. She reminded him she was susceptible to cold and he had promised to go to a 'Do-It-Yourself' shop, buy a piece of draught-proofing and line the door for her. He told himself that he must get it tomorrow. He felt stupidly nervous when he tried to sleep again, and still saw the light. She, too, was awake. Would she ever get over Paul Pryce's death? And if she did, would the scarred memory remain and be always between them?

He turned his thoughts to their honeymoon. He had meant to make her so happy and at that time he had believed she loved him and he had not given a thought to her affair with Paul Pryce. So many girls had serious affairs before marriage, and then put them in the background. Tamara was deeply emotional and there must obviously have been something in particular about Paul that she had found irresistible. So Q. broadminded, and easy-going had not been disturbed by the idea. It was in the past.

Following this unhappy night, he faced up to his own shortcomings. He buried his pride and asked himself where he had failed with Tamara. Perhaps it was just that *his* kind of love and loving had not been right for her. He was to blame — not Tamara alone.

Q. had never imagined himself to be a man who women might find insensitive. But tonight he supposed that was, in fact, the case and why he had failed. He had been so happy himself — until his small daughter's death he had never wondered if Tamara was still in the deep recess of her heart regretting the loss of Paul.

In the early hours of that morning Q. ruthlessly analysed the whole affair and went down into the bitter depths of despair. He lay awake staring into the darkness, trying to prepare himself for anything Tamara might say to him when they discussed the situation again. He was sure he had lost her — this time for good. He wished miserably that he was one of these clever analytical people who study philosophy, psychiatry, and all the latest books that seem to help a man to understand his wife.

He fell asleep just before the house stirred. At half past six, Aunt Liz, ever early, and wrapped cosily in her woolly dressing gown, took Tamara a cup of tea. Her most valued friend was her Teasmade and she never failed to make the early cup. Today in particular she presumed that Tamara would welcome it.

She found Tamara's bed empty. Then she heard the bath running and knocked on the door. Tamara answered, "Good morning, Aunt Liz. Just leave my tea by my bed and thank you, darling."

Aunt Liz, going downstairs again, threw a quick look at Q.'s door as she passed, and sighed. She really didn't understand why Tamara had been so upset and looked so ill when she came home last night. Virginia had seemed a bit strange, too. Liz had mentioned this to her brother. Something was going on. Liz was worried and full of curiosity. But nobody confided in her. She returned to her own room — still wondering what it was all about.

Later on it was Tamara's turn to look at Q.'s door. She

214

took her cup of tea into his room. His bedside lamp was still on. He was asleep. In the lamplight his face looked worn and even old this morning. She had never seen Q. look like this. His face was usually so cheerful. But of course, she realised, there was little to make him feel cheerful just now. She felt her remorse. And a sense of loneliness frightened her. Yet horribly guilty. Her own life was in tatters, and she feared that she had been well on the way to ruining his life, too.

But she had at last reached a definite conclusion. She could not, would not go on hurting him.

She thought of Paul's song, 'Come Back Yesterday'. That nostalgic emotional *cri-de-coeur*. How aptly it described the present, she thought. Poor Paul had wanted 'Yesterday', with no hope of life or love. She had done all she could to make him happy and it had come to a sudden end. She could do no more for him. In the cold dawn, in her own room, she had faced up to an overwhelming sense of personal loss. The loss of both Claire and Paul, and now through her own fault, she was on the way to losing Q. The idea had increased how could she begin to bring back *her* yesterday with Q?

But when she saw him lying there asleep this morning, looking so strangely old and tired, her misery converged into a frantic wish to help him — to comfort him even if she, herself, could not find comfort.

She set the cup down on the table beside him, switched off the lamp, and pulled the curtains. The first grey light of day crept into the room. The shadows began to lift.

Q. sat up. Now he looked flushed and more himself — smiling at her, running his fingers through his thick fair hair, reminding Tamara poignantly of Claire. The little girl used to wake up like that — bewildered at first, but quick to smile. Q. stared at his wife with red-rimmed eyes, and said, "Tam! Good Lord — what time is it? Are you all right?"

Somehow the affection and admiration she had once felt for him found a place in her heart. She ran to the bed and lay down on the eiderdown beside him. She put her arms around his neck.

"Q.," she said, and pressed her face against his. "Dear Q. I've been so awful — so selfish. Oh, Q. how can I expect you to forgive me?"

Amazed and speechless, he took that small shivering body into his arms. At first, the magic and wonder of the moment was almost too much for him to take in fully. He could only hold her in silence and gratitude in this unexpected hour. He kissed the top of her head, feeling her tears against his cheek, and not knowing how best to comfort her. One wrong word, one unconsidered action, and he feared she might disappear like a lovely phantom that had been spirited into his room, but would never be seen again. He shut his eyes and tried to blot out the memory of the past, and to concentrate only on this miracle. For assuredly last night he had lost all hope and confidence in himself.

She lay near him, weeping. He took both arms away from her gently and got out of bed. Then put on his dressing gown and crossed the corridor to her room. He found the pale pink feathery cape she often wore over her bare shoulders when it was cold, and brought it in to her. He put it tenderly around her.

She looked at him, her face blotched with grief. But he saw a new warmth in those dark haunting eyes which encouraged him to feel that all was not yet lost.

"Here — this is *your* tea, darling," he said, "don't let it get cold. It was sweet of you to bring it to me. I want you to drink it."

She tied the ribbons of her cape, lifted the cup to her mouth, grimaced and set it back in the saucer. "It's gone cold, but I don't really want it either, Q., thank you."

"I'll make you some more."

"No, I don't want it. I'd rather talk to you."

"Are you sure? Wouldn't you rather wait till you feel a bit better? I know you can't feel up to much this hour of the morning."

Tamara shook her head and sat up straight. She had made up her mind what she was going to say and do, and she did not waste time. She caught hold of his hand. "Sit down, Q. here, beside me, please."

"Do you mind if I smoke a cigarette?"

"Of course not."

"Do you want one?"

"No thank you."

"Shall I turn on the lamp again?"

"No, only the fire. Switch it on, please, Q. darling. It's freezing this morning."

He turned the electric radiator full on. She gave a deep sigh.

"Thanks, darling."

It seemed so long since he had heard that word 'darling' from her.

"Poor little cold thing — you're always frozen," he said.

"I'm always all the wrong things."

"Rubbish!" he smiled down at her. "You're okay. Things have got a bit out of hand, I know but if we still care about each other, all will be well. Let's not think all is lost."

She gave a watery smile. "Sit down on the bed and let me talk to you Q., please," she repeated.

He lit the cigarette he needed so badly, and sat beside her. "Go ahead, if you really want to talk."

"I really do." Tamara said, and took his free hand and hung on to it as though to a life-belt that had been flung at her in a raging sea.

22

THAT SAME MORNING, Tamara answered two telephone calls in quick succession. The first was from Vince on his way to work.

"I just wanted to make sure you were all right, Tam," he began.

"Thanks, Vince, you're always so kind. Everyone is much too nice to me."

"I don't want you to be too cut up about poor old Paul. He was a pretty sick boy for a long time before he died, you know. He's better off now."

"I keep telling myself that. Don't worry about me. I'm quite all right."

"I'd like to see you some time."

"Of course. I was telling Q. — my husband — about you. How simply great you've been. Nobody could have done more for Paul."

"Except you, Tam. You're the greatest girl I know."

"I'm very much the opposite but I haven't time to talk to you about that now."

"Hang on a moment, Tam. I just want to make sure that you — well — " Vince's voice was embarrassed, "I just want to know that things are okay — I mean I suppose your husband knows about it all."

"Yes."

"Oh, well — super — if it's okay. See you. You know my address Tam. Drop me a line and let's meet some time."

"I'll ask you to a meal here. I'd like you to meet Q."

"Later on — sure. Meanwhile I must tell you that Paul wrote me a letter before he died — I mean after you turned up in his life again — and asked me to inform you that when he'd finished that last song of his and he was gone — I was to give it to you."

"Give it to *me*!" repeated Tamara mystified.

"Yes. He wants you to own it, and sell the rights through

his agents, and they'll deal with you. You're to get the proceeds. I think you know them — Martin Clough, Ltd. You're to instruct them to get in touch with Nick Fearon. Do you remember him? The pianist in the group?"

"I remember."

"I've got his address. Nick will certainly want the song because he's working for I.T.V. and he'll get them to plug it. 'Come Back, Yesterday' — it's a terrific title, Tam, and the tune's great, don't you think?"

Now Tamara shut her eyes because they were suddenly stinging, but she went on talking. "The greatest," she said.

"I'll send you on the score, plus Nick's address, and *you* can write to him, as well as to Martin Clough."

Suddenly she caught her breath. "Vince, won't you do it for me — please."

After a second's hesitation, Vince said, "If that's the way you want it — but I'd rather — "

She interrupted, "It would be best if you'd do it. You're more used to the business side of song-writing. Will you?"

"If you're sure that's the way you want it."

"It is — and we'll work on it together later."

"Okay. The proceeds are to go to you if it's a success. That was Paul's wish."

Her throat hurt and her eyes filled. "Dear Paul! but I shan't take the money. I may perhaps buy some little thing as a memento but I shall hand all the proceeds over to you. No, Vince, don't argue. You're perfectly well aware that I'm not hard up and I know perfectly well that you *are*. Paul would agree with me."

"We'll discuss it some other time, Tammy. I must go now. No more coins for the slot. See you."

She put down the receiver.

Almost immediately the telephone-bell rang again. This time it was Virginia.

"I couldn't leave London without talking to you. Are you all right, Tam?"

"Yes, I'm all right, darling Virginia, but I do rather feel I've been run over by a juggernaut — sort of crushed up."

"Of course you do. Everything's happened so quickly and it's all been a bit larger than you could take. I've been thinking heaps about you, Tam. Henry and I want you to come down and stay with us — really stay this time, and for as long as you like."

"I think I'd like that — if Henry doesn't mind. Doesn't he want you to himself?"

"He has plenty of me, dear, and Henry's very fond of you and we both think you might need a break. He said you can stay as long as you like."

"Thanks awfully, Virginia, I will come. I'd appreciate it. But you needn't worry about me any more. Everything's going to be all right."

"Everything? I've been so upset about you and Q."

"You needn't be. It's really rather unexpected but, Virginia, we sort of got together this morning. I just told Q. everything about Paul and how I felt when I knew he was dying, and how I wanted to be with him, and all that. He already knew most of it, but what he didn't know was whether I had anything left for *him*."

"And — ?"

"And I found I had. I was able to make him believe I'd never really lost my affection or admiration — it was just that somehow after Claire died I had no love left for anyone — not even for him. I was awful. I admitted it."

"Darling, don't go into that now. Tell me more about Q."

"He was wonderful — as you'd expect. He made me feel very small. He even accused *himself* of being stupid and unimaginative and all the things you could think of, and tried to apologise to *me*. My God, I didn't deserve it. He didn't even mention the fact that as a married woman I'd behaved rather oddly — just sliding out of my home in order to nurse my former boy-friend — " Tamara's voice cracked. "But although he was shocked at first, he realised after a bit that there was nothing he really need worry or be angry

220

about — only that naturally Daddy and Aunt Liz are old-fashioned and would be very upset, so we had to be careful how we handled the situation. And of course, he made it clear it had hurt him to feel I'd still cared a lot about Paul even after my marriage. Honestly I thought I'd got over it and Q. attracted me and I believed it would be okay. I was quite honest with Q., Virginia. I told him that even if Paul hadn't been ill and he'd asked me to leave Q. and live with him, I might have gone crazy and gone to him."

"No, you would never have done that," said Virginia quietly.

"Nevertheless the intention was there," said Tamara. "I didn't want to whitewash myself. I told Q. the absolute truth. But Paul died, so there it has ended."

"I know, darling."

"Q. asked me if I could begin again and forgive him for — for the accident to Claire. I said I did forgive him and blamed myself for all I did and said at the time, but I'd like to go away for a little while and sort myself out, then come back to him and try to make him happy again."

Virginia said, "Oh, Tam, Tam, you don't know how glad that makes me. He's such a dear. You *could* be happy again. I'm sure you did love him."

"Yes, and I will again. I also realised that my own life would end if I didn't make more effort to put things right with Q. and make a go of it. For Claire's sake, too, I sort of owe it to her memory, Virginia. I know that now. He *was* her father, and in my way I do care a lot about him — " Tam broke down and stopped speaking.

Virginia said, "Don't be unhappy. It's all going to work out. I've got to go now, darling. I'll phone you when we get home later this evening. Don't regret what you've just told me — it's all for the best. And don't live in the past any more. Q. will do his best to make *you* happy, and I can't help feeling poor Paul would be glad if you had a fresh start with your husband."

"Yes," Tam whispered the word.

After she had replaced the receiver, she pulled a suitcase out of the cupboard and began to pack a few things. Her tears fell thick and fast for a while but soon she wiped them away and settled down to the few things she had to do before leaving town, and going down to Beaconsfield.

She wondered if she ought to run away even for a short time, but after all, Q., himself, had suggested she should stay with Virginia and Henry for a few days. She felt emotionally spent. She knew that she needed a complete rest and break before she could take up the threads of life with Q. again.

As she tidied her bedroom, she remembered what Vince had told her. Dear Paul had bequeathed his last composition to her. She felt a glow of gratitude and pleasure. But she really did not want to benefit by it financially.

It would be wonderful if Nick Fearon could get that song on the air, especially if it meant some money for Vince. She knew quite a lot about Vince these days. They used to chat together when she had a moment or two alone with him while Paul rested. He had been taken on as a partner at the book shop, which was not doing badly, but he had put all his savings into it and times were thin. He needed capital. He was surely the right one to benefit by Paul's royalties. Tamara knew it would be the best thing for her to bring this about.

She felt considerably better by lunch time and telephoned Q. at the office.

"Could you get the afternoon off, Q.?" she asked him.

"I'll try. For anything in particular?"

"Yes. I want you to drive me down to Virginia. I really *am* going down there *this* time for a few days, and I'd like to talk to you on the way."

An instant's silence from Q. then, with a note of anxiety, he said, "You're not going to — "

"No," she interrupted, "I've no intention of staying there for longer than a week. I *want* to come back to you. But I'm just feeling so grim at the moment I'd like to reorientate myself. Am I being an egotist — as usual?" she ended with an unhappy laugh.

He made haste to reassure her. "No — I think it's a good idea. I'll come and fetch you, and after you come back for keeps, darling, we might both take a short holiday together — in the sun somewhere."

She was thankful to find that the idea appealed to her. "Yes, I'd like that. Could Daddy spare you?"

"There isn't a lot doing, with the Market as things are at present, and I daresay I could make him believe you badly need a change. He'll do anything for you."

Now Tamara spoke of Claire in a way she had not done since their child died. "I would like to put some flowers on Claire's grave as soon as I am with you again. I've been so cowardly about it so far."

"Oh, Tam *darling* — " Q. was now so relieved he felt unable to say much more.

She added, "See you later, Q. and thank you — for everything!"

As she put down the receiver, the memory of Paul's last song returned to her.

Somehow in this hour it didn't seem so heartbreaking.

'*Come Back, Yesterday.*' Well — she had accepted the fact that it never could come back. Paul couldn't come back, either. But Q. would be waiting for her to return to him, and life for them would begin again, so there would be a Tomorrow — for both of them.

In her sad, wild, turbulent heart she found it possible to consider that there might even be another child in the distant future. Another daughter, or a son — for Q.

Perhaps that possibility was not so far distant.

They must see.

A SELECTION OF
DENISE ROBINS IN CORONET

☐ 18300 4	Do Not Go My Love	50p
☐ 01065 7	I Should Have Known	50p
☐ 01437 7	Nightingale's Song	50p
☐ 20736 1	It Wasn't Love	50p
☐ 00745 1	Fever of Love	50p
☐ 12792 9	Climb to the Stars	50p
☐ 02435 6	Slave Woman	50p
☐ 20654 3	Second Best	50p
☐ 02920 X	Lightning Strikes Twice	50p
☐ 02922 6	Loving and Giving	50p
☐ 02474 7	Moment of Love	50p
☐ 12784 8	Restless Heart	50p
☐ 01903 4	Betrayal	50p
☐ 20756 6	Twice Have I Loved	50p
☐ 01459 8	The Noble One	60p
☐ 18291 1	The Snow Must Return	60p
☐ 02896 3	Never Give All	60p
☐ 15085 8	Brief Ecstasy	60p
☐ 17850 7	Desire is Blind	60p
☐ 21802 9	Never Look Back	60p
☐ 20809 0	The Dark Corridor	60p
☐ 18877 4	Stranger Than Fiction (autobiography)	75p

All these books are available at your local bookshop or newsagent, or can be ordered direct from the publisher. Just tick the titles you want and fill in the form below.

Prices and availability subject to change without notice.

CORONET BOOKS, P.O. Box 11, Falmouth, Cornwall.

Please send cheque or postal order, and allow the following for postage and packing :

U.K. – One book 22p plus 10p per copy for each additional book ordered, up to a maximum of 82p.

B.F.P.O. and EIRE – 22p for the first book plus 10p per copy for the next 6 books, thereafter 4p per book.

OTHER OVERSEAS CUSTOMERS – 30p for the first book and 10p per copy for each additional book.

Name..

Address..

....